TO DANCE WITH SPIRITS

TO DANCE WITH SPIRITS

BOOK THREE OF
THE LEGENDS OF ARCADIA SERIES

MORGAN HUBBARD

Mystic Lantern Publishing
Visit the author's website at morganhubbardauthor.com

Cover design by Maria Spada
Formatting by Evenstar Books

ISBN 979-8-9863981-4-3

To those who fight unseen battles,
maintain the peace, and work
toward balance and unity.

Author's Note

So, reader, we've reached the end!

A couple notes on this book's folklore if you're curious:

The *micca* were creatures of my design; however, I quickly realized that there's already a being in these mountains. Sometimes called the *Yunwi Tsunsdi'* or *skill'li*, the most common way I've seen it communicated is "the little people". These little guys were about knee-high, very good at hiding, and sometimes seen as tricksters. Other sources I found said they took care of the land and would even plow your field for you at night if they showed you favor. So despite having believed I made up little Appalachian forest tenders, there were already stories of the *Yunwi Tsunsdi'* to draw inspiration from.

The *Nûñnë'hï*, also known as "the people who live forever", are a benevolent race of beings and known for their protective nature. There is some fascinating information out there about the *Nûñnë'hï*, and everyone seems to agree that this powerful guardian race is scattered across Appalachia. There are some locations where they're said to live, but most people passing by will hear music, smell something cooking, and see lights in the distance only for them to disappear when they come closer. Legend says they have aided the Cherokee in battles, and they're known to aid lost travelers or heal the sick. I wanted to weave them into the Legends of Arcadia somehow, and it felt right for the final piece of the trilogy.

The Raven Mocker, also known as *Kâ'lanû Ahkyeli'skï* (anglicized as Kalona by yours truly), is an adaptation of a malevolent creature from the rich folklore of the Cherokee Nation. Said to be a witch or spirit, the Raven Mocker consumes the heart of a sick individual and adds the days or years left of that person's life to its own life. The Raven Mocker travels with the sound of a raven and sparks flying behind. It felt natural to name meteor showers after this dark creature. And while I gave Kalona her own origin story in To Breathe Beneath Stars, it's entirely fictional from my own brain.

With this trilogy, I really wanted to honor my homeland's folklore as well as the werewolf stories from Ireland that are a part of my heritage. In a way, it seemed almost natural. And after all, the Appalachian Trail continues through Ireland, so it's entirely possible that somehow these two lands are connected through stories as well as geology. And I hope this trilogy fused them together just a bit more.

Morgan Hubbard

THE RIVER

BONES.

Piles and piles of bones. The mound of scraps tipped and spilled into my waters, leaving memories to leak and wash downstream. The deer bleated and the bears moaned, the raccoons screeched and the opossums shrieked. Not one creature had been left unaffected.

The merciless master of the Hunt used her talons to tear down and rebuild, crafting a nest of branches and bone by my once-peaceful banks.

Too close to the Arcadian border.

Too close to the human bearing her treasure.

Once, a few of the Guardians passed the place, casting strange glances at the beginnings of her nest, but none truly saw. How clever the master of the Hunt could be.

Now, trinkets dangled from the whip-like branches of the ancient willow. Its fingers grasped rusted railroad spikes, hag stones, carved bones, and glass bottles of all colors. While the wind rippled my waters, it nudged the bottles and bones until they clinked and tinkled in the otherwise quiet holler.

How I wished for a little more noise and conversation. Even the trees were quieter than usual in December, but I suppose snow does that to nature: dampens her until a harsh wind whispering of life spent deep in hibernation is left.

Kalona never spoke to me. I wished many times she would, if only so I could pass a message on, trapping the memory of her in my waters. But I could only wait for the passage of time.

I could only wait to see who would emerge as king, queen, or master of the Hunt.

Who would be forgiven or convicted.

Who would live or die.

A Seer once spoke words over the human on my banks. A night when *kuslar* danced in the dying warmth of *Sliva* along with the ghost beetles and the breeze. A night when *ugals* and *micca* showed deference and honor to the human queen. A night when the king and queen of Arcadia chose love.

These were the words that Seer spoke on that night, not long ago:

They see past the veil. They see what you cannot. And when the time comes for you to be bound to the rock, you will emerge and reign, both beautiful and beloved.

I only hoped he had seen past this veil of darkness, of silence, of sickness. Maybe he spoke of a brighter *Starra* after the ice and snow and despair melted. Maybe the human would waltz with her king and not shift to the Other Realm. Perhaps the *Nunnehi* would be merciful in their meddling with fate.

Maybe it would be Silas and Eden.

Nash and Kalona.

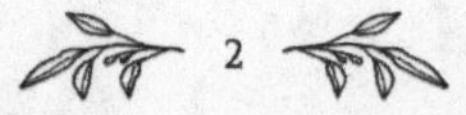

The Arcadians and the Hunt.

But I could only move as fast as the current of time allowed. And it would never be fast enough.

1

NASH

FORESTS HOLD SECRETS.

Or at least, that's what I'd come to realize.

My paws dragged through four inches of snow while flurries danced between the pines. Winter finally arrived, the wind chill dropping the temperature into the teens. The trees, tufted in white, stood silent, and the late morning sun glinted off their frosty branches. I tucked my tail closer to my body and maneuvered around the lodges on the Great Mountain, careful of my footing. Warm yellow lights shone through the windows of the main building, and muted laughter reached my raised ears. The end of the hiking season approached, but even so, I kept watch for human activity, ready to rescue or guide a lost traveler back to the trail or back to somewhere warm to avoid hypothermia.

When we arrived home from Lukosan a few weeks ago, Silas put me with the Guardians to give me a job other than protecting Eden. There wasn't much for me to do anyway. Silas rarely left her side.

That November day we returned, Eden went immediately to bed and didn't wake for eighteen hours. And the next day, she turned groggy and feverish before our midday meal. In the two weeks since, she had only ventured as far as Silas or I could take her. She barely had enough strength to join us for our Harvest Revel. Asa set to work immediately, giving Eden a variety of tinctures, herbs, and salves. Nothing seemed to help. A few days ago, when Silas and I were alone, I'd mentioned taking her to a human doctor in the city. If looks could kill, I would've been dead, so I hadn't mentioned it since.

That bad feeling I'd had when leaving Lukosan? It never left. It wedged itself beneath my stomach, and made itself at home.

The sensation that eyes watched me from the shadows followed my steps. I swore something trailed us out of Lukosan, but I couldn't prove it. Legends of the Appalachians talked about skinwalkers, Mockers, haints, the Whistler, and any number of evil spirits haunting the area. It could be any of them or none at all. Perhaps the situation with Nyx and the Wendigos at Lukosan drove me to paranoia.

Andra occupied quite a bit of my thoughts. She lingered in the corners of my mind, forcing her way through at the strangest of times. I considered her offer to join the Lukosan pack. I had a better place in Arcadia now that I'd been assigned to be a Guardian, but the idea of starting fresh in Lukosan tempted me on the lonelier days—days when I only had my thoughts for company.

Outside the lodges, I sniffed the Trillium Gap trail that would take me back to Arcadia. My job was to return and update Kane on the human activity at the lodges. I raised my head, sight narrowing on the sign for the Alum Cave trail that would take me past Nyx's pseudo-burial spot.

I still hadn't grown any wiser about the past year, that hole in my memories haunting me like a ghost. A disquieting ache settled over me, and I wondered if some part of Nyx still lingered around this ridge.

Maybe I'd missed something.

Maybe something waited for me in the shadows of the Alum Cave Trail.

Do I dare?

Markus, Caroline, and Aubrey had already taken care of the cairn. It's not like it would be dangerous. And Wendigos wouldn't come out in the daytime.

Just a peek.

A door shut somewhere in the cluster of lodges, and I had no time to weigh out a decision. My paws directed me straight ahead and down the Trillium Gap Trail, toward home.

Life looked quite a bit different now that people weren't focused on me, Iain's reckless son. The disapproving looks and mutterings had ceased, and I should've been happy about it. I should have been grateful.

Instead, the people had fixed their gossip on the future queen. I didn't blame them; how could I? While they got used to the idea of a human queen, she returned ill, along with stories of Wendigos and wildfires. Not only that, but they were beginning to notice the signs of the Hunt that Caroline so deftly covered for weeks with the help of some Guardians.

Fear fueled their conversations.

It started so small, a flicker of an ember buried underneath leaf litter. But it only grew. If Silas did nothing to stop it, the flames would soon become a wildfire, uncontrollable and dangerous. And with Lukosan arriving for *Joulo* and the wedding, he couldn't handle having his attention divided.

I stopped a few steps short of the border of Arcadia. I used to sit here in the winter before Mother passed into the Other, freezing my paws off to see the active magic of our kingdom. A line always existed between Arcadia and the valley below the Great Mountain, but it made itself known only in the winter.

Sometimes I would stand in the Great River, half of myself at home and half of myself beyond. Snow floated in the soft breeze, melting when it crossed the border. The green of spring warmed me on one side, and the chill of silent winter shushed me on the other. Even on the banks of the river, the creatures would come to drink, to play, and to bask in the magic of our kingdom.

But winter was different now that I'd grown up. No more imagining or playing pretend.

As I stood on the outside of Arcadia, my mind drifted like the snow. I thought of Mother and Father. Would they be on the Other Side to greet me one day? Would they want to? Would I be proud of my choices when that day arrived? Or would I still be full of regrets?

I had already filled in each crack and damaged part of me with a lifetime of regrets.

With only a tiny slip on the icy banks, I leaped across the border. I scrambled around the base of the bluff where Silas and Caroline and I used to hide—our Rauha—and made my way up the main path that cut near the Tailor's Quarters.

I slowed when I passed by a seamstress. *"How is Eden's ceremony dress coming along?"*

She glanced my way, a light blue Hunter's robe draped over her lap while she mended it. "Almost finished. Will you bring her by soon?" She hesitated before adding, "Whenever she's feeling up to it."

I bowed my head, my ears twitching. *"Of course."*

I trotted on, bowing my head in acknowledgment to the few people who gazed my way. I phased when I approached Guardian's Glade and pulled my silver robe off the hook. I'd told Silas I'd wear light blue to

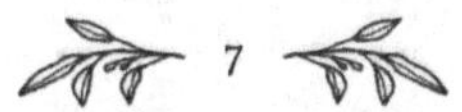

match the Hunters and Guardians, but he'd refused.

"You're still Iain's son," he'd told me.

He didn't know that I felt like an imposter, a wolf in sheep's wool when wearing silver.

After I finished buttoning my robe, I slipped into the Glade. Despite the magic that warmed this place, the sun's pale light barely broke through the film of gray clouds above. The meager rays cast the Glade in a strange dullness.

Kane glanced up from his meal. "Nash, what news?"

"Humans are still day-hiking the Great Mountain. The caretaker, Wildcat, is still up and around, plus he has a few backcountry friends visiting. There are only a handful, and I expect the numbers will dwindle with the temperature in single digits and the wind factor."

"Agreed. Keep an eye out, though. You know how it's been with the Hunt so near. I'd hate for humans in the cities to have another missing hiker case." He swallowed and appeared uneasy, an unusual thing for Kane. "I wish I could figure out why the Hunt set up camp in our valley. They never have in the past, and as far as I know, they've been silent for decades. Is there something we're missing?"

A rhetorical question, though I'd love to be able to give him answers if I had any for myself. Their proximity roused the anxiety in my stomach. I often saw dark shadows in my peripheral vision, but when I turned, I found nothing. They haunted me effortlessly. Even waking, the Wendigo's words from that night in Lukosan lingered.

Son of Nyx.

"Perhaps another wide search is warranted, see if we can find their den." Kane stood, having finished his slice of Spruce bread. "Are you available tonight?"

I lowered my head. "The king needs rest. I'm his night watch."

Kane met my gaze, looking like he weighed his options. "Nash, are you getting enough rest yourself?"

"Oh, I think so."

While not technically a lie, it felt like one.

"Nash, you can tell me when you need a break. You all have a lot of things on your plate right now, and I don't want to add to that. If you don't get enough rest, I'll have to force you to, or you'll get ill."

"Kane, I want this job. I need this job." I hated how helpless I sounded. "Please. And Andra—I mean, Lukosan—is coming. We can't afford to limit patrols now."

He raised an eyebrow. "Tomorrow, take a break for the Passing of the Elders. The next afternoon, head back up to the Great Mountain for another patrol. That way you can get some rest before your night watch."

I nodded. "Have you spoken to Caroline?"

Kane ran a hand through his short hair. "Last I saw, she and Markus were headed to do some research on curses in the Sage Brush. They think it could shed some light on Eden's illness."

I bowed and stepped up on the dais to my brother's bedroom door. Without knocking, I stepped inside. The scent of burning thyme filled the air, and the lanterns burned low.

Silas glanced up when I entered but immediately returned his gaze to Eden's sleeping form. His robe, typically in perfect condition, folded and bunched in places from sitting cross-legged in his chair. His hair didn't look much better; it stuck out in all directions. It needed a good trim, but I'd bug him about it later.

I moved around to the opposite side of the bed and leaned against his wardrobe. His eyes were the worst—sunken in and the skin below tinted blue like he'd been bruised.

I crossed my arms. "*Onni,* you're sure this isn't contagious?"

Silas shook his head. "I don't know anything anymore, Nash."

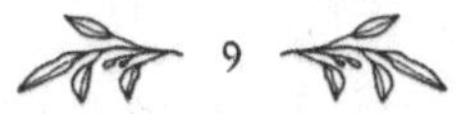

I pushed off the wardrobe and sat on the bed next to Eden. With the back of my hand, I felt her forehead. Her skin warmed my cold hands.

She shifted under the blankets. I watched Silas's eyes dart from Eden's face to her curled-up legs and back again, like sight alone could explain this strange illness that consumed her.

"Si, why don't you get something to eat, yeah? I can handle this." I suggested. "Bring something back for Eden, too. Move your body a bit. You look like bear scat."

He bobbed his head like an obedient child and left without a snide remark.

I hated seeing him like this. It made me nervous. He reminded me too much of myself when Mother had died.

Empty. Wandering. Lost.

When he and Kane were both out of my hearing range, I zeroed in on Eden's heart. It beat steadily, and I counted beats. Too fast.

I tucked her hair out of her face, and she opened her eyes.

"Hi," she croaked.

"The human lives!" I raised my eyebrows. "Is she alive enough to eat a meal? Maybe some bread?"

She smiled. "I love bread. It's my favorite food group."

"I've sent Silas to procure some for you. He's been worried sick about you—almost literally. Can you sit up?"

She bobbed her head, and I helped her move to a seated position, her wooden wedding band a stark contrast to her pale fingers. She winced and set a hand over her chest.

"Anything I can do to help?"

"Can I have some water?" She swallowed. "My throat is really dry."

I moved to the desk. All of Silas's ledgers and notes had been put away on the bookshelf in neat rows. Caroline had tidied while we were gone, and thank Lycaon that she did. The desk was now prime real estate for all of Asa's healing tonics, as well as the jug of fresh water that we kept filled.

I poured a mug and brought it to her, turning the lantern up to brighten the room. "I figured we could surprise Si and give him some encouragement to see you sitting up."

She gulped down the liquid like a water-deprived fish.

"Hey, slow down." I sat next to her again. "There's plenty more."

She wiped her lips with the back of her silver robe sleeve, and I caught sight of the scarring on her arm. Asa had taken great care of her Wendigo wound, promising she'd be back to normal once the wound healed. But weeks later with the gashes covered in fresh pink skin, Eden grew worse.

I considered her robe. The Tailors had presented it to her the day after we returned, and she'd worn it the most since she had little energy to maintain history and documents with Caroline. She'd barely had enough energy to eat.

"Eden." She glanced up at me, so I continued. "What does it feel like? Explain it again."

After taking a shuddered breath, she exhaled. "My chest aches, and I'm incredibly dizzy. Even in my dreams, I can't seem to take a deep breath. And the dreams are unsettling."

"Dreams?"

"Asa gave me valerian to take at night, but it gives me horrible nightmares."

I rubbed the back of my neck, searching for a way to respond. I could talk about my own nightmares, but what good would that do?

Eden shrugged. "Regardless, at least I'm sleeping. My thoughts are clearer than they have been in days."

"Do you feel well enough to do a final dress fitting?" I didn't want to push her, but it would be good to get this over with and encouraging

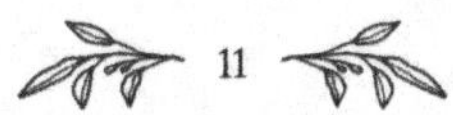

for Silas to see her out and about.

Eden's eyes brightened. "They're almost done?"

I nodded. "We could go today or tomorrow if you want."

Silas opened his bedroom door and stopped on the threshold, staring at Eden. He blinked a few times before setting the tray of food he carried on the table and rushing to Eden's side.

"You're awake. I brought you food. How are you feeling? What can I get you?" His barrage of questions elicited a giggle from Eden, and in their distraction, I stood to leave.

"Nash, wait," Eden called before clearing her throat.

I turned around, an eyebrow raised in question.

Eden's forehead "Are you free the rest of the day?"

"Why?" Silas frowned. "Is something going on?"

"Nash is going to take me to get my final dress fitting." Eden ran circles over Silas's hand that squeezed hers.

"I'll take you." Silas bit his lip. "I want to see."

"I already told you." Eden rolled her eyes; such a human gesture. "I don't want you to see me in my ceremonial dress until our actual wedding ceremony. It's–"

"–a human tradition. I know." Silas huffed. "Please don't wear yourself out. You still have a long way to go until you're back to full health."

Eden's expression soured, but she nodded.

I saluted. "I'll come back to escort you after you eat. I need to talk to Markus."

If they researched curses, maybe they discovered a way to get our queen back.

Lycaon knows we need a miracle.

2
CAROLINE

I T WAS USELESS. I told Markus as much, but he seemed determined to prove me wrong.

"I think it could help." He flipped through a few more pages in a large, dust-covered tome. He sat perched on the edge of a bench at one of the tables in the Sage Brush. This darkness had become more welcoming each time I delved into its depths. Each time, Markus made this place feel a little more like home.

But now, his false hope burrowed under my skin.

"Markus, please listen to me." I tried to keep my tone as level as possible. "Time will not change anything. Time runs like a river, and we're powerless to stop its current."

Maruks inhaled, closing his eyes. "I can at least try."

"You can't study for life like it's a test of mind or strength."

"She's right, you know," Leander piped up from his seat near the crackling blue flames in the center of the room.

Leander had been looking where most of the Seers couldn't look.

The rest of the Seers had sight and Sight, which led to occasional blind spots from the distractions of visual stimuli. Being without his physical sight, Leander had less to distract him from his true Sight. He had more clarity than the eldest of the Seers.

"Thank you for that insight, Leander." I held my hand out to him, raising an eyebrow at Markus. "When are you going to learn that you were chosen for this? There's no cleaning yourself up to appear more Elder-worthy. There's no proving yourself more capable or intelligent. You already *are* the Elder; this ceremony is a formality."

Markus's leg started to bounce. "But what if something goes wrong? What if a *muut* shows up? Owls are basically the death omen. Or what if I embarrass myself and no one trusts my judgment anymore? Or what if I say all the wrong things at the wrong times? What if I can't remember what to do?"

"Markus." I sat next to him, stilling his bouncing knee with a gentle hand. "You already know it. The knowledge is already inside of you."

Markus groaned. "I know. I do, I know. But it's difficult to remind myself of that. I don't feel adequate for this job. I wish I had more time to prepare."

I tucked a strand of his sandy-colored hair behind his ear. "You're going to be fine. I'll be right there with you."

"As will the entire kingdom," Leander called over his shoulder.

"Go fertilize a tree." Markus shook his head.

"Did Ransom say anything about those star charts?" I asked, turning my gaze toward Leander.

He didn't move from his position. "Nothing I couldn't have already said."

"Show me."

For a moment, Leander sat motionless by the fire's edge, the scent of burnt sage ever present. Without a word, he stood and walked to the

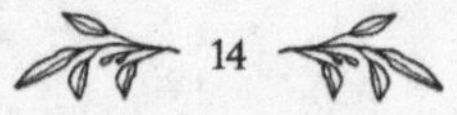

table next to us.

At Leander's table, a large map of the stars lay nailed to the wood.

"Here is the Princess." He felt for the small holes in the map that made up the constellation. "And East of her foot, the Brotherhood. The Snow Moon will fill the Bull, and the light of the Brotherhood will dim before *Joulo*. But not before the Raven's sparks fall upon us. And they will come again, the second night of *Joulo*."

Markus furrowed his brow.

"So you're saying what, exactly?" I peered over Markus's shoulder. "The meteor showers are going to start more wildfires or something?"

Markus shook his head. "It's metaphorical. A new beginning at the foot of the Princess, an entry into the kinship of sorrow, but new beginnings will be found in the love born from the darkness."

"How in Lycaon's name did you get that from a star chart?" I rubbed my temples. Seers had a way of confounding me in every way possible.

"The black moon," Leander explained with a shrug. "It's obvious."

I shook my head. "Please enlighten me."

"The month passes away under the black moon, a symbol of fresh beginnings." Markus ran his hands through his hair, leaving it sticking up in many places. "It looks like a curse bred from the dark, but it's actually a blessing."

"What is the curse, exactly? Eden's illness?" I stared down at the Brotherhood constellation. I stuck my hand in my pocket and let my fingers brush against the small stone I carried from Nyx's cairn. It had become almost soothing to me, a reassurance to know that his cairn could never be rebuilt. But I kept it hidden from the others, afraid of what they might say. Could it be bad luck to carry it around?

Leander shrugged. "Time will tell. The curse could be her illness or something of another nature."

My thoughts drifted to the blood-splattered stone. Surely it wasn't the issue. Wouldn't everyone be affected by it if the curse attacked by proximity? Unless it only targeted humans…

"Knock knock."

I turned to find Nash at the threshold, his intro to a bad joke pushing me out of my thoughts.

"No one's going to say 'who's there'?" He held his hands out.

"Who's there?" Markus sighed.

"Wafer!" Nash rubbed his hands together like a little kid.

"Wafer, who?" Markus rolled his eyes at Nash but grinned at me. He'd been putting up with my brother's antics since the trio returned from Lukosan.

"I've been a *wafer* a long time, but I'm here now."

"Boo!" I called. "Too soon."

Nash smirked and plopped down on the empty tabletop, propping his feet up on the bench. "So, give me all the juicy details. How is the curse-breaking coming?"

"No curse-breaking, but a lot of nonsense about the black moon and Raven's sparks." I leaned against Markus, resting my chin on his shoulder.

Nash perked up. "Meteor showers?"

Leander inclined his head. "We should probably talk to Aubrey and see what she suggests."

"Why not Ransom?" I ran my thumb over the stone in my pocket again.

"Aubrey will know more about the stars, though it might be smart to talk to both of them." Markus turned and kissed my forehead. "But I have to get back to studying."

A loud groan escaped my lips and joined Leander's mumbles as Markus moved back to his colossal tome next to my brother.

Nash peered at the book. "Are you seriously studying for this

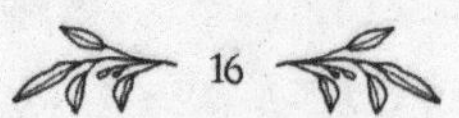

ceremony?" He stole the book from Markus and closed it.

"Give it back." Markus reached for it.

Nash held it out of reach. "Nope. No more studying. Go take a nap. I find they help me much more than reading the same thing over and over."

Markus turned to me to defend him, but I shrugged. "He's right. Go rest."

Markus groaned in response.

"*Ja rakassen,*" I said in a sing-song voice.

"I love you, but I don't like you right now." With an exaggerated frown, Markus disappeared down one of the darkened hallways of trees to his room. After today, he'd be on his own in the Elder's Study.

"I believe I'll go find Aubrey and Ransom to discuss the celestial movements in the next few weeks." Leander disappeared down a different tunnel of trees.

"And then there were two." Nash pursed his lips. "How are you doing, sis?"

The thought of Nyx's stone flashed in my mind, but I pushed it aside, willing my heart to stay steady. "Fine."

He raised an eyebrow in response.

"What? It's true! I've been helping Markus prepare for this ceremony and checking on details for Eden and Silas's wedding. I've also taken on management of Kane and the Guardians since Silas has been busy, but it's not too much work."

Nash leveled me with a glare. "Along with the preparations for Andra and Lukosan's arrival, managing the Kitchens for wedding prep, and organizing *Joulo* celebrations? Not to mention, you'll be getting married come *Starra.*"

All of the things he listed were approaching at an unbelievable speed. With Silas practically absent, given how much time he spent

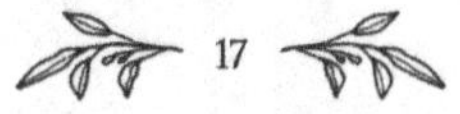

away from his duties so he could care for Eden, people dumped responsibilities in my lap. I could handle one or two things, but so much rested on my shoulders that I'd barely had time to breathe.

I hadn't even considered my wedding in all of this. I'd only thought of the well-being of Arcadia and Silas.

"All right, it's a lot. But I'm holding it together," I grumbled. The light shifted, the blue-tinted Sage Brush flames flickering in Nash's glossy eyes. I wondered when he'd last slept. "But how are you doing? How's the patrol going?"

He shrugged. "Lots of snow and trees and stones. Nothing out of the ordinary on my end."

"And you're eating enough and sleeping and getting time to rest? Aren't you taking the night shift for Silas most days?"

"Lycaon, you sound like Mother." Nash laughed, but it rang hollow to my ears.

I moved to sit next to him, shaking him gently with one hand. "I'm worried about you."

"Don't waste what little free time you have worrying about me. I can take care of myself." Nash chuckled. "Why don't I take over communication with Andra? She and the pack will be here in a few days, so I won't have enough time to screw anything up."

"Are you sure you'll have enough time?"

He dipped his head. "Positive. It'll be a breeze."

I chewed on my bottom lip. "And you're sure you'll be able to manage? You'll tell me if you can't handle anything?"

He rolled his eyes. "Yes, Mother."

I took Markus's book from Nash and pulled out the loose paper at the front. "This is the last correspondence I received from Andra. They should arrive the day after tomorrow, so you won't have to worry about them at the Passing of the Elders tomorrow evening. If you can, ensure that there's ample space for them either north of Mender's Heath or south of the Boneyard."

"Easy as breathing." He grabbed the letter. "Should I respond to Andra?"

I shrugged. "If you want. You can tell her where you'll wait to receive them, that way she'll know to expect you and not me."

He nodded. "Caroline?"

I hummed in response, straightening the other documents from the book.

"Do you think we'll figure out what's going on with Eden? I mean, without outside help? Do you think she'll be able to heal before... before–" He swallowed.

"I don't know." I stuck my hand back in my pocket and held the stone in my fist. I breathed deep and wondered again if the stone had anything to do with Eden's illness. "All we can do is pray something is discovered and that Eden is as strong as we thought."

"She's already stronger than I thought she'd be in the beginning." Nash smiled. "She's perfect for Silas. I'm happy for him. And I'm happy for you, too. Markus is a great choice."

I tousled my brother's unkempt hair. "One day, you'll find someone. It'll be unexpected and intense. And nothing else will matter after that."

"Maybe. But I tend to be a lone wolf." He howled a wimpy, fake call.

I bumped his shoulder with mine. "You know I'm always here for you, right?"

He averted his eyes. "I know."

I worried about Nash. I wondered if he would be happy in the end, if the bruise color under his eyes would become permanent, and if I'd always be able to see his ribcage through his skin and fur.

Only time would tell.

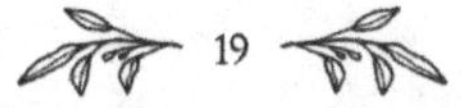

3

SILAS

"**T**HERE HAS TO BE AN HERB OR ANTIDOTE.**" I paced the row of jars at Mender's Heath, out of sight of anyone in the rooms with illness or injury. "We're missing something, that's all."

"*Je kunan*, I've tried everything I know." Asa watched me, one hand propped on his hip. "Maybe it's time we considered taking her back to a human healer."

"No," I snapped, freezing in place. I opened and closed my fists a few times. "No. There has to be something else we can do. The Seers are researching curses, and Nash mentioned that humans get some sort of lung illness in the winter. It'll pass—she needs time. Have we considered the scarring on her arm from the Wendigo?"

Asa sighed. "Yes, and it's healing beautifully. It's not infected or inflamed, and the scar isn't growing. It might not even be visible in a year or two."

I massaged my forehead, head throbbing with pain. "It's my fault she got injured in the first place, and now she has to live with the memories and a daily reminder on her arm. But even if the scar isn't an issue, maybe there's something a Wendigo could tell us. If we found one, we could capture it and question it."

"*Je kunan.*" Asa frowned. "I really must protest."

I straightened. "If you won't keep trying all options, I'll relieve her of your care."

I hated this—hated fighting a man I regarded in the highest esteem. But I wasn't about to give up on Eden. She'd been so lively when I brought her lunch. She ate her meal and talked with me about our wedding and human wedding traditions. Eventually, we ended up lying down and talking quietly about the adventures I would take her on someday. And at some point, she drifted to sleep. When she breathed even and deep, I touched the back of my hand to her forehead. But even to me, her skin burned, illness boiling underneath.

She'd been coughing more often, getting fatigued from simple things, and struggling to keep her breathing steady. She covered it up with laughter and listening well while she walked among our people.

Treading carefully to not wake her, I snuck out and made straight for Asa.

"Silas." Asa sounded stern. "I will continue my care, but please consider the idea of taking her to a human healer. One day, that may be your only option."

He waved for me to follow. I hesitated, but stalked after him. He led me down a short path and stepped into his personal room. Two shelves were full of books and scrolls and jars of herbs. He reached for the first book on the shelf. "I've flipped through these thousands of times, but maybe your eyes will see something mine do not. Help yourself to any of these books, and tea if you would like."

"Thank you," I breathed, flipping to the first page.

Since our return to Arcadia, I'd fought an uphill battle. My people

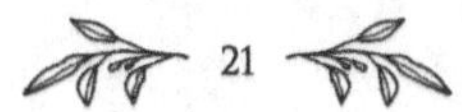

began to ask questions about Eden's illness, and they all assumed she'd never be well again. I addressed them all together only once and spoke of Eden's harrowing encounter with a Wendigo, how she showed courage, and how she'd faced it and survived. But rumors started to spread about a curse, poison, and someone even brought up Nyx again.

There'd been so much to do and catch up on when I returned that it'd been difficult to manage the people's view on Eden. They didn't know her like I did. They didn't love her like I did. And love wasn't something that gave up when terrain grew difficult. I would bear this, endure it, and outlast it like I carried the illness instead. Because she and I would never be separated again.

But what if she does need a human healer?

I shook the thought away and flipped to another page. I didn't trust the humans to take care of Eden. I'd put her in such a precarious situation, stealing her away from the human world to come live and be loved in Arcadia. If I returned her—even until she healed—they would take her from me. I wouldn't be able to fight it without exposing all *virlukos*, and I would lose her forever.

I couldn't. I would find another way.

Asa piddled behind me in his room. "I take it that preparations for the Passing of the Elder ceremony are complete?"

"Almost," I muttered, eyes scanning old words on brittle paper. "Getting finishing touches done tonight while Eden is getting fitted for her ceremony robes one more time."

"So long as she's strong enough." Asa grumbled.

I turned to meet his eye. I needed him to have the same conviction I did about Eden, that she would overcome this. "She will be."

I only hoped I would be right in the end.

4
EDEN

“**T**URN AROUND.”

Nash blinked. “It’s not like I haven’t seen you before. We went skinny-dipping in the lake with Archer, or did you forget?”

The Tailors glanced up at me from my position on a low table.

“That’s not the point, Nash, it’s just–” I held my head in one hand. “I’m not there yet, okay? It’s still a bit strange.”

“Fine. Turning around.” Nash made a big show of covering his eyes and facing away.

“Thank you,” I murmured before dropping my silver robe that marked me as royalty. Wild to believe that I would be a queen in less than two weeks.

Despite the magical barriers between Arcadia and the chill of the Smoky Mountains in December, I felt the cold prickle over every inch of my bare skin. I had a fever again, but I couldn’t show it. I needed to show the people of Arcadia that I could handle this. Two Tailors pulled the fabric of my ceremonial dress up past my chest and helped me slip my arms into the sleeves, covering the jagged scar on my arm.

The fabric settled over my shoulders, but a breeze cut through the gaps in the sides, eliciting a shiver from me. I peered down at my side. "Is this going to stay—"

"Oh, no. One more thing." One of the Tailors unspooled a long piece of white fabric.

"Can I look?" Nash mumbled behind his hands.

"Not yet," I chided while the Tailors gently wrapped the fabric around my waist like a belt. I glanced over my shoulder to see them tie a bow in the back.

"Final touches," one of the Tailors said, buttoning the ends of the sleeves where they met my wrists. The other Tailor placed a woven crown of juniper on my head.

I raised an eyebrow, and the Tailors beamed. "Okay, we're done."

"I can turn around?" Nash clarified.

I hummed, and he turned to face me. His face softened and a smile lit his face. "You look like a forest nymph."

"Don't tell me those are real, too." I crossed my arms, noting that I could move easily in the sleeves and belt addition. It resembled human fashion more than Arcadian, and I was grateful for that small gift.

Nash picked a juniper berry off the crown and rolled it around between his fingers. "Wood nymphs are rare, yet Andra swears they met one further east. But seriously, E, you look beautiful. Silas won't be able to speak for a week when he sees you."

I smiled and wondered what the ceremony would be like, if it would feel at all like a human wedding or if it would be unrecognizable, perhaps uncomfortable.

"Do you think that if…" I started, but whatever question I'd meant to ask disappeared like the last rays of a sunset. Mentally, I reached after it, scrambling to hold on to the thought of *something*, but my hands emerged empty.

"If what?" Nash tossed the juniper berry and crossed his arms.

I held my head in my hands, squeezing my eyes shut. "I don't know, my brain is a bit hazy right now."

Nash's contentedness slipped into concern. "Are you feeling okay? Do you need to sit down?"

I shook my head, but the motion tossed my stomach like a boat in a stormy sea. I blinked a few times as my vision darkened around the edges and a ringing started in my ears. I crouched to avoid a fall if I passed out.

Nash's arms were under mine in an instant, and the Tailors soon after. I could hear Nash's panic, but none of his words penetrated. I leaned my head back, but I felt a strong hand push my head toward my knees.

Nash's words sloshed through my semi-consciousness. "Slow, deep breaths. Come on, deep breaths, Eden."

I obeyed, but felt the swimming sensation come over me again.

"Is it too tight?" I heard Nash ask.

Suddenly, the warmth of the belted sash disappeared, and the cool breeze chilled my sides. I trembled, and my body seemed to twitch in parts of its own accord. I couldn't stop the shaking. The Tailors unbuttoned the sleeves and removed the juniper crown. And after a moment, I lifted my head. I felt Nash's fingers graze my cheek, cupping my face.

"The human lives!" He smiled, but I could see the concern behind his eyes. "Tell me what hurts. What's different?"

"Dizzy." I swallowed, but my throat felt tight. "Sorry."

He tucked a thumb under my chin before pulling his hand away. I missed the warmth.

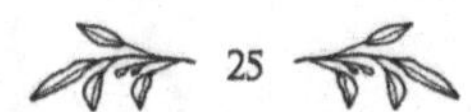

Nash frowned. "Don't apologize. You've been sick, and you're still recovering."

I caught a glimpse of the Tailors, making themselves look busy on the far side of the clearing. The whole kingdom would soon know about my fainting spell. But worse, my bones ached, and my limbs shook. I tried tensing my muscles and curling into the fetal position, but nothing I tried controlled the tremors for long.

"Let's get you back, yeah?"

I nodded weakly.

"First, we have to get your robe back on, okay?" Nash pulled at one of the sleeves, and I didn't protest. The whole forest spun. Pain riddled my body, waves of aches flooding my system. It hurt to move, to feel the air brush against my skin, and to draw a breath.

The Tailors and Nash lifted me enough to pull the dress down and fit me back into my silver robes, fastening the last few buttons before I stumbled off the low table and vomited in nearby bushes.

Nash mumbled something behind me to the Tailors, and soon, I had a mug of water. Nash held my hair back, and we stayed until nothing else came out.

"I'm sorry. I'm so sorry." I moaned, leaning against Nash.

"Hey, stop apologizing. This isn't your fault."

"Whose fault is it? I have words for them." I wiped my lips with the back of my hand.

Nash's chuckle rumbled against me. "Even ill, you have a sense of humor. Do you feel well enough to ride?"

With effort, he helped me stand. He disrobed and phased, bowing to give me an easier time of climbing on. I held his robe in one hand and grasped his fur with the other, my wedding band standing out against my pale skin and his dark fur. He didn't complain, though I knew I must've been pulling tight. He was my lifeline in a swirling sea of trees and an endless ocean of pain.

Silas wasn't around when we returned, and a wave of gratitude washed over me. I'd been so careful, so good at pretending I'd been all right. I couldn't bear to let him down. But I wasn't getting any better.

Nash handed me water, along with a bite of bread to help settle my stomach.

After a minute or two, Nash left and returned with a steaming mug. "Doctor's orders." He passed me a hot cup of tea. "Pine tea with mint and mallow. Best for healing the stomach."

"Add that to my list of illnesses," I groused.

"Are you keeping a list of symptoms?" Nash moved around the room, straightening things while he went. He fixed the bookshelf, the rack of crowns, our wardrobe and the minimal clothes within, and the desk, before settling in Silas's chair.

"In addition to nausea and vomiting, dizziness, difficulty breathing, abnormal heart rate, fatigue, and brain fog? At this point, this illness could be anything, and I think that bothers me the most. I wish I had the stamina I had before all of this." I inhaled deeply before sipping at the tea. My throat still burned from the stomach acid. "I mean, it's not like I lived my life on a couch before coming to Arcadia. I hiked for my job. I paid attention to my nutrition."

Nash propped his chin on his palm. "Hopefully, we'll have answers soon."

I set the tea on the side table and gazed up at the darkening branches. "I wish I had something to read. I used to fly through books when I got sick. But not having a library or bookstore to visit really does put a damper on my reading goals."

Nash perked up. "Oh, I miss bookstores. The smell, the atmosphere, the quiet reverence. It's magic."

I chuckled at the image of Nash in a bookstore. "I forget you

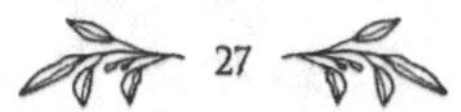

mingled with humans. Did you read any good books?"

"Oh yeah. I'm a big fan of the *Lord of the Rings* because of the dragons. I also enjoyed the lore of *Lake of Glass*. And the last one I read before–" he swallowed. "Well, before my memories go blank for a while, was *Divine Rivals*. I really connected with the characters in that one."

"Really?" I giggled. "I didn't think you'd be one for romance."

He put a hand to his chest like I had injured him. "Hey, just because I didn't fall in love with a royal werewolf king doesn't mean I can't dream of my own sweeping romantic saga someday."

"You'll have your moment, Nash. And she'll be one special woman."

"Enough about my nonexistent love life. We need to get you books."

"Really, Nash. I don't want to add any stress for anyone."

"Nonsense." Nash leaned forward. "How about this—on my next patrol near Pigeon Forge, I'll look for one of those little book birdhouse things and grab a few I think you might like."

"It won't be dangerous that close to the city, will it? I don't want to get you in trouble."

He scoffed. "Me? Get into trouble? Never. I'm the king of the human world, thank you very much. I'm the only one from Arcadia to spend an extended amount of time in their company. I'm practically a *virlukos* ambassador to humans."

"You have a point." I sighed, feeling guilty for asking so much of him. "If it won't be too dangerous, it would be nice to have a few books to read that aren't the history of Arcadian law. But don't forget that this was your idea."

"You have my word." He bowed his head. "In the meantime, since I don't have any exhilarating fantasy novels, how about I tell you a story?"

I grinned and snuggled down under the blankets.

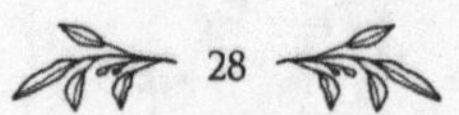

Nash cleared his throat. "Once upon a time, there lived a wolf boy who discovered a city named in his honor."

I sat up. "You've been to Nashville?"

"Hush! Don't spoil the story. Now..."

Nash began telling the tale of the first time he discovered Nashville, its neon lights and loud country music. The boots, the denim, the line dancing, and everything in between.

It reminded me of the time my parents brought me to Nashville for a work event, but they left me at the hotel while they explored the city. I visited later on my own to look at Belmont University, but that night alone in the hotel room as a young child stuck out the most in my memory.

What a contrast to now have a family that loved me and wanted me around. A family that would go out of their way to care for me when I was so ill. It wasn't lost on me how special that was.

In the haze between consciousness and slumber, I worried what would happen if I needed a medically trained doctor to kick this sickness. Would I lose this family I'd grown to love so much? Would I have to say goodbye to Arcadia? It had been almost a month of progressively worse days, the nightmares being the worst side effect. While I drifted into the dark, I wondered when it would end.

I sat at Rauha, my back against a large boulder while I gazed over the valley below. The sun had risen over the far-off mountains, and I swore I could see my childhood house in the distance.

It was Christmas. Someone opened a gift under my grandmother's decorated tree. I wanted to see, but the valley stood in the way. The house was too far away.

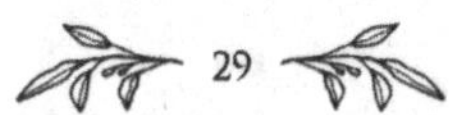

"Wait." I coughed on the word, forgetting that it hurt to speak.

I blinked a few times, but my vision never cleared enough for me to be sure. I knew that wasn't where our house had been. Had it moved? And why had I not been at Christmas dinner?

"AHK!" A croak startled me to my feet.

Among the branches of a yew tree, a white raven perched. I'd heard of the phenomenon, but had never beheld it with my own eyes. It peered at me with sky-blue eyes.

I cleared my throat. "Where did you come from?"

"Who?"

"No, where?"

"Who am I?" The raven cocked its head to the side the way that birds do. "Don't you know?"

I spoke to a raven, a white raven, and it spoke back. Could it be a Spirit? Did I know it already?

"Why are—" I dissolved into another coughing fit.

The white raven spooked, pale wings fluttering through the thin branches of the yew tree. The noise of its wings echoed and amplified. And I realized I hadn't spooked the raven, but something unnatural cracked behind me. I spun around, and the valley below submerged in thrashing waves from behind the Great Mountain—the Flood.

I tried to run, but my limbs didn't respond. I heaved one leg up at a time, pulling myself farther into the trees, but the water burst over the boundary, racing straight for my legs.

I tumbled into the abyss.

All I could think, the only words my brain could conjure weren't even mine. They were words questioning my identity, where I belonged, and what place felt like home to me. They were the white raven's words:

Who am I?

5

NASH

RELIVING THE PAST had a strange way of healing old wounds. For years, I'd run emotionally and physically away from reminders of the pain. But grief is like a river flooded by *Starra* showers: if you don't watch your step, the current could swallow you whole and drag you under.

I eyeballed the honey collected by our kitchen hands. They often gave the task to the pups, encouraging bravery while allowing them to learn another piece of what it meant to be a *virlukos*. It meant taking great care of the other creatures, big and small, ensuring their safety and prosperity in relation to the rest of *Shaconage*.

I set a pot of water to boil while I dug around in the pots and baskets for what I needed. I pulled out this season's persimmons; baskets on baskets had been filled. I chopped the fruit into small chunks—a tedious task—stopping only to pull the water away from the heat.

I slipped one of the seeds out, wiping the pulp off with my robe sleeve. Legend went that the persimmon seed predicted the winter.

I nestled the seed sideways between my back teeth and squeezed until I heard it pop. Pulling it out, I slid a nail between the two sides of the seed and opened it, revealing the shape of a knife.

Bitter cold.

As expected with the intense chill we'd had so far.

As I continued work on the *kulas*, kitchen staff flitted in and out, all busy drying or pressing or crushing or folding or roasting or sorting. Some returned with freshly picked maypops, spicebush berries, and dock, their hands coated in a thin layer of dirt and soil under their fingernails.

I watched them move around each other, a dance almost like the bees when they work on the hive. Guilt, fresh and sticky, dripped down my spine. I chose to leave this, to forge my own path and forsake the family I'd been born into. I left to flee from my pain, but I didn't realize the gift I'd left behind. I left the dance, and now I struggled to find the steps again.

I owed that to my lack of memory. The more I grasped at the lost memories, the darker that void appeared in my mind's eye. Each time I tried, it felt like recalling a dream only to come up short, wondering who you dreamt of, where you were, or if you even dreamt at all. I cursed Nyx each time my thoughts fell short, teetering at the edge of the void.

I thought back to that pull, the curiosity that burned through me on the top of the Great Mountain. That voice saying, *Do I dare?*

What would I run into down that trail where dark creatures laid that beast to rest? Would I find the reason why the wild shunned me? And though I was Iain's son and not Nyx's, wasn't I a son of the wild, too?

"I think your water is cool enough." Lilah smiled at me from where she folded dough, her things scattered near the pot of water I'd heated.

"*Bene.*" I dipped my head in gratitude. "Is this bread for tonight?"

Her smile grew wider. "One loaf of many. We're all proud of Markus. He's done so much work to get to where he is today. And he cares about the pack."

Another few drops of guilt trickled their way down my spine, sending a chill running over my shoulders. Logically, I knew her words only had one meaning, but it felt like a cut. *I* should've cared more for the pack. *I* should've done more work to prove myself. *I* should've made them proud.

Deep down, I feared they would turn on me, and I waited for the other paw to drop, to cast me to my fate in the wild all alone. I feared that they would give me exactly what I'd asked for in the first place: isolation and freedom from pack responsibility.

But where would that leave me?

"Nash?" Lilah's flour-coated hand waved in front of my eyes. "You okay?"

I blinked myself back to the present moment. "Yeah, lost in my thoughts."

"Why don't you finish this batch of *kulas* and take a break? It still needs the final touch from the *kuslar* if you don't mind getting them to come help."

A break isn't what I needed, but a distraction...

"Yeah, that might be nice." I forced a smile, reaching around her for the water.

Lilah returned to her loaf, and I added a little bit of the water to the batch of *kulas*, swirling the liquid to mix the honey into the water. Once it had all incorporated, I tossed in the persimmons.

"I'll be back." My feet crunched across the pebbles and shells of the Kitchen clearing before settling into the cool, soft moss and soil of the forest.

I picked my way to the riverside, keeping my eyes peeled for the telltale signs of *kuslar*.

As I walked, I thought back to the morning, swimming with Silas. I finally worked up the nerve to pitch an idea I'd considered since my return to Arcadia. I knew I stood on shifting sand with Silas, so I figured this might turn the odds of staying in my favor.

I saw a future where the packs of *virlukos* scattered across the continent were united. A future where interpack relations were a common occurrence rather than a rare one. Once, long ago, Arcadia and Lukosan had been one pack. But somewhere amidst the rapids of time, the packs split and separated for good.

But did it have to be that way?

That's the question I pitched to Silas, the idea that maybe my job is to bring the packs back together. And not just Arcadia and Lukosan, but all of them. Surely I could invite other packs to Arcadia. If it worked with Lukosan, who's to say it wouldn't work with other packs of *virlukos*?

Silas promised he'd think about it, and I'd been running the conversation over in my head ever since.

Listening to the soft rippling of the river's current, I crouched by a hollow stump. I peered inside, but I found nothing. Instead, I cast my gaze over to the undergrowth near the river. I ran my hands through grass and winterberry before I found what I sought.

Ferns danced in the slight breeze, and I spotted a white-belled foxglove in their midst. I heard their whispers before I glimpsed their forms. Humans never listen long or hard enough, but I'd always had better patience in the silence. The *kuslar* whispers melded with the rustling of the leaves, but I could catch their soft words spoken in the Ancient Tongue.

They were hosting a party tonight while we were busy working.

Kuslar and their festivities.

"*Onni, carakuslar?*" I whispered.

The forest grew quiet, and the only sound was the water slipping over the stones. Beneath the bells of the foxglove, tiny hands pulled the flower out of a small elfin face. The petite, winged creature stared up at me through delicate lashes.

"*Onni!*" I bowed my head. "*Rauha ussen. Sen vene usslava lo kulas?*"

The single *kusla* fluttered forward. She whispered something that I didn't quite catch.

"*Ja doleo?*" I scooted forward and she jumped back. I froze, trying not to move a muscle.

Eventually, she spoke. "*Varte rikassen sur vaara innusu?*"

Why do you still live with danger inside of you?

"I-I don't know. I can't..." I shook my head. "*Ja nisur rauha.*"

"*Rauha nisen. Rauha nivene. Senus vanni surmyt rauha au onni Kanati, lo dumahn.*"

Peace isn't yours. Peace has left you. Bid farewell to the peace of the past, and welcome the Hunt, the future.

The conversation felt so similar to the *micca* in Lukosan. So why did it scare me more?

"*Panni.*" I whispered.

"*Lo Lyco e Vapolukos venetem allamyt. Vene auori.*" More of the *kuslar* emerged from hiding, tiny hands and feet and wings appearing from behind twigs and mushrooms and ferns. They all raised their eyes with a mix of fear and awe.

Whispers upon whispers filled my senses, thrumming with the beat of my pounding heart.

The Son of Nyx will rise again. Come and see.

The Son of Nyx will rise again. Come and see.

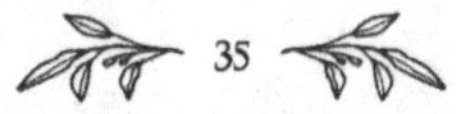

"No. I won't. I'm not him." I stepped back once and twice. The void grew around me, threatening to swallow me whole. But I couldn't let it. I couldn't let what happened to me in the past define who I could be in the present. I couldn't let the *micca* or the *kuslar* or whatever other nettle-brained creature tell me my identity.

But how could I prove my innocence?

How could I show them when I had no idea who I'd been for the past year?

I tore through the forest, desperate to disappear and run away, but I had a job to finish in the Kitchen. I rerouted, slowing my pace, though no doubt my heart would betray me.

"Uh, Lilah?" I started, stopping at the edge of the clearing. "The kuslar refused to come with me. I don't—I don't understand, but they won't help."

She dusted her hands off. "Typical *kuslar*. I'll go talk to them. Why don't you take the afternoon off?"

I exhaled, relieved to hear those words. "Thank you."

Lilah walked back the way I'd come, but I turned toward Guardian's Glade. I poked my head inside, hoping no one would be present. My luck continued when I slipped into Silas's room and it was just me and Eden.

"Hey, *pilukos*." I crouched next to her. "You still getting your beauty rest?"

Her cheeks were rosier than normal, darker against her pale features. Her curls, once springy, lay limp around her face, some sticking to her forehead.

She stirred, smiling sleepily. "Not anymore."

I brushed her hair away from her forehead, her skin burning against my fingertips. "I'll let you get back to sleep so you'll be ready for the ceremony tonight. I wanted to come and tell you that I'll be gone this afternoon. But I'll come back before dusk with a gift for you."

"Promise?"

I locked my pinky with hers. "Pinky promise, E."

After a quick muss of her hair, I left, depositing my robe on the hook outside of the Glade's double doors.

I was on a mission. I only hoped it would prove distracting enough to get the *kulsar's* words out of my head.

The Son of Nyx will rise again. Come and see.

6
CAROLINE

I KNOCKED ON THE TREE I knew would open for me. In the middle of the densest part of the valley stood the Elder's study, a safe place within a secret kingdom. Markus had locked himself in there sometime this morning after our morning meal. Darkness fell, and I still hadn't seen him.

Ransom sent me to find him, to make sure he was still within the boundaries of Arcadia. A sassy remark from Ransom about Markus not being great under duress, but I knew better. And so did Ransom, but Ransom had a lot of pressure on him regarding the root cause of Eden's illness, so I understood why he needed to let off some steam.

We'd all been reading and searching for solutions. We'd studied herbs, rituals, and ridiculous myths, but nothing had healed Eden or lessened her symptoms. She grew worse by the day, and I wondered what state she'd be in for her and Silas's ceremony in less than two weeks.

Eden had suggested pushing it back, but Silas wouldn't hear of it.

He kept saying she'd be better by then. But the people closest to him could tell those words were only to convince himself she could pull through. I knew it must be difficult for him, but pushing the wedding back to focus on getting Eden well again seemed a better option at the moment.

I knocked on the tree's bark again, this time harder. "Markus, I know you're in there! Open up."

I ran through my mental checklist of all the preparations for the Passing of Elders, Lukosan's arrival, and finalizing the dinner plans for the wedding as well as setting the celebration schedule for *Joulo*. I checked with Nash to make sure he cleared everything with Andra and knew where to meet Lukosan when they arrived in Arcadia. They'd be in our valley tomorrow morning, which meant I had to double-check what Nash did because ultimately my neck lay on the line if something fell through the branches.

The tree rippled and stretched until a small window appeared. I saw Markus's blond hair first, visibly disheveled.

"I can't," he groaned.

I straightened his hair through the window. "You can. Let me in."

"No, I mean I can't do this. I'm not ready."

I rolled my eyes. "Fox spit. Open this tree immediately."

His brow furrowed. "Why?"

I stepped back and folded my arms. "Royal business."

Markus groaned again, louder this time. "Fine."

The tree bent out of the way, and I stepped inside. The study was a disaster. "Did you set off a tornado here?"

"No, I've been panicking. I've reread all of the histories, and I don't think I'm the ideal candidate for Elder. Ransom would make more sense, or even Leander. Pick anyone else."

"Markus, sit." I pointed to the chair that had a stack of books in it. My eyes roamed over the room, the shelf sat empty, and books scattered over every other surface. I started picking up while Markus cleaned off the chair to sit down.

I shelved a few books before rounding on him. "You need to stop wallowing. It's not attractive."

"Wallowing? But—"

I held up a hand. "I'm not finished. Elder Macon began training you for a reason. He chose you. Who are you to disregard his last wishes? Aren't you supposed to take any order the Elder or the King gives you?"

"Well, yes—"

"So," I said, raising my voice. "That means you're going to do this whether you feel ready or not. Markus, you are the ideal candidate for the position. You follow the order, you clean yourself up, you do the ceremony, and you become the Elder that Elder Macon saw in you. Whether you like it or not, this is your life now. So what are you going to do about it?"

I could tell he was steaming. I hated tough love, but sometimes people need a swift kick in the tail to do the right thing, to accept their fate.

"Hmm?" I questioned, propping my hands on my hips.

"I'll be at the ceremony," he mumbled.

I crouched in front of him, taking his hands in mine. "Now, I'm taking off the royal robe and putting on my historian robe."

Markus rolled his eyes, but I felt him shift forward. "Am I getting a lecture on history now?"

I shook my head. "Nope. Hi." I smiled. "You want to know what your fiancée thinks?"

He shrugged, but he couldn't fight the smirk on his lips.

"I think you're ready. You've studied and trained and taken wisdom and instruction from one of the best Elders that Arcadia has seen. No one is more fit for this position than you."

He swallowed. "What if I screw up? What if I'm not wise enough?"

"Your predecessors will give you wisdom when you need it. Lycaon knows you'll do the best you know how." I squeezed his hands. "And that's enough."

He nodded.

"Now." I stood. "I'm going to clean up in here while you put your ceremonial robe on."

He raised an eyebrow. "You're staying?"

I smirked. "I'll be too busy cleaning up your mess to pay too much attention to you."

He rolled his eyes and stood to kiss my forehead. "Lycaon, I can't wait to marry you."

I shoved him away with a laugh. "You're so sappy."

He shrugged. "I'm a sappy guy. Practically a sugar maple."

After replacing all the books and scrolls on the shelves and straightening the cot and desk, we left the Elder's study and headed north toward the Yard. Markus's robe was the color of shadow and the first phase of the moon. Mine shimmered bright in the pale light of night.

Moonbeams cascaded through the foliage and bathed the path ahead in a hazy blue. A few wolves meandered down the paths to take their place for the ceremony. I hadn't had too much time to consider how historic this event was, Markus being the youngest Elder in over a century. I had been too busy prepping for Lukosan's arrival, assisting with wedding planning, and working with the Seers on digging for a curse to explain Eden's state.

Worst of all, I spent most of my time with the people of Arcadia dodging questions and stifling rumors about Eden. People started to be concerned for the well-being of Arcadia with such a sickly queen.

Would she be able to rule? If trouble arrived in the valley, would she be able to hold her own?

I kept these comments from reaching Silas. He'd been a shadow of himself since returning from Lukosan, and I feared the doubts would set him off. He rarely got angry, but when he did, it was ugly. Things would break, and he'd start shouting in Ancient. So I kept the peoples' doubts a secret from him to protect him and everyone else as best as I could.

"You ready?" I whispered as soon as I caught the flicker of firelight from the Yard.

Markus swallowed, but I could still hear the hammering of his heart. "As I'll ever be, I guess. Do I look okay?"

He stopped and stepped back, looking down at his charcoal robes. The oiled buttons gleamed in the moonlight.

"You look incredibly handsome, actually, and I'm glad you'll be wearing this one for our wedding."

Markus smirked. "Oh really? You like this one more than the white or violet robes?"

I bobbed my head. "Much better."

"So I walk in when the drums start, Silas paints my face, the Seers chant, and I start the dance."

"See? You know everything." I squeezed his shoulders before nudging him onward. "And we all cheer, the people present you with gifts, they fatten you up with bread and *kulas*, we shower you with blessings, and we go to bed."

Markus exhaled through his lips, shaking out the nervous tremor in his hands. "Right. Easy. Quick and easy."

I kissed him on the cheek. "And this is where you have to do it alone, love."

I walked the rest of the way on my own. To my surprise, Eden sat

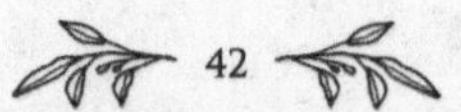

in a chair between Silas and Nash, her two loyal Guardians. Silas had been painted again like *Sarva*, his year of mourning almost complete. After that, his symbols would change.

I took my place on Silas's right side.

"Is he freaking out?" Silas whispered.

"Wait until you hear his heart." I stifled a giggle. "He's nervous that he won't be wise enough."

Silas glanced at me with incredulity. "You're kidding. But Elder Macon chose him."

"That's what I told him!" I rolled my eyes. "He came around—eventually."

Nash cleared his throat. "Let's put him out of his misery and get this party started."

Silas dipped his head to the line of musicians. The two drummers picked up a rhythm that mimicked a heartbeat. Besides a chosen few and us royals, the rest of our people were in wolf form, sitting, standing, or pacing at the edges of the clearing.

Markus stepped into the firelight, heart matching the steady rhythm of the drums. He was meant for this position, for this moment in time. And I marveled, knowing he was all mine.

Proud didn't come close to describing what rushed over me.

Markus stepped up to Silas, glancing at me before closing his eyes. Nash held a mortar with dark paint in front of Silas. Coating a wooden tool with the paint, Silas held Markus's chin and began to paint the elder tree rune on the new Elder's forehead. Markus wouldn't wash his face until the mark disappeared over time.

A solid line with five slanted lines.

Life and death.

Rebirth.

Protection from evil.

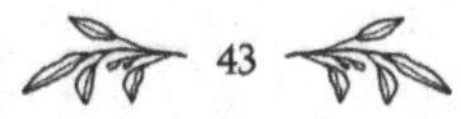

Silas followed this with a series of dots and lines that represented each Elder in our long history. When he finished, Markus's face had been covered in swirling lines and dots, his eyes shadowed by spiraling figures.

Silas bowed to Markus, and the drummers ceased. Everyone followed suit, showing respect to their new Elder. Around us, dozens of heartbeats continued the rhythm of the drums.

Silas stood. Somewhere in the crowd, Ransom—now in human form—began the chant in the Ancient Tongue, an old and distinctive chorus. The other Seers phased and joined in until my ears were full of the confirmation that Markus no longer belonged solely to himself.

He belonged to the pack, and we belonged to him.

Markus stepped back, silhouetted by the firelight. The wolves paced, restless for the start of the dance. The drummers began again, steady and fast. With a determined air about him, Markus began to move with rhythmic, sharp movements. I never had the pleasure of watching him practice. This was a sacred and weighty thing, something only Seers were taught. And we all witnessed history with his dance.

He chanted along with the Seers, and soon they joined the dance. Our people howled. Silas and Nash beat their chests, joining the call, and I picked up the old kulning tune we were taught as pups.

Eden pushed to her feet and moved to stand next to me, taking my hand in hers. My fingers stung at her touch, her body ice cold despite the warmth of the fire. I faltered in my call when I glanced at her. Her eyes sparkled, but not from curiosity like usual. They'd glossed over, and I realized the fever hadn't left her. Lycaon bless her for being at a ceremony, showing face despite feeling so ill.

I gave her hand a squeeze and turned back to Markus who'd been surrounded by Seers, branches of the elder tree held aloft in the dance.

Silas inhaled. *"Rauha!"*

The wolves stood at attention, and the Seers placed their elder branches at Markus's feet, a wreath that would someday pass to the next Elder. Markus's shoulders raised and lowered with each breath. He fixed his eyes on his king.

"*Visun Arcadia, lo surin municci ealla,*" he shouted.

Eden glanced at me, still holding my hand. I leaned over and whispered in her ear as quietly as I could, translating. "We are Arcadia, the greatest pack of all."

"*Autem sir rauha vene roka au vaara e lo feru.*"

"And yet, with peace comes hate and danger from the wild."

"*Vitem ar rikassur rakas au carasur suralla feruna.*"

"We, then, shall live with love and friendship among all creatures."

"*Vionni surlo Gichi, vi Lyca.*"

"This begins with the Elder, our Father."

Silas placed his fist over his heart. "Markus, *ar jeslava avias sennu cara, lyco, au Gichi.*"

"Markus, it's my honor to have you as a friend, brother, and Elder."

The wolves began to howl, the people shouted, and Markus bowed serenely. The Seers reclaimed their elder branches, falling in line behind the chosen Elder. Markus couldn't hold back his grin. He'd managed to get through the tensest part of the evening. Everything else would be easy, like I told him it would be.

"If you will." Silas held his hand out to the path leading to Guardian's Glade. Markus took the lead with Silas following, and the rest of us royals filed in. Behind us, the Seers followed with their branches, and the rest of the pack joined behind.

I threaded my arm through Eden's, and Nash mirrored me on her opposite side. We managed to get her to the throne room without incident.

In Guardian's Glade, Markus hesitated a few steps from the throne.

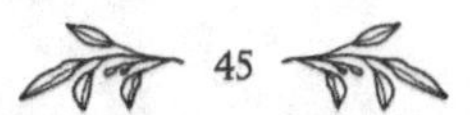

Silas stood beside him and Nash. Eden and I stood behind them while everyone else filed into the open space.

"Are you ready?" Silas whispered.

Markus inclined his head and he stepped forward to assume the throne.

Again, Silas bowed to Markus, and we mirrored the action.

"Let the offerings begin," Silas called.

The crowd thinned while each person left to retrieve their blessing or gift for Markus. Silas slipped into his room and returned with a special robe he'd commissioned before he left for Lukosan. In addition to Eden's ceremonial gown, silver robe, and Historian robe, Silas had requested a garment to be crafted in secret for this occasion.

"A piece of silver for your bright future." Silas grinned when he passed the silver robe to Markus. "Not to be worn until the day *after* you marry my sister."

Markus chuckled, holding the robe lightly in his hands. "Of course, *je kunan.*"

I stepped forward and kissed his forehead, pulling my gift from the pocket of my robe. "Stones to wear so you'll always remember where we will return."

I passed him a necklace I'd made myself from a few stones I'd found from the Great River, holes bored straight through by countless years of passing water. Stacked on top of each other, they resembled a cairn.

Markus immediately draped it around his neck. He kissed my hand and pulled me in for a hug. *"Bene, je rakas."*

Nash approached along with Eden. Nash cleared his throat. "It's not finished yet, but Eden and I—mostly Eden—have taken it upon ourselves to craft a special batch of *kulas* for your wedding. Elderberry, of course."

Markus gazed up at me, nothing but love and confidence living in his eyes.

Each person or family unit from the pack brought gifts to their new Elder. Some lay yew and elder branches at his feet. Others gave him tobacco or ginseng. Some brought teas and breads mixed or baked by hand. And others brought natural gifts from the earth—stones and bones and wood. All would be beneficial for life as the Elder.

But my thoughts linger on the *kulas*. Tradition was to brew enough for every guest to have a few glasses, and if you ran out, it was a bad omen of a lack of joy in the union. And the more I thought about how many batches of *kulas* had to be made for Silas and Eden's ceremony, the more I dreaded my own wedding preparations.

If Silas would give us his blessing, maybe Markus and I could have our own small, moonlight ceremony at Rauha or the Great Mountain instead of having it at Guardian's Glade. And maybe we only had to invite a few important people from the pack—people that meant something to us.

But that would be a conversation for later down the road. First, we needed to get through my brother's wedding and get Eden back to full health. My wedding plans would have to wait.

7

ANDRA

I WOULD DIE IN THIS INFERNAL WINTER. Not from freezing solid or starvation or even sliding off the cursed bluffs surrounding Arcadia's valley.

My best friend was going to murder me.

I didn't have hope that it would be swift or merciful. I expected white-hot fury that melted the snowcapped mountains and smashed them to rubble. I planned for cursed words and shouting in the Ancient Tongue. And I would accept my fate with grace and shame, knowing that I deserved every insult, every wound, every sting. And it would almost be worse to leave me alive.

Because I was about to murder my best friend's bride. Indirectly, of course. And if things went my way, maybe I wouldn't become a murderer and therefore wouldn't need to die to reset the balance.

"An, I know that look." Archer raised an eyebrow. "That's your scheming face."

"This is my normal face."

My brother smirked. "Further proves my point."

I jabbed an elbow into his side, knocking him off his log and into the snow by the crackling fire. We had one more night in the bitter cold before I could peel off my hoodie and enjoy rolling in warm grass and wildflowers.

Archer dusted the snow off with a laugh. "Messing with you never gets old."

"You're lucky I like you." I rested my chin in my hands. "I don't have to keep you around, even if you are blood."

"Come on, you love me. You'd never kick me out." He plopped back down on his log. "I think I'd have to die for you to get rid of me, and even then, you'd come and pester me beyond the grave."

"Don't talk like that." I frowned. "My mind is too overrun with thoughts about death for that. And I'll definitely die first."

He scoffed. "Sure, like you'd be stupid enough to die."

I sighed at his peace offering. "But serious, Arch. What should I do?"

He groaned, letting his head drop back. "I've told you I disagree with you. You need to tell him the truth immediately regardless of the outcome. You need to accept your consequences, whatever they may be."

I sighed. "I can't tell him what I did. He wouldn't believe me, first of all. And second, even if he did believe me, he wouldn't let me near Arcadia ever again."

"Not like we visited much before now anyway."

Archer had a point.

"But we're in an amiable position, and Nash visited us last year!"

My brother's eyebrows shot up. "Oh, I see. Mmhmm."

I sat up. "What?"

He grinned and turned his gaze to the fire.

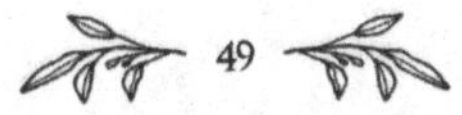

"What?" I scrambled to my feet. "What do your mutt eyes see?"

Arch chuckled. "Not even your insults can dampen my mood now."

I grabbed a quick handful of snow and chucked it right at his face. He blocked most of the blow, but some of the snow managed to stick to his caramel hair.

"What demure actions from a queen."

"Please." I rolled my eyes.

"And an eyeroll! Folks, we have hit a nerve." Archer's smile lit up his face. "Is it because I know something you don't? You'd hate that, wouldn't you?"

"What don't I know?" I folded my arms.

Archer smirked. "You have a thing for a prince."

I rolled my eyes. "I told you, I'm over Silas."

He raised an eyebrow. "Did I say king?"

I opened my mouth to reply, but nothing came out.

Archer said *prince*.

"I don't–" I shook my head.

"She's speechless! What a feat!"

I didn't even have the brain power to throw more snow at him.

He said *prince*. Surely that wasn't true. Surely I would know if I was even remotely drawn to Nash. Surely...

"Well, unfortunately for me and you, once Silas knows the truth, you might not have a shot with Nashville."

"Oh, shut up. His name isn't Nashville. And I won't be telling Silas the truth, so that won't be a problem."

Archer sobered. "Andra, please tell him you ripped a branch off a Mocker tree, had it fashioned into a wedding band, allowed it to be gifted to the human queen of a neighboring pack, and doomed her to a slow and painful death. I'm sure he'll forgive you eventually."

I paced on the other side of the fire. "There has to be a way I can get the ring from Eden and return it to Kalona before she realizes something has been taken from her."

"From the sound of Nash's letter, Eden isn't doing so hot. I'd say Kalona already knows."

I growled. "I could steal it from her while she's sleeping. Or I could ask to try it on."

"Like that would go well, given your past–"

"I could offer to clean it for her. Or get someone to do an engraving on it. Maybe she takes it off when she's cooking or swimming or whatever, and I can snag it."

"Tell him the truth!" Archer threw both hands out in front of him. "Swallow your nettle-brained pride and tell him tomorrow first thing. If Silas turns us away, we go east."

I groaned and dropped back to my seat in defeat. "Anything but that, please."

Archer leaned his elbows on his knees. "Well, keep asking the same question and you'll get the same answer from me. Your friends deserve the truth. Anything else is betrayal in the worst form."

I chewed on my lip for a moment, trying to calculate any other option. "What if they hate me?"

"That's your consequence. My guess is they'll still love you, and they'll love you even more for coming clean before any more damage is done."

"I don't know."

Archer stood. "You don't have to listen to me. You don't even have to have me around if you don't want me here. But if you ask for my advice, at least consider it before rejecting it."

With that, he ducked into his tent.

I sighed. Maybe I would sit here and consider his suggestion until the fire burned out. But I doubt it would ever be as easy as waiting for

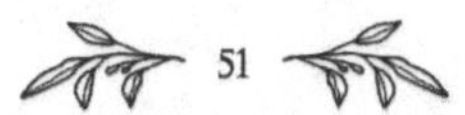

the right answer to come to me. I'd have to decide soon, and I knew whatever I decided would shift everything forever.

Not a big deal.

Just one decision:

The truth or another lie?

8

SILAS

I GAZED UP AT FERU FALLS, relishing the chill of its spray on my fur. It hadn't frozen over yet, but we expected it to after last year.

I gazed down the river where the path to Arcadia meandered through the valley floor under the shadow of the Great Mountain. Snow covered stones and bushes and trees and logs, everything patched together in a white-and-gray quilted wilderness.

I awaited Lukosan's afternoon arrival. Nash was supposed to be here. Eden mentioned he'd come by our room last night, but I must've been fast asleep. For the first time in weeks, Eden seemed capable of recovery, and that knowledge helped me sleep restfully. She'd been to the Tailors, sat up in bed for a few chats, and made it through the Passing of the Elders ceremony. She even stayed awake—and alert—for the entirety of the gift giving.

Concern still lingered, though. I had to be missing something, if only I knew what troubled my Spirit.

Without warning, icy mountain water doused me from head to

claw. Shaking the moisture from my fur, I turned to find my idiot brother pulling himself from the frigid river. Clearly, our morning polar plunge didn't satisfy his masochistic nature.

"*Sorry I'm late.*" Nash shook out his coat, throwing hundreds of water droplets on me.

"*You're always one for an entrance,*" I huffed.

"*No sign yet?*" Nash gazed down the path, his tail wagging slightly behind him.

I shook my head. "*The birds have settled, singing their territorial songs. And the squirrels are starting to go into hiding.*"

"*Humans.*" Nash's ears twitched. "*They'll be here soon. Markus did well last night. One ceremony down and another to go. How's the wedding planning going?*"

A sigh escaped me. "*As smoothly as it can go. Eden's ceremonial robes are almost finished, my ceremony robes are getting touch-ups, the kitchen staff are working on meals, and the kuslar have already communicated about lighting. It's going really well.*"

"*But?*"

I eyed him. "*I'm worried she won't be better by Joulo. We could push off the ceremony, but neither of us really wants that.*"

Nash bowed his head. "*She's resilient. We need to give her time.*"

I shake my coat again, trying to rid myself of the chill that settled over me. I wasn't sure if it had been Nash's antics or the conversation. "*Well, how's the kulas coming?*"

Nash tucked his tail. "*It was going well, but–*"

A collection of laughter and footsteps sounded close by. I turned and waited a few moments until a group of humans and a few wolves rounded the bend.

The wolves noticed us first, picking up their speed to give Nash and me a proper greeting. When Andra and Archer made their way to the front, they both nuzzled under our chins, tails wagging, and the air around us filled with happy yapping. Many of the humans dropped the backpacks they carried.

"You made it." I stepped back, tail wagging while Andra bowed her head. Gratitude surged through me that things weren't awkward between her and me after all that went down last month. With her confession, the kiss, and chaos that ensued after, we'd patched all the damage—emotional and physical—before Eden and I invited the whole pack to Arcadia for *Joulo* and our wedding ceremony. I worried that there might be lingering tension, but it felt like old times again.

"The whole pack is in one piece." She cast a glare at Archer who wrestled Nash near the riverbank. *"Or at least for now."*

"Come on, I'll show you all in."

I took the lead, guiding the procession up behind the waterfall and through the hidden cleft in the stone.

"So you fared okay on the journey?" I craned my neck, ears back to hear Andra behind me.

"As good as expected with the Hunt on the prowl."

"We've had a few issues around Shaconage, but nothing serious. Did you all have any altercations with them?"

Andra snorted behind me. *"Sent a few of them to the Other Realm. Not exactly pretty or what I'd prefer, but when it comes to protecting my pack, I'd do it again."*

I bristled at the thought. It dredged up memories of Nyx and the Wendigo encounters in the past month. I wasn't sure how long this would last. Any time the Hunt appeared, they never stayed for long. Would that ever change?

"Apart from that, the humans struggled with the dropping temperatures and snow, but that's normal for Suya weather. The seasonal snow always slows our moving progress down, and it takes

twice as long to reach our destination. So I'm happy to be here. I can already feel my paws defrosting."

"Did you all have any more wildfire issues before leaving?" I turned the last corner and we filed out into the clearing of my valley, my home.

Andra followed me to the edge of the clearing, stopping to wait for her pack while they spilled out of the cleft in the stone wall onto the green grass of *Starra*. *"Wildfires are always an issue during Suya when it's dry. The snow helps, but as soon as it dries in the valleys, there's always the potential for another deadly fire. Y'all had a bad one several years ago, right?"*

I scrunched my nose at the memory. *"Almost a decade ago. Eight years, maybe? Mother was still alive. She even helped with some of the rehabilitation of the wildlife."*

Nash and Archer trotted over, tails wagging and nothing out of place besides a few slobbery chunks of fur from their tussling.

"Si, good to see you! And grateful to defrost a bit. Where would you like us to set up camp?" Archer's ears pinned back for a moment.

"Good to see you, too, Arch. Bennett will show you to your home for the next month or so." I turned to find Bennett trotting out of the trees. Right on time, as usual.

"Welcome, Lukosan. It's wonderful to have you here." He bowed his head, ears and tail straight. *"If you will follow me, Nash has ensured a clearing for you near Mender's Heath and the Boneyard."*

Archer perked up, bumping Nash's shoulder. *"Perfect for late night sparring."*

Nash nipped at Archer before the latter trotted after Bennett, leading Lukosan to set up camp.

"Are you going with them?" I shifted, watching Andra hesitate.

"How's Eden?" she asked, surprising me with the change in

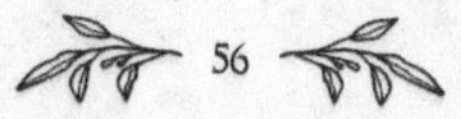

conversation. *"I would've expected her to be here."*

"She's all right." The lie tasted stale on my tongue.

"You don't sound convinced."

I made sure everyone but Nash had moved on with Bennett. *"I'm not convinced."*

Andra shifted her paws in the grass. *"Meaning?"*

Nash rubbed against my shoulder. *"Meaning, he's worrying himself sick over her. She's been ill since we left Lukosan, nightmares and fevers."*

Something shifted in Andra's expression that I couldn't quite catch. *"She's not getting better."*

It was a statement more than a question. Was it that obvious in my face how nervous Eden's illness made me?

I flicked my tail, ears twitching. *"At first, we thought she was improving. She slept a lot, but she'd chat and dance and laugh with us. Then Caroline caught her clutching a tree for support one evening. All of her so-called improvements are really good acting."*

"She's good at putting on a mask," Nash added. *"She musters up enough strength to do what's necessary, but even that reserve of energy has been less and less as the days pass."*

"Can you help her?" The words slipped out before I could stop them. *"Your mother–"*

"Silas, I don't know what illness my mother had. She started getting steadily worse, fatigued and struggling to be present. And she got injured the day before she passed." Her face fell, but her ears perked up. *"If it would make you feel better, I'd love to see Eden. I can talk to her more about everything that's been going on."*

My heart soared. If anything, Andra might be able to see something we've overlooked. And maybe Andra would be my wife's savior.

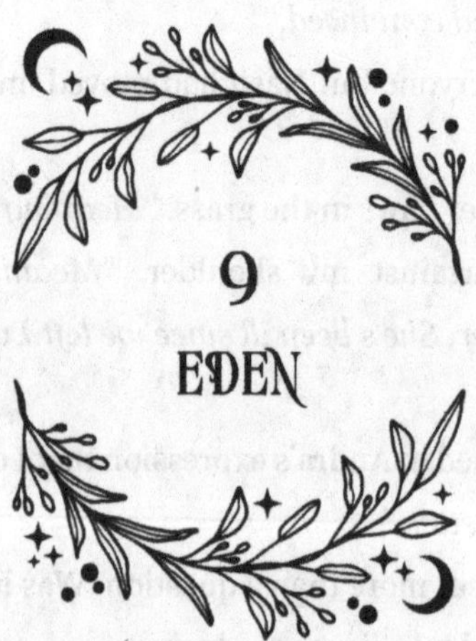

9

EDEN

I'D BEEN ANXIOUS since before the Passing of the Elders ceremony. Nash told me he was leaving for the afternoon but would return with a gift. He'd come in while Silas was sleeping, and I shooed him away. It had been the first time in a while that Silas had fallen asleep so quickly. I didn't want to wake him, but I was curious to know what Nash brought me.

Lukosan had been set to arrive any moment, so my gift would have to wait. I'd been able to sit by the river this morning, a way I could prove to Silas that I could heal. But it was a farce on my end. I'd used all of my strength to get to the river that I had to wait there until I gathered enough energy to crawl back into bed.

In the beginning, putting on a front was easy. I covered up my lack of breath or exhaustion by listening more than speaking or finding a seat while everyone else stood. But each day proved more difficult than the last.

When I woke up from a nap this afternoon, Asa brought me tea and a small meal. I'd picked up a book written in Ancient Tongue and translated a page before having to lie back down. Breathing still hurt, and I was prone to coughing fits when I tried to talk too much. Trying to protect me from questions or in fear of my condition worsening, Silas didn't allow many visitors. The ones that did come by, like Aubrey and Bennett, were only allowed to stay for a short time.

This chronic illness doomed me to a life of isolation.

I stared up at the foliage, listening to the Carolina wrens and woodpeckers chatter back and forth, trying to spot them in the branches.

A knock at the door surprised me. I cleared my throat, which led to a few coughs. "Come in."

A face I didn't expect poked around the door. "Getting your beauty rest?"

"Andra!" I pushed myself up to sit, coughing a bit more with the effort. My lungs burned and lit my chest on fire, but I was so grateful to see someone else. Even if things still felt a little off kilter with Andra, she wouldn't look at me like I would pass at any moment. She'd treat me normally and wouldn't speak fox spit about this illness.

"Hey, you. Can I sit?" She pointed at Silas's chair and Silas and Nash followed her in.

I nodded. She wore a beige robe, something like the one I first wore when I arrived in Arcadia. She sat in the chair while Nash propped himself on the desk, and Silas settled next to me on the bed, both men in their silver robes.

"How are you?" I held my hand out, and she took it. I watched her eyes catch on my ring, but she didn't mention it.

"Good. We're all good. Glad to be here where it's warm." She grinned conspiratorially like warmth was a secret to be kept. "How are you doing? These two told me you weren't feeling well."

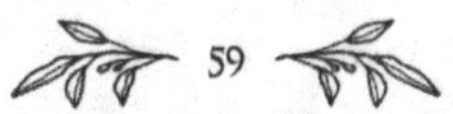

I shook my head. "I've been better. I haven't felt well since we returned home. But I feel better today. I even walked by the river for most of the morning."

A look passed between Nash and Silas. They knew I held back and probably that I hid a lot of the truth, but I wanted to be strong and prove that I'd be okay. If not for my sake, I did it so they would stop worrying over me so much.

I shivered involuntarily.

"Do you need another blanket?" Silas jumped to his feet. "I can go get you another."

"It's okay." I stifled a yawn despite it being early afternoon.

"How about I come hang out with you at breakfast tomorrow?" Andra squeezed my hand before standing, casting another glance at my hands.

"That sounds great, actually. They have me locked in here like a prisoner." I rolled my eyes, smiling at Silas. His shoulders relaxed a bit, and I desperately wished I could ease his tension.

"It's a date." Andra gave me a wave before ducking back through the door to Guardian's Glade.

"I'm going to go find a blanket." Silas started for the door, but Nash caught his arm.

"No, you're not. I'm on patrol duty for the midnight shift, but I can stay and keep Eden company so you can be a king for the afternoon."

Silas clenched his jaw, mulling it over. Eventually, he assented. "Yeah, okay. But please come get me if you need anything at all."

"Absolutely." Nash nodded and turned to me. "I'll go find an extra blanket just in case, and a few more things, but I'll be right back."

The brothers left me to my own devices, and I thought about breakfast tomorrow. Was this Andra trying to reconnect and start over? It would be nice to have that connection, to have a home away from Arcadia and another pack to call friends.

I shivered again, nestling deeper under the covers when Nash returned, a bundle in his arms.

"Merry Christmas! This is for you." He passed me the blanket. "And so are these."

As I wrapped the blanket around my shoulders, he pulled a small stack of books out from behind his back. I recognized a few and stifled a laugh.

"You actually have books for me?" I held the blanket tight around me.

"Of course. We have to keep your mind occupied since you can't run around asking a hundred questions every day." Nash settled into Silas's chair. "I chose this one because it has a full moon and a magical realm that you can get to by dancing. I chose this one because I've heard it has werewolves in it. I chose this one because I loved the main characters. And I chose this one because the main character sounds a lot like you with your art notebook thing."

He passed me the stack of four books in the order of his list. They were a little loved, but he'd found a good little free library to have decent copies of decently popular books. I held *Wildwood Dancing*, *Twilight*, *One Dark Window*, and *Emily Wilde's Encyclopaedia of Faeries* in my hand.

He leaned back and ran a hand through his loose curls. "Now, which one would you like me to read to you?"

I passed him *Twilight* for kicks and giggles. "Maybe I'll dream I'm in Forks instead of lost in Appalachia."

"Bad dreams again?" Nash moved the other books to the desk and dropped into Silas's chair with *Twilight*.

I sighed. "They never stop. I dream nearly every time I sleep, and I remember strange pieces. I think all of them feel like nightmares, but

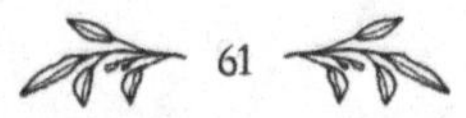

sometimes it's a dream that turns into a nightmare. I wake up feeling even worse."

"Maybe a nice bedtime story will help ease your worries." Nash opened to the first page. "Settle in, *pilukos*. We're about to read about the werewolf and why they're the coolest creatures ever."

I tucked the blankets under my chin and smiled to myself.

"I'd never given much thought to how I would die—though I had reason enough in the last few months—but even if I had, I would not have imagined it like this..." Nash raised an eyebrow. "Very ominous— and it's probably spoiling the ending."

I laughed, which morphed into a slight cough. "Shush! Keep reading."

Nash picked up where he left off. "I stared without breathing across the long room, into the dark eyes of the hunter, and he looked pleasantly back at me. Surely it was a good way to die, in the place of someone else, someone I loved. Noble, even. That ought to count for something."

It seemed comical to me that I sat with a werewolf reading about vampires. Some days, it felt like I belonged to Arcadia, that I'd been here since time began. And other days like this one, I felt untethered, like a fly watching someone else live in my body and doing things I could only have dreamed of.

At some point, I must've fallen asleep, because a mist—thick and rolling—consumed *Shaconage*. And it swallowed me whole.

My body ached and swayed in the tide of the forest. Trees protruded from nowhere, looming large above me. I could sense that I was in danger, though I didn't know why. Something dark and sinister lurked in the shadows, but I couldn't see. Was it the vampire from the book Nash read me? Or did his talk of werewolves make me dream of Jacob Black? The thought made me think of Jacob and Claire from Lukosan, and I wondered if I could find them in Arcadia.

"Can't–" I choked.

Why can't I breathe?

"Can't see," a voice croaked. It was deep and throaty.

Where did it come from?

"I can't–" I swallowed, but it stuck halfway down my throat. I tried to cough, to fight, to do anything. But I couldn't get air in.

I was dying.

"Did we win?" the voice croaked again.

"Help," I gasped, falling to my knees, the mist scattering around me. The ground was all moss, but pain shot through my body from the stone hiding underneath.

The ruins at the heart of Arcadia.

Why am I here? Am I dying?

A shadow shifted in the forest, a body dangling next to a looming figure. The figure threw the body to the ground. I tried to scream, but no sound escaped my lips. Not air, not even a whimper.

"More," a voice called from ahead of me.

"Never," another voice answered to my left.

"More," a third voice demanded to my right.

Pushing to my feet, I felt for the crown I knew was on my head, tall and bent, branches stretching to the heavens like the trees they originated from. I staggered forward, holding its weight in my hands.

The voices continued heckling me.

"Never."

"More."

On and on and on.

"Nevermore! Nevermore! Nevermore!" The disembodied voices squalled in a haunting chorus, one that chilled me to my bones. Their sounds didn't die immediately like I thought they would. Instead, they echoed.

On... On... Onward.

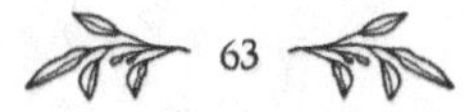

"Nevermore...more...more."

And as strange as it began, the voices died. They left me drowning though I stood on my feet. I choked on fumes I couldn't see.

I'm dying. Why can't I breathe?

A flash of movement drew my attention to my left. Black in the mist, shadow in the fog, darkness in the light. Something had been born of my fears, my agony, my lack of breath—a flutter of wings.

The Raven.

10

CAROLINE

"LYCAON, YOU THINK IT'S THE STARS?" Aubrey asked while tidying up the common area in the Sage Brush.

"I'm not saying anything." I threw my hands up, the perfect picture of a *virlukos* pup throwing a tantrum. "I'm out of other ideas. All I can think about is how *virlukos* get a little strange with the full moon."

Aubrey leveled me with a glare.

I scoffed. "Come on. You know it's true."

"We don't go crazy and eat people!" Aubrey threw a handful of leftover herbs into the fire. They burned with a whoosh and sizzle. "Don't spew that human fox spit at me about werewolves."

"No, we aren't werewolves, but we're restless. During the Beaver Moon, Nash stayed awake for over thirty hours and started messing with the black bears like the nettle-brained catfish that he is. Meanwhile, Silas started hiding from the *micca*, trying to prove he was better at stealth. But he was too distracted to notice the beggar's lice, and it took me an hour to pick all the burs out of his fur."

Aubrey groaned. "I see your point. But Eden shouldn't be affected by it. That's *virlukos* behavior."

"Exactly why I've come to consult the star expert."

She rolled her eyes, but I caught a hint of a smile at the corner of her lips. "Okay, what are your theories?"

"Leander and Markus mentioned the Princess. That was her constellation, right?" I started pacing. "So what if celestial objects around the Princess are affecting her body?"

Aubrey shook her head. "Can't be. It would affect everyone if that were the case. Next?"

I grunted. "She has some human illness that lingers. I've heard of things like this before, and Nash mentioned something about a disease after flying. It can be your stomach or your lungs. And a lot of humans get the flew disease in the winter. Maybe it's a strange human thing?"

I caught Aubrey chewing on her lip.

"What, you don't think that's it?"

She frowned. "Eden would know what that disease felt like, right? So she would've told us by now. We could ask, but it seems unlikely." She grabbed a basket and passed it to me. "Come with me to collect some spicebush?"

I grabbed the basket and followed her east through the Yard and down the river to Feru Falls out in the bitter, cold valley beneath the Great Mountain. We followed the river, careful to avoid the ice and slick patches between the trees.

"Does it feel warmer than normal to you this season?" Aubrey gazed up at the trees.

It was true that it had been a mild winter compared to the previous year, but I didn't like to linger on the events of last year, not with the anniversary of my father's death looming.

I shook my head to clear the bad memories. "It's difficult to judge

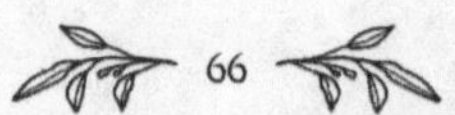

since last year was such a harsh winter. The freeze and all that." I ran my hand over a snowy branch, sending chunks of snow to the forest floor. I ran into Aubrey, catching myself from slipping by grabbing onto a small birch. "*Silva*, what is it now?"

I followed her gaze and caught a flash of something green in the dull landscape. It flickered in the slight breeze.

"Is that glass?" I whispered.

Aubrey approached with slow steps, and I followed a step behind. With each step, my eyes found new things hanging from the switches of a willow. Bottles dangled from the bare branches, clinking against hag stones, railroad spikes, and, to my horror, bones.

I had been on this path less than a week ago, and this tree hadn't been decorated before, and certainly not with such strange ornaments. *Virlukos* always treated bones with respect and would never use them for anything other than burial. Dark hands hung these bones, bottles, and stones.

"*Je slava*," Aubrey hissed.

I jumped back and caught a shout in my throat as a group of deer ran under the willow and crossed the river, disappearing behind a hill. Something must have spooked them.

"Lycaon," I whispered, my heart hammering in my chest.

"Hush!" Aubrey hissed, continuing her path forward.

A cold feeling rushed through my center, something separate from the chill in the air from the thick snow. My eyes scanned the treeline for an invisible foe, and I wondered if I, too, would flee like the deer. This place gave me the creeps, but I couldn't put my finger on why.

When we came within a few paces, I could tell that the mound around the willow wasn't solely snow but snow-covered piles of bones to match the ones dangling from the tree's switches. Piles and piles of bones.

I reached out and pushed a piece of metal that swung and clanked

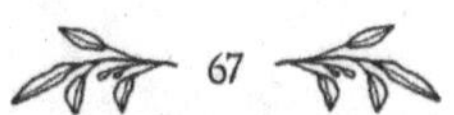

against a fox skull with a hollow thunk.

"Caroline," Aubrey reprimanded in a low voice.

I'd never seen her afraid before, but this place upended her calm demeanor.

A gust of wind shredded past the river, the tinkling sound of bottles and stone and metal and bone rang through the silence of the forest. The snow quickly absorbed the sound, leaving Aubrey and I in the unsettling quiet of the willow.

Aubrey hissed again, her hand wrapping around my wrist like a rope. Her nails dug into my skin.

"What is it?" I pulled at her hand, but she didn't let up.

"I thought—" She swallowed. "I'm not sure. But something dark is here. I don't—"

"Afternoon, ladies." A shirtless man I unfortunately recognized hopped down from a tree on the far side of the willow, stepping lazily toward us. "Fancy seeing you again, mongrel." The cursed catamount directed the insult at me. I'd run into him while Silas had been gone and the resupply party ran into trouble with the Hunt. He'd been injured, and I wondered if it had healed.

And what was *he* doing here?

"It's the tomcat," I snarled, Aubrey loosening her grip. "And here I thought you might have died from the embarrassment of losing your prey last time I saw you."

He hissed, shoulders rippling with tension. "You shouldn't be here. This is sacred ground now."

"All ground is sacred in the shadow of the Great Mountain." I moved my hand to my middle, unbuttoning one button slowly, hoping to avoid his notice. If I could phase...

He tsked, folding his arms. I finally noticed the wound he'd had at our previous encounter started to scar. "Fighting won't help you now, *rakas*. My master has roots too deep now. We're long past squabbles."

"Who is your master?" Aubrey asked, finally finding her voice.

The catamount smirked. "I am surprised you do not already know. Tell me, how is your future queen?"

Aubrey's nostrils flared. "What do you know of our queen?"

He moved behind the trunk of the willow, peeking out on the other side, yellow eyes bright and feline. "Much."

I shifted to face him. "She is well-protected. You won't make it far trying to get to her."

He laughed, a sharp sort of sound. "She is already our daughter. There's no need to reach her now."

"All you speak is lies," I hissed, but Aubrey held my wrist tighter.

"Do ask her about her dreams. I'm sure they're insightful." He grinned wickedly before launching onto one of the willow's branches and swinging into the river with a splash. He shifted and bolted north.

"We need to find Silas." Aubrey tugged on my sleeve. "Now."

11

SILAS

I SAT IN GUARDIAN'S GLADE on my throne, a small line of people waiting with questions that I'd been putting off answering for days. I hadn't had the energy to decide anything. But now that Lukosan had arrived, I couldn't evade them any longer.

I decided the meals for the week with the kitchen, answered a few questions for Bennett about arrangements for Lukosan's human population, conversed with Kane about recent activity as well as Nash being on patrol tonight, and decided on *Joulo* festivity scheduling and how that would operate around Eden's and my wedding ceremony.

Finally, I received my updated ceremonial robes from the Tailors and sent them away with the promise of Eden going to visit one last time before our wedding. The only two left were Asa and Elder Markus.

I shrank in my throne, shoulders crumpling like my fortitude.

"*Je kunan*, you need to sleep." Asa smiled at me in his grandfatherly way.

"It's barely afternoon. I need answers." I rubbed my fists into my eyes, eventually running my hands back over my scalp. My hair had grown longer in the past few weeks, and I did little to tame it into submission. But Asa was right—I hadn't slept in almost a full day. I stayed awake all night with Lukosan and then watched over Eden until Andra had arrived for their breakfast. I'd barely sat down in Guardian's Glade before a line formed this morning.

"That's what I'm here for, Si." Markus knelt in front of me. "We're working hard on this."

I perked up. "Any news?"

He shrugged. "We're doing our best."

I pinched the bridge of my nose. "It's not good enough."

The silence was heavier than the fresh blanket of snow that the night had given us.

I sighed. "I'm sorry. I didn't mean to snap."

Markus shrugged. "It's okay. You have a lot going on."

I met his gaze and shook my head. "It's not okay, Markus. This pressure is getting to me. I don't have the luxury of making mistakes, you know? Everyone is expecting something of me, and I don't have anything left to give anymore. I'm not allowed to break."

"Silas." Asa set a hand on my shoulder. "Can I make you some tea?"

I raised an eyebrow. "Is it going to knock me out for a full day?"

Asa grinned. "Perhaps."

"Sure." An airy laugh escaped my lips. "Bring two, please." After Asa left, I stood and embraced Markus. "I really am sorry I'm not a better king for you. Or a better brother to you."

Markus moved back. "As your Elder, I advise you to shut your mouth."

Rolling my eyes, I shoved him. "Yeah, yeah. Great advice. I'll think about it."

Markus's smile faded. "On a serious note, I wanted to discuss the

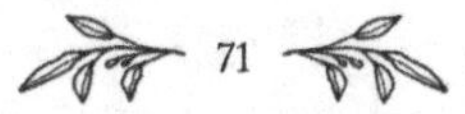

star charts and some celestial events. But seeing you like this…"

His sentence trailed off, leaving a weighty space in its absence.

I shifted my weight to the side. "Can it wait until tomorrow morning?"

He hesitated, and I could tell he wanted to protest, but he nodded instead. "Yes, of course. But we have to discuss it first thing tomorrow morning."

"It's a plan." I forced a smile. "I think I'm going to lie down. Send Asa in whenever he's brought that tea."

I inhaled deeply before pushing myself out of the throne and stumbled my way to my bedroom door. Laughter sounded from inside, which warmed me to hear.

"I swear." Andra laughed from her position folded up on the corner of the bed.

I watched silently from the doorway.

"There's no way. It's like all *virlukos* love that song." Eden shook her head. Despite being paler than I'd seen her, she grinned at Andra. "That's Nash's favorite song."

Andra froze. "Really? I had no idea. He—He never said."

Eden shrugged. "You should ask him. He promised to show me some of his dance moves for the wedding, so I'm hoping that one of the humans in your group has a working phone and Bluetooth speaker."

Andra smirked. "That can be arranged. I'm sure Jacob and Claire can figure something out."

The remnants of their breakfast sat on the desk, and I pushed them aside to lean against it. The sound of rattling plates drew their attention to me.

"Silas." Andra moved to stand. "I didn't know you were back. I can leave y'all alone."

I bowed my head. "Thank you. Come find me if you need anything."

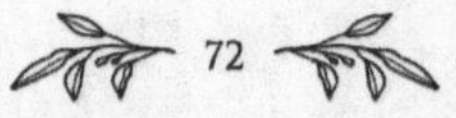

She shook her head and ruffled my hair. "Nah. I'll pester Nash. See ya, E!" She waved at Eden before slipping out of the room.

"Well, that seems like it went well." I raised my eyebrows. "Are you all friends now?"

Eden thought about it for a moment. "I think so, or at least on our way toward friendship. She acted a little strange, wanting to see my ring. I think she tried to take it off, but I may have been misreading things." She shook her head. "Weird, I know."

"Why'd she want to take your ring?" I furrowed my brow, finishing a piece of spruce bread left on their plates.

Eden shrugged. "She said she wanted to see how it was holding up. She wanted to make sure Rory did a good job making it for me. She even said she'd get him to make me a new one from Arcadian wood if the Lukosan one wasn't holding up."

Odd. Nothing felt strange between us when she arrived, but maybe Andra wasn't over my engagement. Maybe some of those emotional ties lingered. Or perhaps she only wanted to ensure her Seers worked with excellence.

Eden picked up her journal from the table next to the bed and began sketching again.

"What are you working on?" I moved to sit next to her, craning to watch over her shoulder.

"Oh, nothing." She tilted her head sideways, adding shade to a drawing of a bird I knew well. "I woke up thinking about ravens. I think I've been dreaming about them lately."

The way she'd drawn it, the raven perched on top of a skull and a pile of bones.

"What is it you wrote under the skull?" I squinted, trying to read the curly script.

"It is the darkness where wild is born."

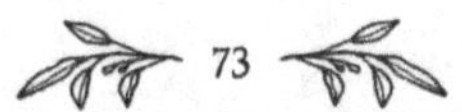

So strange. I'd perused Eden's drawings dozens of times, and they were always logical and academic. This raven unnerved me. I wondered what her dreams were about since the raven represented communication between realms and transformation. Had she interacted with the Other Realm? Did that mean she wouldn't get well?

I kissed her forehead, not wanting her to see my concern. Her forehead scalded my lips. "Please get some sleep, okay? Asa is bringing us both some tea to help. He said—"

Eden rolled her eyes. "That I need as much rest as possible. I know. But I feel like all I do is sleep these days."

I rested my chin on her head, giving her shoulders a squeeze. "But rest will help you feel well again."

Eden groaned.

"I love you." I gave her forehead another quick kiss before standing.

"I love you too, you silly king," Eden hummed, setting her journal to the side. "Have you slept much yourself? You look a bit worn."

I chuckled. "That's human for I look like bear scat, right?"

She rolled her eyes, but she was smiling—that was a good start.

"Don't worry. I'll go find our tea and we can take a long nap together, all right?"

She gave my hand a squeeze before I retreated to Guardian's Glade. When I walked down the aisle, I glanced back at our room. She seemed in better spirits the last day or two, but she burned like a torch and dry wood.

I shook my head free from the cobwebs of negative thoughts that surrounded me. I couldn't keep them at bay for long, but maybe I could shake them off long enough for me to find Asa and get that tea.

I slipped out of the double doors to Guardian's Glade, casting one last glance at the door to our room before colliding with hands.

"Silas." Caroline's wild eyes met mine, Aubrey looking pale beside her.

My mind jumped back to about a year ago when my sister and I stood outside these doors, her face looking just as ashen from shock and despair. The cobwebs of negativity were ropes now, panic synching me in until I almost couldn't breathe.

"Caroline. Aubrey." I stepped back. "What's wrong?"

My sister cast a wary glance at Aubrey before turning back to me, hands still clutching my shoulders. "Has Eden had strange dreams?"

12
ANDRA

I PACED IN THE AISLE OF KINGS while Archer lounged near Ellie and Iain's cairns. "It has to be Kalona. I can't imagine it would be anything else." I tucked my hair behind my ears, turning to walk back down the path past Archer again.

"Talk to Silas," Archer said.

"He won't believe me."

"You won't know until you try."

"Say he does believe me." I turn again, walking back down the aisle. "Then he'll blame me since I chose the wood for the ring in the first place."

Archer shrugged. "He might, but he also might not."

"He could kick me out. He'd kick our entire pack out." I turned on my heel, walking again.

"You won't know until you tell him the truth." Archer sighed. "I really don't see another option, An."

I stopped in front of him, holding my head in my hands. "There has to be another option. There always is. It's just hidden still. Somehow this will work out where Silas doesn't hate me, our pack still has a place to stay for the winter, and we save Eden from Kalona."

Arch pursed his lips. "That would take a lake full of luck."

"Yeah, well, your idea sucks and will end with him murdering me."

Archer rolled his eyes at me. "What do you keep me around for? I'm dead weight if you never even consider my advice."

I dropped to the ground next to him with a sigh. "I wish this were easier, but it's my own fault for being such a snake about the engagement. I know it's because of Mother, but I–"

Emotion clogged my throat, so I swallowed, trying and failing to keep it at bay.

"Yeah." Arch squeezed my knee. "We all heal in different ways. Yours happens to be making everyone else miserable like you."

I shoved him to the side, careful not to disturb Ellie and Iain's cairns. I studied them while Archer dusted the soil off his hands. "I wonder if Mother and Father are waiting in the Other Realm for us or if they've forgotten all about us."

"They'll be waiting." Archer bobbed his head with conviction and stood. "I can feel it. We're still tied to them, an invisible rope that keeps us grounded while we're in the Present Realm. And we have tethers to everyone we love which is why it's even harder when an Alpha passes to the Other. She had so many strong ties with so many wonderful people. So yes, I think she's waiting on all her tethers to join her in the Other."

He offered a hand up which I accepted, trying to stop the tears. "It still hurts."

"I think it will for a long time." Archer smiled sadly. "But I'll always be with you."

I snorted. "Yeah, because even when I foist an eligible woman on you, you somehow find a way to set her up with someone else."

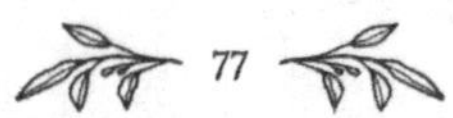

Arch chuckled, leading us back toward the Yard. "If Lycaon has a woman out there for me, she'll find me. But if not, you're already too much to handle anyway."

He dodged the elbow I'd aimed at his stomach and ran before I could try again. I followed, close on his heels until he stopped at the edge of the Yard.

"Still faster than you, even in robes." He smirked.

I snorted. "You had a head start."

His eyes caught on something past me. He waved and mumbled, "Don't look now, but I'm about to foist you upon someone."

"What–" Before I could get my question out, Archer wrapped his foot around my ankle and purposefully tripped me into two strong arms.

"I am so sorry, An." Arch ran a hand through his hair. "I never know where my feet are."

I would've shot him a glare, but I stood pressed into Nash's side.

"You all right?" Nash asked, making sure my footing was secure before taking a step back.

I nodded. "Fine."

Nash lifted a hand and, with a thumb, gently wiped away a tear. "That's a lie. But I can pretend I believe you if that's what you want."

I scoffed. "You're a terrible liar, Nash. You can't pretend to be anything you're not."

A muscle feathered in his jaw, and I caught that look of shame in his eyes before his mask slipped back into place with a grin. "Guilty as charged. I'm headed to the river for a bit before my patrol shift. Y'all want to come?"

He glanced over at Archer, who shook his head. "I have to find Nyrah and Milo to check on how their training is coming along. I'll catch y'all later!"

I wanted to curse Archer for leaving me, but deep down, I liked having Nash to myself. His personality was magnetic, which meant everyone wanted him to themselves. But having his undivided attention made me feel hopeful and wanted.

"Guess it's just you and me." He smiled. "Sucks for Arch because I brought snacks."

13

NASH

I TOSSED A DRIED MUSCADINE UP TO ANDRA, who caught it in her mouth. We sat along the border next to the Great River, half frozen with the split of the seasons. Andra was only an arm's length away.

I thought about our friendship, a strong tie between us that had been there since... forever. And I thought about how angry I'd been at Red River Gorge when I knew she'd lied to me, to my brother, to Eden, but *silva*, I couldn't pretend that our borderline flirtation had sparked part of the relationship I didn't know was present. One part devotion, the other desire.

With her in my spaces, walking between my trees, I couldn't stop thinking about her.

"You're messing with me, right?" I ran my hand over my hair that I'd tied back in a bun.

Andra leaned back on her hands. "I'm serious. *Je slava*. 'Rasputin' is my favorite song in the entire world."

"*Silva*, this must be some elaborate way to get back at me for being a nettle-brained catfish all those years. Eden told you to mess with me, right?"

Andra shook her head, barely containing her laughter.

I popped the last dried muscadine in my mouth, talking while I chewed. I didn't have to be a prince in front of Andra. She knew me too well. "I don't mess around when it comes to 'Rasputin.' I'm serious."

"So am I!" Andra leaned forward, arms propped on her knees. "Two summers ago, Jacob was talking to one of the humans we'd run into at a popular rock climbing park, and they mentioned some dance thing from over a decade ago. I asked about it, and the climber couldn't believe I'd never heard the song. So they played it, and I've been hooked ever since."

"No kidding." I matched her pose, which put our faces closer.

"Nope." She shook her head. "There's something about that beat and the clapping and the melody that envelopes my whole being."

I dropped my chin to my chest. I couldn't hold her eyes for too long. Her words inviting me to stay with Lukosan still floated to the surface every morning when I woke alone. I thought about it more often than I'd like to admit. And sitting with her now, laughing and playing in our own peaceful pocket of the forest, I couldn't help but think of how fun that change might be.

I couldn't help but think of how nice being with *her* would be.

I swallowed.

Cold. I needed cold water.

I rolled over and dropped right into the river, gazing up at the long branches stretching over the banks.

"*Sen sun feru*, Nash." Andra laughed, and soon, she was in my field of vision, peering at me with those hazel eyes. Her short hair hung down, leading my gaze to her beaming face. I had the urge to say yes, to give myself to Lukosan—to Andra. Instead, I snagged her wrist and pulled her down with me. I made sure she landed on the *Starra* side of the border instead of the *Suya* side so she wouldn't be so cold.

Lycaon, her laugh was infectious.

"You really are wild, you know that?" She propped up on her elbows, gazing down at me.

Even the freezing knives of the winter river couldn't chill the warmth inside of me from this moment. *Silva*, I could–

"What in the shadow of the Great Mountain are you two doing?"

Kyla.

I groaned as quiet as I could, frustrated by the interruption. Instantly, Andra's brightness dimmed. She turned to face her pack member. "Cooling off. Arcadia's warmer with the extra bodies."

I was grateful for her response, because I couldn't find my voice yet.

"What's up?" Andra asked as she climbed back onto the bank, squeezing water out of her borrowed robes.

"Almost meal time. Figured I'd come find you, and some of the *micca* saw y'all headed this way." Kyla crossed her arms. I knew she didn't approve of me after the incident I'd had at Lukosan and blowing her off for a year, but in my defense, I wasn't myself. Literally.

"Thanks for letting us know." Andra dipped her head. "I'll catch up in a bit."

Kyla glanced between us and shook her head, heading back toward the main paths of Arcadia. I silently thanked her and Lycaon and whoever else was listening that she hadn't said more or made it a big deal that her queen and the rejected prince—Omega of Arcadia—were seen, soaking wet in the river like otters.

It wasn't even about the past as much as it was about propriety. I was an Omega, and she was a queen and Alpha. Who was I compared to her? How could I ever belong in her circle again? I couldn't do that to Andra.

I vowed to be better, to keep myself in check next time. To stop myself from going too far.

Next time. I hoped against all hope that there would be a next time, another moment of peace with Andra.

As friends. Just friends.

I pulled myself out of the river, clenching my teeth to stop from smiling at the way the sun played with the drops on Andra's cheeks. It reminded me momentarily of her tears earlier. She and Arch had spilled out of the path heading to the Aisle of Kings.

"About earlier–" I started.

"I have a question," Andra said simultaneously.

I chuckled. "You first."

"No, you." She chewed on the inside of her cheek. Whatever she had to say seemed to worry her.

"Earlier, you were crying." I swallowed. "Is there... Do you want to talk about it?"

Confusion flooded her features before understanding wiped it away. "Oh, you mean– Yeah, I'll be okay. I miss my mother a bit extra today."

"Can I give you a hug?" I raised an eyebrow with open arms.

"You don't have to ask me that, Nash. You give the best hugs." She tucked into me like she'd done it a thousand times. She nestled her cold nose against my neck. "You used to want to hug everyone when we were pups. You'd spend all day curled up at Father's feet while Mother did her Alpha duties. He could never resist you."

"Oh, *silva*, that's a lifetime ago." I rested my head against hers. "I loved your father. And your mother."

"He loved you like a son."

Son—that title followed me everywhere. My thoughts drifted back

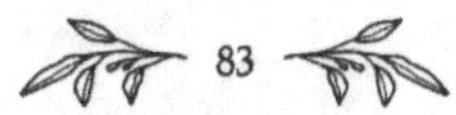

to the *kuslar* inviting me deeper into the shadowy place within me, to become the Son of Nyx. I still couldn't fill in the gaps of my memory, so how could I possibly figure out how to avoid becoming that monster?

I cleared my throat. "I'm sure they loved y'all way more than a scrappy pup like me."

"Listen to you, using human lingo." Andra laughed, and the sound rattled through me.

"What?"

"Y'all? It's like you're a born-and-raised East Tennessean."

"Technically, I am."

Andra pushed back slightly, barking a laugh. She stopped when she met my gaze. Only a breath separated us.

"You sure you're okay, An?" I whispered, afraid if I spoke too loud I'd break this moment.

"I am now." She glanced at my lips and back to my eyes. "Come with me?"

"I—"

"To midday meal." She swallowed. "Sit with me?"

"Andra, I can't."

She worked her way out of my arms, a chill filling the space where she'd been seconds ago. "Right, you're busy."

I ran a hand through my hair. "I'm patrolling Mt. Leconte this afternoon. It's my regular route now."

"Oh." Her tone shifted, and she tucked her wet hair behind her ear, eyes sparkling again with that adventurous spirit of hers. "Can I come with you? Not that you need accompanying, but I haven't been in so long. It would be fun, you and me."

I hesitated, letting myself consider for a moment. If I only needed to patrol, it wouldn't be half bad to have the company. But I needed answers about Nyx, and I wanted to see where his cairn had stood. .

I had a dream —a vision of sorts in Lukosan—that I stood by Nyx's cairn while it disassembled itself. Three Spirits watched me gaze in awe, standing in the swirls of their light. And then Nyx, back leg broken and eye wounded, limped into the clearing. He told me the Hunt will come for all in the end. He made it seem like the truth would hurt worse than the gaping hole that blotted out part of my past.

I needed to know.

I needed to go alone.

Finally, I shook my head. "I wouldn't want to draw too much human attention. And besides, you have better things to do than hang out with lowly *virlukos* like myself."

She opened her mouth, but thought better of whatever it was she meant to say. She nodded. "If that's what you want."

What did I want?

If I could be honest with myself, I wanted whatever we had a moment ago. I wanted peace and a lack of a regular schedule. I wanted picnics by the river and laughing in the sunlight. I wanted that smile on Andra's face forever.

She held out her hand. My eyes moved from it back to her eyes. "What?"

"I can take your robe back for you so you don't have to go out of your way."

I stared at her, my chest burning at the thought. It meant nothing day to day to go without a robe, and it still wouldn't if it wasn't for that fire in Andra's eyes. I knew she could hear my heart and I could hear hers. Both hammered in their cages.

I unfastened each button. It took everything in me to hold her gaze, knowing I may be trapped in her vision forever. I shrugged off the wet fabric, passing it to her waiting hand and phased before either of us could speak.

Andra cleared her throat while she busied herself folding my silver robe. "Next time you're not working, I'd like to visit Mt. Leconte, just you and me."

She lifted her eyes to mine, and I huffed in her face, her hair rippling back behind her. She laughed and ran a hand through my fur. I froze at her touch, and she noticed but didn't remove her hand.

"Nash?" Her voice seemed so small. "I'm still sorry about everything back at the Gorge. Mother's passing sort of broke me. I'm still trying to–to heal. But I swear, I'm trying."

She swiped at her resurfacing tears. Regret laced her words, and I hated how much she reminded me of myself.

"*I know.*" I lay my chin on her head. "*So am I.*"

She shuddered, doing her best to wrap her hands around my neck.

Careful not to knock her over, I stepped back and swished my tail twice before taking off towards Mt. Leconte. I hated to refuse her offer to tag along, but knowledge waited for me on that ridge. I didn't want anyone present to witness the tether I had to the Alum Cave trail. I hadn't stopped thinking about it for the past three days. Would I find the answer to unlocking my memories? Or did something darker wait for me?

14

EDEN

THEY MUST HAVE LEFT ME ALONE for a long time, because I finished the first raven drawing and moved on to another—this one of the white raven I'd seen in one of my other dreams. It sat perched in a dark green conifer, its blue eye staring out from the page.

Silas returned with tea on a tray, followed by Aubrey and Caroline, both of whom looked like they'd seen a ghost. Maybe I was the ghost. I felt thin enough to dance between realms, the Spirit in me pulling away from the body like the skin of a leaf from the veins.

"Here we are." Silas set the tray next to me on the bed and fussed with the cups.

I glanced at Aubrey. She wouldn't meet my eyes. I turned my gaze to Caroline. She stared at the drawing in my open journal.

"What were you drawing?" she asked, coming to stand closer.

I shrugged. "A raven."

I caught the look that passed between the two women, but I couldn't even guess what it meant.

"We don't get many ravens in these parts anymore." Caroline sat in Silas's chair while he passed me my cup of tea. "Did you see one?"

I shook my head. "No, I dreamt of one. Although I can't remember much of the dreams. They're a bit hazy."

"Would you tell us about one?" Aubrey stood behind Caroline. "I'm quite good with dreams, you know. Most Seers are."

I sipped at my tea, the scent of valerian hitting my nostrils. "I dreamt of a white raven a few nights ago. A white raven and a flood in the valley below Rauha."

Silas sucked in a breath beside me.

"What else have you dreamed of, Eden?" Aubrey knelt by my side, holding my free hand in hers. "Try not to think. Just feel."

I closed my eyes, straining to remember the other dream, the one I just had. What was it that scared me so much? Why was I afraid of dying?

I opened my eyes. "I'm sorry. I can't remember. I was in a dark forest with a raven, but I can't remember anything else."

As I dissolved into a coughing fit, Aubrey backed away. Silas pulled the tea away from me and set it aside, then wrapped an arm around my shoulders.

"I think we need to rest," Silas said, but I could hear the command in his voice, the underlying demand for them to leave us alone.

I wondered what they said to bother him so much, or maybe it was something they'd done that I wasn't aware of. Caroline and Aubrey muttered their goodbyes before slipping out into Guardian's Glade.

Silas handed me my tea again and picked up his own mug. "Tea and then a long nap?"

I hated to deny him the opportunity to care for me, so I nodded. I didn't want to sleep, didn't want to relive those nightmares and ghoulish meanderings of my feverish mind. That's all they were—fever dreams. They'd go away as soon as my fever disappeared and I felt well again.

But how long would that be? It had been nearly a month now of illness, of dancing around the subject. It didn't feel like the flu, despite the fevers and body aches. Unless I'd developed some chronic illness while at Lukosan, I couldn't begin to understand this sickness.

I'd considered tick diseases, mononucleosis, and a dozen other things, but I wouldn't know for sure unless I went to a human doctor. And I didn't know if Silas would even entertain the idea. Did I even want to go? What would the repercussions be of me going to the doctor and giving them my name? And with what money would I pay for the visit? My things from my human life had been stowed on the top shelf of Silas and I's wardrobe, but I doubt I'd have what I'd need. It wouldn't be possible without risking everything I'd built here.

There wasn't a clear answer to the illness, and I think that's what bothered Silas the most. He must be used to easy answers and traditional ways of fixing things. But now that I was ill with something no one in Arcadia had come down with before, traditional ways didn't seem to be working. I was past fixing, and it ate Silas alive that he couldn't help me.

I wondered if that's how it had felt before his mother died, and his father. How hard did Silas try to control things and keep the people he loved within arm's reach so that nothing bad could touch them? In his mind, if he could touch them, speak to them, and see them, everything would be okay.

He could touch me, speak to me, and see me all he wanted, but I wasn't getting any better. He had to at least see that.

"Silas, I've been thinking–" I started, clearing my throat, but it turned into a cough.

Silas squeezed my hand. When my coughs started to lessen, he

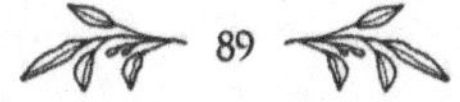

brushed my hair out of my eyes. "You're going to be fine. You'll be good in no time once you get some uninterrupted rest and no Seers messing with your dreams. And Caroline told me that your ceremonial robes are finished. She has it under control, and she'll make sure Nash isn't in the way of the *micca* so that everything still gets done. Especially during the wedding. It's going to be perfect."

Another coughing fit interrupted me, and I downed the entire cup of tea and some of Silas's to calm my lungs.

"Please get some rest." Silas rubbed circles on my back while I wiped away tears from not being able to breathe properly.

Why can't I breathe?

"My dream." I mumbled, bracing myself with a hand on my forehead. "I couldn't breathe, and there was a raven there—an impossibly large raven. And I was in the Heart of Arcadia."

"You're safe here with me, E." Silas brushed my hair back from my face. The once-silky curls hung flat and lifeless, oily and coated in sweat from my fevers. I had never craved a bath more.

"Do you think someone could help me with a bath tomorrow? Like a human type of bath—is that possible?" I turned to face him, a wan smile on my lips. "I think it would help me feel a lot better."

He inclined his head. "Say the word and it's done."

"I may need help. Maybe Andra could help me?" The words slipped out before I could think better of it, but at the moment, I was tired of being monitored every hour of every day. Plus, Andra had more insight on possible human and *virlukos* transmitted diseases, if that was even a thing. Hadn't she mentioned her mother got sick near the end? At the least, she wouldn't look at me like I was a Spirit already.

"A bath first thing when you wake up, okay?" Silas gently pulled me down next to him. He propped himself on his elbow and began sorting out the tangles of my hair, one by one, with such careful attention. He hummed a song I'd heard Caroline sing once before. It was apparently an old song that Ellie used to sing to them when they were only pups. It sounded reminiscent of an old hymn my grandmother used to sing, but there was something about the way that Silas and Caroline sang it that sounded like those eerie calls that Elder Macon and Markus made during the funeral ceremonies.

There are Spirits in the Other Realm who wait for me.
When I lay my body down, will I join them across the sea?
Will the Kingdoms continue ruling on and on? (On and on.)
While my better home awaits me with Lycaon. (With Lycaon.)
I can imagine gleeful feasting by the fire a long time past
And I cry o'er heavy grievings being the only king to outlast
Will the Kingdoms continue ruling on and on? (On and on.)
While my better home awaits me with Lycaon. (With Lycaon.)

15

SILAS

I HUMMED *WILL THE KINGDOMS* and played with Eden's hair until she fell asleep. It pained me to see her this way—this weak. I'd known her for a little over two months now, not long in the grand scheme of things, but I'd learned so much from her in that span of time. And it went beyond that, all the way back to that stormy afternoon on the Little River.

I thought back to that moment, my annoyance with Nash since he bested me again, and being the one responsible for a human while my siblings relaxed with our mother. I remember the feeling of anger rushing through me nose to tail when I realized the girl's parents hadn't even cared that she'd almost drowned. She would have died without help, and they wouldn't have known.

In a way, I felt justified in keeping Eden from them now. She'd expressed her disinterest in returning to the human world, but the moral part of me tried to reason that maybe Eden was trying to make things easier for both of us.

One day we can visit, go back, and see how the city moved on without her.

The city did its job raising Eden, but it was time for change. The forest needed her. *I* needed her. The thought of the city reclaiming her or if this illness claimed her...

I shook the thoughts away and tucked the blanket around Eden's body, settling down beside her. I could hear her steady heartbeat, the rhythm of her life beating away. I lived in fear of hearing her heart stop or Caroline's or Nash's, or anyone close to me. I had to listen and watch while my father's heart stopped its marching pace. I sat there, helpless as Elder Macon's heart ended its long journey. But I expected my own heart would shudder to a stop the day Eden breathed her last.

A rogue tear slipped down my cheek, and I was grateful to be alone, even hidden from Eden's empathetic eyes while she slumbered. I tucked my nose against her head and kissed her hair, attempting to steady myself.

"I love you. How can I live without you?" I tasted salt on my lips. "Please stay with me."

She shifted toward me in her sleep, her eyes never even fluttering from her dreams. I rested my cheek against her forehead and felt fire.

But she'd been sitting up. She'd attended the Passing of the Elders. How long could she continue living and masking this illness? Weeks, months, a year?

How many beats of her heart did I have left?

16
NASH

ON TOP OF THE GREAT MOUNTAIN, cold seeped through my skin despite my thick, winter fur. Ice clung to the pads of my feet and the fur between my claws. After the fresh snow, the world resembled a snow globe or a winter postcard.

The Wildcat was out taking his daily photo of the lodge, but it seemed the other humans had all left, presumably before the snow hit. I turned around the last building when I heard someone's heartbeat coming up the trail in front of me.

I needed to be fast if I was to avoid notice, and I needed to be careful with my tracks.

I launched into the snowdrifts away from the mostly clear path and pushed through the trees, sticking close to the laden branches, knocking snow down to cover my tracks. I kept my huffs and breaths to a minimum until I slipped onto the Alum Cave trail.

Not pausing to listen for the hiker's heartbeat, I sprinted through the corridor of trees, my own heart pumping steadily in my chest until the view spilled out in front of me. Clouds blanketed the valley below, my only view of the next ridgeline through gaps in the mist.

I tried to slow my pace but slipped on an icy patch of the rocky trail, sending me sliding and clawing for purchase. I skidded to a stop into a tall pine, its branches shedding their weight and dousing me in wet snow.

I growled, pushing back onto my feet and shaking off as much as I could before resuming my hike, this time with a slower pace.

I shouldn't be doing this.

But I'd made my decision. And I still needed answers.

The miles disappeared as I trotted through the tight tunnel of trees, stopping to rest when the foliage opened, and I could see *Shaconage* in all its beauty, frosted in white. It mirrored my own Spirit, dormant and cold. The barren trees no longer whispered their stories to me. Instead, they kept secrets and played coy.

My breath lingered in the air, the puff of cloud causing droplets to freeze on my whiskers. I needed to keep moving, but the itching doubt halted me.

Should I cut through the forest over the ridge and go back to Arcadia?

It would be easy to turn around and find my way back home on a different path. But would I regret not at least exploring? It would most certainly be nothing, just the paranoid thoughts of an amnesiac.

If nothing is there, why turn around now?

I continued down the trail, the icy path fading into frozen earth. A lift in temperature accompanied the steep downhill portion of the trail with the cable for humans to hold onto for extra stability. I scrambled down the switchback with ease, finding myself at the wooden stairs.

Mile after mile, my thoughts circled.

Nyx, cairn, answers, fear, Father.

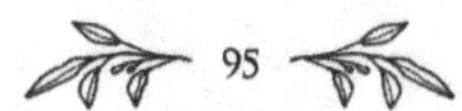

Nyx, cairn, answers, fear, Father.

I found myself slipping down a sandy bank underneath what the humans called a cave.

Nettle-brained humans.

Large, thick icicles stretched toward me, hanging precariously off the edge of the bluff. I hadn't seen or heard a single human the entire time I had hiked. I lay down underneath the salty, frozen bluff facing the view, taking a breather to rein in my thoughts.

I knew I was close to the cairn site.

I could feel it pulling at me—a gnawing, biting thing.

If I stopped lying to myself, I'd say the thought of finding something terrified me as much as not finding anything would crush me. The gap in my memories loomed over me daily, like an ever-present reminder of my failures. If I stayed still too long, it would consume me.

The quiet eroded me from the inside out. After a minute or two of utter silence, I had to move or else I would freeze—not from the cold, but from fear.

I stumbled down more stairs between slabs of slate and chunks of limestone. After what seemed like a thousand more stairs, I arrived at the sweeping view of Inspiration Point, a dazzling view of the surrounding knife-like ridgelines.

Now if I were an ancient, evil presence like Nyx and needed a burial ground, I'd make it here. Always a beautiful view.

Each fold of the foothills below had been dusted in white, contrasted to the dark and cracked trees poking into the sky. The world was still and the silence oppressive. Each conifer had been dressed in silvery ice, a precious decoration for the regal mountains I called home.

But their shade recalled memories of my childhood, of my father's eyes with a backdrop of snow. His steel eyes that he gave to me. His eyes which I would never see again in the land of the living.

I have to keep moving.

My pace slowed even more when an aching pain settled in my chest. The cairn site no longer pulled but clawed at me. Its remnants screamed in my mind from somewhere nearby.

I headed down the trail a little farther until I felt called off the path, into the trees. I could tell where the fires had ravaged the trees in November, life charred and lifeless teeth poking through the snow drifts. Under the blanket of snow lay the corpses of countless other trees, sleeping in their wintery graves.

I lowered my head and pushed through the undergrowth, maneuvering through a small opening through a thicket of briars. A dreary clearing stretched out before me, the same one I saw in that dream only a month ago.

I glanced across the space, expecting to find the three odd, antlered Spirits waiting for me and Nyx to follow them. But the forest around remained silent in the way only snow could produce.

The clearing lay undisturbed, so I pushed through the foot of snow that had collected around the edges of the undergrowth.

Join the Hunt, Nash, je lyco.

I heard the echo in my head and scrambled back into the tangle of thorns. A yelp escaped me, and I stumbled forward once more into the center of the clearing.

"I thought you might come," a smooth voice called with a huff.

Jerking my head around, I met the burning, red eyes of a Wendigo.

"Your kin was here two fortnights ago. Have you spoken to her?"

Caroline.

I nodded.

Silas and Caroline both had too many questions for me. Honest questions, and important ones, too. Lycaon only knew why they still trusted me. I had no answers, no memory of that bear scat of a year.

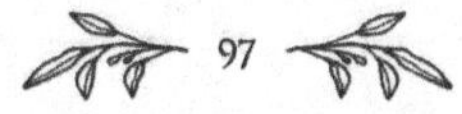

I couldn't even promise them that I didn't have blood on my paws. But their questions echoed my own.

Why did the *micca* and *kuslar* shrink from me? What had happened with Nyx that my soul was now marked as his son? Why did the Wendigos know my name?

I had heard their riddle, knew it by heart. It was something my mother had taught me so many years ago, before the heartache of death had the chance to touch me.

Remember the Wendigo as you pass by.
Remember that as you are, so once was I.
To hunt, to chase, to trail, to track;
Beware the eyes behind your back.
As we are now, so you all must be.
Prepare thyself to follow me.

But that knowledge shouldn't have implicated me in anything. Neither should the opinions of *micca* and *kuslar* and anything else that roamed these mountains. But what did they know about me that I didn't? Why did this Wendigo expect my arrival?

I worked desperately to regain my reputation around Arcadia, but none of that good faith had passed to the other beings around our kingdom.

I tucked my tail under myself, keeping my distance from the lanky monster in front of me. *"Caroline and I have spoken."*

"And she knows of your fate?"

"What do you know of my fate?"

The creature huffed, a rattling sound emitting from it when it tilted its large antlers. *"Do you not know even now?"*

My breath fogged in the air. *"Tell me."*

A whistling cry sounded far away, the Wendigo staring me down. *"No."*

I stepped forward. *"But–"*

The dark creature's antlered mask pressed close against my nose, barely touching. I hadn't even felt the air shift when it sped toward me in the blink of an eye. *"I will not tell you. But I will show you."*

Its eyes blazed, and the scent of rotting flesh filled my nostrils. Its claws slashed out and pricked my paw, like one of the thorns from the brambles behind me. I yelped and watched the snow around me grow steadily red with the flow of my own blood.

"Lyco." The creature tilted its head with a rattle.

"I'm not your son. I'm Iain's son," I breathed.

And suddenly, it was my father's voice instead of the creature's. *"Lyco. Nash."*

And the world spun, growing dark.

And the snow melted in a flash.

And the taste of iron filled my mouth.

And pain—tormenting pain—overwhelmed my senses.

Grief—my old friend.

Join the Hunt.

17

CAROLINE

"**E**XPLAIN AGAIN." I paced the length of the space around the blue flames at the Sage Brush, worrying my hair at the bottom, combing through the tangles and twisting it around my fingers.

"It's only a theory, but it stuck more than any of the others." Markus leaned forward on the bench, his broad shoulders hunched as he leaned over the star chart with Leander. "We talked of symbolism before, but after the run-in with the catamount and Eden's dream, we're starting to see connections where there weren't any before."

"But it's just a theory?"

Markus shrugged. "Nothing confirmed yet."

"Tell her." Leander's voice was steady, so I wondered why it made my insides shake.

Markus shut his eyes, hand flat over the section of the stars where I knew the Princess shone her brightest. "We theorize that Eden has somehow drawn the attention of a Raven Mocker."

My instinct was to argue, to dare Markus to speak lies again. But after the initial chill passed, the words settled like I'd swallowed stones. "Have you warned Silas?"

"No."

I swallowed, my mouth and tongue like sand. Lycaon knew I should be there when he did. Who knew how Silas would react when there was nothing he could control, nothing he could do.

"So Eden is as good as gone." I clenched my hands into fists, not daring to speak above a whisper for fear of the Spirit haunting our dying queen.

"No," Leander said, voice still steady—almost amused. "There's more yet that we can do to help her."

I pinched the bridge of my nose. "Like make her comfortable before it takes her?"

Markus wrapped his arms around my shoulders, and I leaned into his warmth. He'd been dreading this, I could feel it. He knew how heavy this would be for me—for Silas.

Leander stepped back. "Elder Markus, I'll fetch Aubrey and Ransom."

I leaned my forehead against Markus's chest. "What else does he think he can do for her? She's out of our hands now, like that stray cat said."

He shushed me, pressing a kiss to my forehead. "There may be a way out of this."

"How?"

Leander returned, flanked by flowing robes of violet. Aubrey dropped a dusty book on the second table, sending dirt in all directions.

"Not all Raven Mockers are death omens," Ransom said, and exhaled. "Some are mere nuisances of a bygone era, trying to make sense of a world with less magic."

"So how do you know the difference?" I fit myself into Markus's side, desperate for some sort of comfort.

"That's where we come in." Aubrey flipped through the cracked pages. "Ransom can climb into Eden's dreams, try to get a glimpse of the Raven Mocker and figure out where it's hiding, or which one it is. Maybe one of our own has met it in the past."

Leander picked up his tea, forgotten so long that it no longer steamed in the chilly air. "I will use my own enhanced ability to communicate with the Mocker."

"We'll try to figure out what it wants." Ransom leaned up against the table next to his wife. "Sometimes they get tied to places—physical objects, memories, or songs. If we can figure out why it's latched onto Eden, we can send it away."

Markus squeezed my shoulder. "And ask it to maintain a safe distance from Arcadia."

"Is that possible?" I scanned each of their faces, searching for a hint of doubt or concern that this might not work.

"It's our best chance." Leander tilted his head in thought. "And possibly our only option."

"And what memory or place is it connected to?" I frowned. "There hasn't ever been a Mocker connected to Arcadia that I can recall."

"I think it's a song." Aubrey frowned. "She's listened to a lot more music than we have, which means a lot more of an opportunity to attract a Mocker's attention."

"I think it's a memory that she uncovered while in Lukosan. Eden fell ill when she left their encampment." Ransom rubbed his chin in thought. "If we could map a detailed day-by-day of what she did there..."

Markus cleared his throat. "I think it's a place. Ransom, it's like you said. She only started getting sick when they left the Gorge. What if the Mocker attached to Eden by accident, and now it can't find its way back to its home?"

"I don't want to rule out a physical item," Leander chimed in.

Ransom shook his head. "But that doesn't make any sense. The only clothing she has is from Arcadian Tailors. And the Mocker isn't attached to anything she already owned before. We would've known."

"What about Silas?" I gazed up at Markus. "He would want to know."

He shook his head. "I meant to tell him this morning, but I'm afraid he'll snap. He needs to rest. I'm concerned his exhaustion will have long-term effects if he continues to wear himself out like this. Telling him about the Raven Mocker now would be disastrous."

I couldn't count the times I'd see Silas snap, but there were only a handful he'd truly lost it. Most of them happened around the time Mother passed, when Nash returned to Arcadia, or when Father passed. If he had any idea that Eden was doomed to die, he might destroy the whole kingdom.

Ransom shrugged. "And besides, it's a theory. We don't even know if we're right."

"There's a way we can find out." Aubrey ran a fingernail along the words, scratched in Ancient Tongue, and read, "Raven Mockers are part-woman, part-raven, gaunt with talons or beaks. Occasionally, they appear in flames in the sky. But Mockers are only visible to the ones they haunt, though some accounts speak of Mockers being visible to healers and gifted Seers."

"It must not be a Mocker if I can't see it." Ransom's sigh turned into a grunt when Aubrey's elbow connected with his stomach.

"Just because you can't see it doesn't mean the theory is incorrect." She blew a stray hair out of her eyes. "Not being a Gifted Seer means not specifically blessed. It doesn't mean you're unintelligent."

Ransom rolled his eyes, but I caught the hint of a grin on his lips. "Okay, so we talk to Asa and see if he's noticing anything suspicious."

"And when will we tell our king?" Leander asked and finished the last of his cold tea.

Markus shook his head. "I don't want to tell him until we know for sure it's a Raven Mocker. No need to worry him if we're not certain."

"So we talk to Asa." Aubrey closed the book, keeping a finger between the Raven Mocker entries.

"It's settled." Ransom clapped his hands together.

I relented, though I feared Silas finding out the truth before we told him. "We hide the theory from Silas, ask Asa if there's anything suspicious, and climb into Eden's dreams. Easy as breathing."

"Easy for you to say." Ransom ran his hands over his knees. "You're not the one risking injury to invade Eden's thoughts. I can't say I'm looking forward to it."

"Is it dangerous?" I met Markus's gaze.

Leander sobered. "Not fatal, but certainly risky. It's prickly and fatiguing."

"You could still try, you know," Ransom offered.

Leander turned to face him, milky eyes unblinking. "You and I both know it would be a wasted trip for a blind man to try to see someone's nightmares."

"There's a first time for everything," Ransom muttered.

"What about Nash? Should we tell him since he's been taking care of Eden? Maybe he'll handle it better than Silas would." Markus's brow furrowed.

I shook my head. "He's probably off gallivanting with Andra and Archer, having a good time. Best leave it that way so he can entertain our guests."

18
NASH

I TRIPPED OVER MY PAWS for the hundredth time, stumbling across Arcadia's border well after reporting time to Kane. I could easily excuse it, say that I had to help the Wildcat or avoid the day hikers, but then I'd have to explain my sorry state and why I limped.

The wound wasn't that bad. It would heal within a week. But a deeper wound existed that might never heal, one that threatened to swallow me whole.

How could I?

I shook my head and kept moving, one stumbling step and another, until I threw myself at my father's graveside in a sobbing heap. I phased, curling my hands in the moss, wanting to feel anything but the cold, yawning emptiness that awaited me.

I screamed, the ferns near me quaking in the path of my anger. Let people wonder who cried in mourning. Let them come see for themselves the mess I had become.

I screamed.

And screamed.

And screamed.

My throat burned. My chest ached. My head thrummed.

I couldn't deny what I'd seen. I couldn't deny it any more than I could deny the sun's warmth or the Great Mountain's roots.

It has to be a lie—a trick.

But memories rushed back to me, memories that lay dormant for a year. Each moment ripped back in startling clarity, and my head ached from remembering.

Walking alongside Nyx in the *Washita* Mountains.

Feasting on the flesh of roadkill somewhere in West Tennessee.

Glimpses of *Atagahi*, the fabled lake of healing.

What strange places my feet had taken me without my knowledge or consent.

How many times had I prayed to Lycaon for recollection of that cursed year? How many times had I reached deep into the recesses of my mind, trying to grasp the slippery tendrils of memory?

I'd give it back if I could. I'd do it if I could take back my innocence. Unfortunately, that was long gone.

Body-wrenching sobs engulfed me, leaving me wrung out and limp. I collapsed in the dirt, soil sticking to my wet face and palms, mingling with the dried blood from the Wendigo's attack. I cursed at myself and that infernal creature. The words did little to heal my shattered self.

That beast left me in that clearing, a stain of red on the purest of white snow. At least the sharp cold pushed me into motion. Had it been *Starra* when this happened, I might have stayed in that clearing until the worms devoured my flesh, a warm meal after a harsh winter.

But by the time I clawed myself to safety and warmth, the shock had dissolved into pure rage and fury at the Wendigo, at the world, at Lycaon for allowing this to happen... But mostly at myself.

This was all my fault.

I pressed a hand to my chest, pushing and pushing until only a sliver of the ache remained. And behind it, there was nothing, only a yawning darkness inside of me with the truth like a beast hiding from the light.

I rolled to my side, eyes glazed and unfocused.

How will I face this?

Voices drifted toward me, and before I could hide in the undergrowth or amongst the cairns, Andra and Archer stepped through the gateway and around the bend in the path. They froze. I wasn't sure if they could smell my tears or the reek of my sins. Perhaps both.

"Go away," I muttered. I couldn't look them in the eyes.

"Nash." Andra stepped tentatively toward me.

"Get away from me!" I scrambled back, my dirt-and-bloodstained hand held in front of me.

"Nash, what happened to your hand?" Archer moved past Andra.

"Stay away!" I roared. The effort sapped the remnants of my energy, and I sagged in a heap in the center of the path, curling my body around myself. The sobs returned in full force.

Both of them stood so still that, for a moment, I could've imagined I was alone.

"Nash," Andra murmured. Her voice was closer, only a breath away.

Too close.

Too close.

"I'm sure whatever has happened isn't all that bad. Let me see your—"

At the touch of her hand on my own, I crawled backward again. "I'm not who you think I am."

The tension in the air sizzled like bear grease dripping into a

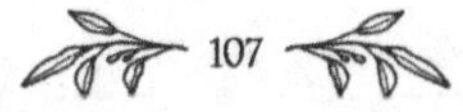

campfire, volatile and painful. I could hear their heartbeats, but nothing compared to the thrashing of my own in its cage, begging to be released like the wild animal I'd been suppressing all this time.

"I don't understand." Andra held a hand up like she was calming a feral creature. "I'm listening, so please clarify it for me."

I growled, and the ease with which I transformed to a beast startled me so much that I never fully phased, only scrambled backward on fading paws. Shaking my head, I whispered the only word that seemed to form on my lips. "No."

I repeated it a dozen times before curling in on myself and threading my hands in my tangled hair.

No, no, no, no, no.

My life was a spool of thread, beautiful and brimming with potential. And ever since I breathed my first breath of Arcadian air, I'd been unraveling. What a strange sort of destiny to unspool before I could find my way in the world.

I flinched from the warm hand on my shoulder. I could smell Andra from a mile away, but her proximity overwhelmed me. "Nash, if you're not who we think, tell us who you are. We're here for you."

I heard the shift and shuffle of feet on the path when Archer dropped to the ground on my other side.

"Don't make me wrestle you," Archer grunted.

"I'd still win," I grumbled.

"There he is! That's my best friend." Archer chuckled.

I rocked forward on my heels, bracing myself with my hands in the dirt. Cold, hard ground despite the warm barrier around Arcadia. My eyes glazed again, staring into the forest but seeing only shadows. "I don't know who I am anymore."

"Is it about the *micca*?" Andra rubbed gentle circles between my shoulder blades, and it brought some spark of warmth back to the numbness that had stolen over me. "You know how the forest talks. Beech trees are notorious gossips."

A dry chuckle tried to escape me and failed, trapped in my throat. "What do they have to say about the Son of Nyx?"

The hesitation spoke volumes, and the buzzing tension returned.

"Well, uh…" Archer cleared his throat. "They say he's in Arcadia. That he's working to take back what belongs to Nyx. And the Hunt is behind him." He chewed on his bottom lip.

"Say it." I swallowed. "Please."

"They think you're the Son of Nyx," Andra stated, so matter-of-factly that my stomach dropped. She knew the rumors—but did she believe them? I couldn't tell, but I couldn't bear to look her in the eye when I told her what I'd done, what I'd seen.

Maybe I wasn't the son of Nyx by blood, but each step seemed to echo his history. I wondered if the Nunnehi—the deciders of fate—planned for this all along. I wonder if this had been my immortal legacy, my destiny from my first breath. Was I becoming a monster with each passing day?

"I think you can put together the rest." I knelt all the way down and rested my forehead in the dirt, trying to calm the thoughts fluttering like birds taking flight. A murder of crows and a cacophony of noise in my skull.

"I don't believe any of those rumors. Not even for a second." Andra's typical stubbornness flared.

"And why is that?" My voice hissed out, too venomous, too cruel. I didn't mean it, but I couldn't stop myself. "Are you too prideful to believe in the gossip of foolish trees or some fox spit? Too important to listen to the talk of forest peasants?"

"I don't believe them because I care about you, all right?" Andra snapped.

I deserved it. I deserved every ounce of her anger. And maybe I was a masochist for enjoying it, but it felt a bit like penance.

Even then, it will never be enough.

I clenched my teeth, holding back the sea of emotions that threatened to escape. "You shouldn't do that to yourself. It's pointless to care for someone like me."

"And who are you, Nash? Or do you have another name you'd prefer?" She was on her feet now, and I watched her—barefoot here in Arcadia—pacing between the ferns.

"If I tell you, you'll kill me." On second thought, it didn't sound half bad to die, not when I deserved it. But I was so afraid. All this time I thought I was invincible, that death would have to run to catch me. But here was the moment, my time. Was I ready?

"I could kill you now for being insufferable, but thank Lycaon I have self-control." She threw her hands in the air, exasperation apparent in each movement.

I stood, drawing both Andra and Archer's attention. Good. This is what I needed—what I deserved—after what I'd done. Full attention to the sins I'd committed.

I knew as soon as the words left my lips, it would be permanent, fixed, unalterable. And in a way, I knew the River had already changed its course a year ago, but I hadn't quite admitted it to myself yet. Not when today marked the anniversary of my father's death.

Not when today marked the stark divide of who I was before and after.

I could see his eyes, the color of fish scales. His hair, like mine. I could hear him call my name, calling me son. He was gone.

I inhaled deeply.

"I killed him."

19

ANDRA

The call of an Eastern Whip-poor-will cut through the silence, the only sound I could hear past the beating of three hearts. For a moment, Nash stood there blinking, his eyes darting between Archer and me.

I shook my head. "Impossible."

He took three swift steps to me, holding out his wounded hand. "Don't you see this? Can't you see? It's blood magic. My blood. And it's a stain on this valley.

Archer moved closer to me, and I could feel his unease. "Nash, let's take a seat again, have a conversation about what you think is going on."

"I wish it was only in my head. I wish... I wish–" Nash crouched, rocking slightly.

"Hey, you're safe with us. Promise on the River." I placed a hand on his knee.

Nash froze and gazed down at my hand. "You don't believe me."

I stole a glance at Archer. "It's a bit difficult to comprehend."

"What don't you understand?" Nash hissed. "I killed my own father."

"Nyx *forced* you to kill Iain," Archer corrected. "Those are two separate things."

"But my father is dead, and it's because of me." Nash sobbed, a moaning sound escaping his lips. "I can taste it."

"Nash." I shook my head. "Don't do this to yourself."

"I can hear him screaming. I can feel him pulling. I can smell the iron in his spilt blood."

"Nash." Archer held a palm out. "Stop torturing yourself."

"He called me his son, for Lycaon's sake," Nash cried. "He called me his son after I ripped his flesh from his bones. What kind of person does that?"

"A man who recognizes that someone used you like a pawn." Arch grabbed Nash's shoulder. "You are not your actions. It's not your fault."

"He's dead. He's gone." Nash repeated the words over and over.

If what Nash said was true and not a cruel trick of the Hunt, a year ago, he'd killed his own father under the control of Nyx. He'd walked for quite some time under Nyx's control, going where Nyx went and doing what they asked of him. And one day, they set him free.

Why? What had changed their minds? Why didn't they kill him? Unless...

I met Archer's gaze, raising an eyebrow. I knew he'd ask me later what I'd been thinking. But it all made sense. If the Nunnehi decided to shift destiny for good or bad, they would've needed powerful players. They would've needed people who could cause a scene. They would've needed something or someone to be the catalyst to shift the decisions and destinies of hundreds of people or creatures.

Nash, Nyx, and Iain all played huge roles, but Nash's wasn't over.

"It's like Eden said about our favorite song." Nash wiped his nose on his wrist. "The cat isn't really a cat. A man went missing because someone murdered him for being corrupt and too influential. I don't want to end up like Rasputin. I'm afraid to die."

"You're not going to die." I removed his hands from his face.

He appeared hollow. I nudged him to sit and drop his knees. With as little awkward fumbling as I could manage, I climbed into his lap, my hands cradling his face. His whole body froze at my touch. "Nash, I need you to look at me, okay?" He blinked.

"There's a thing some of the human pack members talk about in relationships. It's a way to recenter when things are unbalanced and off kilter. So I need you to put your arms around my waist, and I'll hang onto your shoulders."

He swallowed but obeyed.

"I want you to breathe with me really deep, okay? And hold it for a few seconds before breathing out."

He breathed with me for a few moments. I could hear his heart rate slowing, his shoulders visibly relaxing a bit.

"You aren't going to die because of this," I reassured him. "I won't let that happen."

"But I have to tell Silas. I have to–"

"We'll figure that out when we get there, but in the meantime, you need rest." I ran my fingers through his loose hair, working out any tangles I caught.

He closed his eyes, leaning into my touch.

"I'll even walk you to your room if you want."

"You're already doing more than enough," he murmured.

I couldn't say it out loud—not yet anyway—but I could never do enough to show him how much I cared for him. No amount of praise or doing things for him out of my way or sneaking any sort of touch would be enough to prove to him that he was so worthy of love and care. Despite what he'd done and the things done to him, I loved him. But I couldn't say it out loud.

20
EDEN

I woke to Eastern Whip-poor-will calls, distinctly aware of their connotation of death.

Where am I?

My eyes adjusted to the dim room, making out the faint outlines of the desk, the books, the shelves, the rack of crowns, and the sleeping king beside me. I was in Silas's room. I was safe. I was alive.

I shifted to my other side, running a hand lightly through Silas's messy hair. It had grown so long since I'd first arrived in Arcadia. I wondered if he would cut it for our wedding, if I would even make it for that long.

Silas stirred, wrapping his arms around my torso and pulling me close like a child would his favorite blanket. I rested my chin on his head, nails combing through his tangles.

"Is it morning yet?" he whispered, voice hoarse.

"Not yet, love."

"Why are you awake? Are you feeling okay?" He moved back, but I pulled him close again.

"I'm fine. Not even a nightmare. Asa's tea must have worked. Or maybe your singing kept me sleeping peacefully."

"You're drinking that tea every day until you're well again," he mumbled, squeezing me tighter.

A chuckle escaped my lips, and I wondered how long it had been since I laughed properly. "Whatever you say, *je kunan*."

Silas tilted his head to look at me. "When you speak like that—with the Ancient Tongue—it's like you've always been here, like you've waited for me all this time."

"Is it what you hoped for?"

His eyes flicked back and forth between mine. He swallowed. "No."

"No?"

I knew I wasn't most people's idea of a good queen. But I wouldn't question Iain's judgment. He'd chosen me regardless of what Silas hoped for in a wife, a mate.

Silas ran a hand through my hair, tucking it behind my ear. "It wasn't what I hoped for, but it's been so much more. I can't imagine anything else anymore, E. My life wouldn't be the same without you."

I leaned into him, pressing my lips to his. In the dark hours before dawn, he held me like I was fragile and kissed me like my skin was porcelain instead of flesh and bone. He held me like I was his, and nothing could've been more true.

I rested my chin on his head again, relishing in the warmth he brought to my chilled body. "What about that bath you promised me?"

His laugh reverberated through me, the echoes filling the gaps inside. "I'll go see if Andra is awake and willing to help out. We'll start boiling some water for you, and I'll come get you when it's ready, okay?"

He kissed my forehead before stealing out of the covers and out of the room.

I wondered if there were *micca* about, tending to the forest in the wee hours of the morning. I wonder if they'd sit for me and let me sketch them if I asked nicely. Maybe I could bribe one of them with the prospect of new clothes.

Would I still have the time to sketch regularly after they crowned me queen? Or would I have duties like Silas, managing the valley and handling business. For a forest kingdom, paperwork and rules consumed a good portion of his time. And as much as I'd come to love Silas, what did it mean to be his wife? Would I be paraded around in front of other packs? Would I be held for ransom by some darker force wanting to weaken our kingdom? Or would I just be a human girl in love with a wolf king?

I held my left hand up, squinting to make out the wooden band around my ring finger in the dark blue of predawn. The ring may be simpler than the ornate diamonds and gold that humans received when getting engaged, but this one fit me well. I couldn't imagine a better one.

I dozed, dreaming of swimming in the river with Silas, like that first day we kissed on the bank in the light of the kuslar, but better. That day, his words hurt me, his confession at the dinner table that night that he didn't want me. And how could I blame him? At the time, I'd only been a nuisance that his father foisted upon him.

He'd chosen to love me anyway.

And I'd chosen him right back.

"*Je rakas.*" Silas's voice pulled me up from the waters of drowsiness that rocked me. "Do you still want to bathe, or do you want to keep sleeping?"

"Bath," I mumbled.

"Come on." Silas held both hands out to me and easily helped me out of bed. He walked with me, offering me an arm when I needed it.

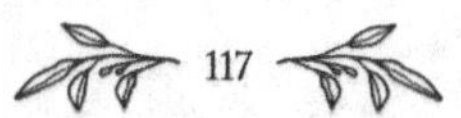

We walked out near where we'd shared our first kiss, close to that place I'd dreamt of.

A basin of wood sat in a small clearing, the trees draped with curtains and *kuslar* lounging in the branches.

"All this for me?" I took a moment to really look at Silas. Standing before me was a lover, not a king or a brother or a grieving son. This was a young man in love with a woman whom he thought the world of despite her weakness.

"All this for you." Silas held my hands and kissed my pale knuckles, rubbing a thumb over my wedding band. "I'll have breakfast waiting for you."

I squeezed his hands. "You're making my breakfast, right?"

Silas smirked. "Only if you're okay with oatmeal. I fear it's all I know how to cook."

I gasped dramatically. "But oatmeal is my favorite!"

Silas rolled his eyes. *"Sen sun feru, pilukos."*

"Ja rakassen." I kissed him on the cheek, inhaling the familiar scent of rain and soil.

"I love you, too." He kissed my hair. "Don't hesitate to call for me. I'm not far away. Andra should be here soon."

And with one last kiss on my forehead, he slipped away, stealing glances over his shoulder while he made his way toward the kitchen.

Finally alone—save the kuslar dozing in the foliage—I unfastened my robes, only struggling with a few of the last buttons. The watery fabric slipped from my shoulders to the ground, and I stepped out of it. In the low blue light of dawn, tendrils of steam drifted to the canopy of leaves, the scent of rose and honeysuckle drawing me to the basin. I draped my silver robe over a branch, vowing to get it laundered soon. I'd been wearing it for a week without changing for lack of energy.

I couldn't remember my last real bath with warm water, but I knew it would ease some of the ache in my body. Nothing could beat a hot bath on a sick day.

I swirled the water experimentally, fingers grazing over petals.

"Need any help?"

I spun to face Andra, folding my arms across my bare chest. But her eyes were closed, hands in front of her while she stumbled toward me.

I snorted. "How long have you been walking with your eyes closed?"

Andra caught her toe on a root, cursing quietly. "A while. I didn't want you to feel embarrassed. I know how humans can be."

I swallowed and inhaled. "Well, I'll have to figure it out sometime, right? And I think I'll need help getting in."

Andra opened one bleary eye. Maybe it was a wolf thing, but she didn't even glance down. "So, only a bath or are we washing hair, too?"

"Hair, please." I thought for a moment before furrowing my brow. "I'm guessing you don't have any shampoo I could borrow?"

Andra helped me into the basin, keeping me balanced until I could sit down. "Nope." She stepped over to a collection of bowls to the side. "But we have something better."

She brought one of the bowls over, and I caught a whiff of something minty. "What is that?"

"This is nature's soap. Go ahead and get your head wet, and I'll wash your hair for you."

I grasped the sides of the basin. "Andra, you don't have to do that."

She waved a hand. "Think of it like a spa day before your wedding. But you might want to take your ring off to be safe. I'd hate for it to get damaged from the bath."

I glanced at my hand. "Do you think it might?"

Andra shrugged. "If it were me, I'd rather be cautious than have to get a new one made."

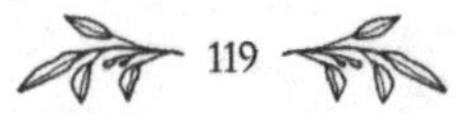

I slipped the ring off and passed it to Andra.

"I'll put it in your robe pocket for safekeeping until you're done." She tucked the ring into the pocket of my silver robe and returned with the bowl. "Now dunk. Time for some R and R."

I submerged myself in the hot water, the sounds of the forest disappearing for a moment as I ran my hands through my tangled and oily hair. I pulled myself out with help from Andra. I could already feel the tension leaving my body.

"Growing up, my grandmother on my father's side would wash mine and my cousins' fur." Andra rubbed her hands together over a piece of what appeared like pickled ginger slices, but it bubbled like a foaming soap. "She'd gather all of us together early in the morning like this before the sun broke, and we'd stumble into the river. Sitting there quaking like a birch tree in *Starra*, we'd wait our turn. She'd comb our fur with a brush of stiff grass and wash our hair with yucca root."

Andra ran her soapy hands through my hair. It wasn't like the shampoo I bought from the store, all sudsy and thick. It was runny with chunks of the yucca getting caught in tangles.

"You have a thick head of hair, E." Andra pulled out tangles, rubbing her hands with yucca before diving back into washing my hair. "Lycaon bless you and Silas's pups. The mats you'll have to pick out..." She shook her head.

Her words brought a jolt of fear back that I hadn't considered since September. If I did feel well again, what of children? What of heirs and the throne? Why would Iain choose me if he knew there was a chance I wouldn't produce *virlukos*? What if they only took after Silas's human side and inherited no shapeshifter genetics?

Oblivious to my fear of the unknown, Andra continued. "Anyway, my grandmother would rinse out the yucca and slather on some bear grease or something similar to get that nice shine and softness. We'd lay in the sun, warming ourselves and taking a little nap before returning for breakfast. I'd forgotten how much I miss her." Andra grew quiet and rinsed off her hands. "Funny how that happens. You think you're past something, and suddenly you're sixteen again and your grandmother's not coming home." She shook her head, moving to the set of bowls again, and she returned with a bundle of sticks. "Brace yourself."

I held onto either side of the tub while she worked through my tangles from the bottom to the top until my hair lay flat down my back, the ends curling in the water. She repeated the same thing again in comfortable silence, washing my hair with the root and rinsing before combing back through my hair.

Andra passed me the bowl to wash my body. "Have you thought about your future family?"

I paid careful attention to lather everything, washing my arms and torso before working down to my legs and feet. "I don't know, it seems impossible—daunting, at the least. And the unknowns are a little frightening to dwell on for too long."

"Like what?"

I shrugged before washing the dirt from between my toes. "Like what if I'm a terrible mother? Can I even have *virlukos* kids? What if they turn out like me and not like Silas?"

"The usual questions, huh?" Andra smirked. "And for the record, I think you'll be an amazing mother. But forget about those questions. Whatever happens, Silas is with you. And that will be enough."

I nodded. She had a point. I knew Silas would stand by my side, but the guilt would nag at me for as long as I lived if I ended his family line by not bearing an heir.

"Enough about my love life." I rinsed in the water. "Tell me about you and Nash."

Andra scoffed. "What do you mean *me and Nash*? There is no me

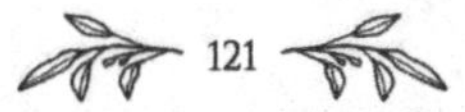

and Nash. There never has been, but especially now with– Or at least it's not like that. We're just friends."

I rolled my eyes.

"I'm serious! Besides, I think we're both too hurt from…" She shook her head. "Anyway, I don't think there's anything there. If there had been, that spark is gone."

"Oh." I didn't agree. There was something there, but maybe it was residual tension like between her and Silas. "It still couldn't hurt to talk to him about it," I offered.

"What, and say, 'Oh, hey, despite everything we've been through, I've had a massive crush on you since we were little, and I can't help but notice we're both single and lonely and broken. Want to kiss me?'" Andra froze. "If I thought there was anything there—which I don't. Because there's nothing there."

"I think you should sit with him for a meal today and talk. See where it goes and try it out for a while. If it doesn't work, at least you'll live the rest of your life knowing that you tried." I ran my hands over my face. "You'll regret it if you never try."

She chewed on her lip. "Maybe, but he's… Well, it's difficult to explain. He's not what I thought." She pinched the bridge of her nose. "That's not what I mean, I just– He's going through some things, grieving his father's death. *Silva*, I'm still grieving. How could I possibly add to his troubles like that?"

As Andra shifted to the side of the tub to better reach my hair, she furrowed her brow. She worked on the tangles at the ends of my hair. Her face seemed pale, but maybe that was just from the low light of morning.

I cleared my throat. "You know, we're never complete. We're always growing, changing, phasing into new people moment by moment. You don't know who you'll be after all that growing up, but at least you can try to be with the people you love."

I had been blinded by jealousy and fear at Lukosan—so blinded that I couldn't see the obvious truth hidden by the lies. Andra didn't love Silas. She loved Nash. She wanted Nash, not his brother, and it was so painfully obvious to me now that I really saw her. She lived and breathed to see him happy and unburdened, but she didn't believe that she could make him happy.

"Where is Nash?" I asked, picking some of the rose petals out of the water. "He's been reading *Twilight* to me, and he missed last night. I haven't seen him since breakfast yesterday actually."

Andra swapped the yucca bowl for a smaller one that had a substance with a soft lotion-like texture. "Oh, he's probably asleep now. He had to patrol yesterday and ended up being out super late."

"So you saw him?"

Andra twisted my hair and wrung out some of the water, brushing it once more. "Only for a moment. Archer and I ran into him last night when we went to pay respects to Iain and Ellie."

"Oh." I had forgotten how well Andra had known them. "Was he okay?"

Andra shrugged. "As good as he can be, I think, given the circumstances. His position is... rocky, I guess?"

"Silas would disagree, but I'm sure it's difficult coming back after all that time, not remembering the past year. It has to be frustrating."

"Terrifying, probably. I can only imagine the pain he must be feeling." Andra ran her fingers through my hair. "But what about the wedding? I haven't heard much about it yet. What are we eating? What's the *kulas* like this year? And who's doing the ceremony with Elder Macon gone?"

I shared all the details while she massaged the minty, yarrow salve into the tips of my hair, climbing all the way up to the roots. Bennett stopped by at one point—bringing me tea from Asa with fennel and licorice—and dropped off my Historian robe, swapping it so he could launder the silver one.

Andra groaned over the stew Silas had chosen—clearly a fan favorite—and complimented my choice of pastry—a pan-fried dessert with marshmallow root and cherries. She listened and chimed in with opinions, but mostly kept quiet when I mentioned Nash had struggled to get the *kuslar* to assist him in making the *kulas*.

Andra rinsed her hands in the water before working the style. She scrunched my hair section by section, my curls springing to life again. "I'm excited to see your ceremonial dress." She braided my hair and tied it out of my face. "It'll be a first for Arcadia for people not to be matching in their ceremonial robes. Good for you to shake up tradition a bit."

"Only a bit." I smiled.

Andra held out her hand for me, but I pulled myself out of the basin with ease. "Look at you! You don't need my help after all." She smirked. "That bath is working wonders already."

"I feel better. Like a human again." I dried off with the cloth she handed me. "Do you know about any strange illnesses between *virlukos* and humans? I did wonder if maybe I'd contracted a rare disease shared between us or something. I figured you would know more, considering how close you live with humans."

"Well..." Andra cleared her throat. "The thing is, this isn't a *virlukos*-and-human-transmitted disease or anything. It's definitely not human."

"But not *virlukos*? How do you know?" I pulled on my Historian robe, relishing in the water-like texture. I buttoned it with ease and wondered at how quickly I started feeling better.

"It's not something I've seen before. I mean, I heard about it, yes.

But seen it with my own eyes–"

"You've heard about this happening before" I froze, eyes pinned to Andra.

She tucked her short caramel hair behind her ear. "It's said in legend that–"

"There you are!" Archer jogged through the trees, beige robe fluttering behind him. "I thought I'd be lost forever in this forest. All the trees were starting to look the same."

"You poor thing." Andra clicked her tongue mockingly. "We would've found you after a few hours claiming you hadn't eaten a thing in decades."

Archer rolled his eyes and threw an arm around Andra's neck. He mussed her hair before turning his attention to me. "You're looking as stunning as ever, *pilukos*."

I blushed, knowing it was just a compliment but recalled how nervous Nash had been about Archer in Lukosan. Archer's flirtation had all been part of the plot to separate me from Silas, but the tension lingered in the back of my mind.

"Silas is a lucky dog." Archer smirked, releasing his protesting sister.

"And you'll be a lone wolf if you touch me again," Andra snapped, straightening her robe and fixing her hair.

"She loves me. Couldn't live without me," Archer whispered, like he and I were in on the same secret.

"I can think of a few things you could live without," she grumbled, folding the cloth I'd used for a towel and placing it with the yucca and yarrow. "Is breakfast ready?"

"Yes, ma'am." Archer bowed his head. "I've come to retrieve you both."

He held his arm out for Andra, but she held out her hands. "Not

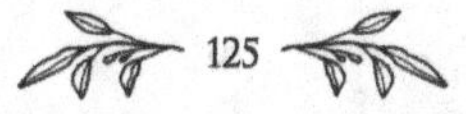

a chance. You'll wrinkle my robes even worse than you already have." She rolled her eyes, shooting me a grin before starting down the path.

Archer raised an eyebrow at me. "Come on. Don't let me walk alone. I'll get lost again and never get to eat Silas's famous oatmeal."

"I can't say no to you, can I?" I laughed, threading my hand through his arm. "But it's Ellie's famous oatmeal. A mama's recipe is always better."

"Agreed. Plus, I think Silas mainly directed the Kitchen hands. I don't think he'd know where to look for a pot."

I chuckled, remembering Silas's ignorance with cooking. "It takes a while, but eventually he finds what he's looking for."

Archer squeezed my hand. "Like he did with you, right?"

The question caught me off guard. Archer always seemed to do that, bringing deeper meaning into such trivial conversations.

"Yeah, I guess you could say that."

We lapsed into silence, skirting around the Yard on our way to the Kitchen. We passed lots more people than usual, a mix of Arcadians and Lukosans mingling on their way to breakfast. Most who recognized me waved or greeted Archer and I, and some of the Arcadians seemed surprised to see me out and about.

And it surprised me, too, how easily my calloused feet remembered the paths. My muscles strained, but remembered the rhythm of a short walk with someone dear. Most surprising of all, my lungs remembered their routine of breaths without fits. It was almost like I hadn't been sick at all.

Maybe I needed to take a bath every day.

Or maybe I needed friends like Andra and Archer to help me through.

21
SILAS

I HADN'T HEARD FROM EDEN OR ANDRA YET. I sent Archer to find them, but if they were gone for too much longer, I'd need to make sure someone covered breakfast before I went to find them myself.

Maybe Eden's illness grew worse while I was away.

I wiped the thought away as I dabbed sweat from my brow. The heat wafted from the large, steaming pots of oats, stirred by several different Kitchen hands. I'd walked them through my mother's recipe, dropping in thyme at the last moment.

I turned to Lilah, who ran the kitchen this morning. "Are you okay if I—"

Someone cleared his throat at the edge of the kitchen. "Announcing her darling majesty, queen of the valley realm of Arcadia, and elected high Alpha by his majesty Iain... Queen Eden of Arcadia."

I turned so fast that I bumped into Lilah and knocked a spoon straight into one of the pots. I watched helplessly while it sank beneath the oats.

"It's fine." Lilah laughed. "Go on. I've got this."

Archer stepped away from Eden's side and to the pot where the spoon disappeared. "Don't mind if I do. Mother always nagged me for playing with my food. This is the dream job for me."

I straightened my robes, turning my full attention to my bride-to-be.

Eden practically glowed. Her Historian robes shimmered in the early morning sun, perfect curls escaping her braided bun.

My Eden.

"Hi." She smiled.

I swallowed, breath hitching. "Hi." I caught glances of kitchen staff hiding their giggles and smirks causing a blush to creep up my neck. Clearing my throat, I bowed my head. "You're glowing, *pilukos*."

"Who knew a nice bath in the light of a sunrise would do the trick?" Eden grinned. "I heard you made our pack breakfast."

My heart stuttered at the words *our pack*. Of course it was true, but hearing her say it out loud gave me a flutter of excitement. I hadn't allowed myself to think of much past *Joulo*, a part of me afraid I'd lose Eden to whatever illness plagued her. But standing in front of me now, how could I doubt her?

"I haven't done much of the work." I turned to Lilah to give her compliments on managing a tight crew, but she and Archer laughed over sticky hands and something he'd said to make her smile.

Returning to Eden, she gave me a look that said she knew exactly what was going on. If I wasn't careful, Archer would have my entire kingdom wrapped around his paws from his charm and flirtatiousness alone.

"Shall we?" I held out my arm for Eden, who slipped her hand around my elbow. I walked her to the recently renovated dining area. We'd added a few more tables to the pebble-coated clearing to accommodate

Lukosan. I feared it might feel too tight and claustrophobic, but instead, the clearing felt cozy, like the Lukosan dining tent. We had succeeded in bringing out Nash's vision to make Arcadia a blend of the two packs while Lukosan visited.

He brought the idea up to me over a swim the other day. He surprised me with a well-formed plan to strengthen the bond between the two packs. He surmised that we could replicate the same accommodations for other packs, making us the first pack or kingdom to create intercultural communications and integrations. Nash asked to be the head of communications for future pack relations, but I asked him to wait until after *Joulo*—after Eden felt well again—and we could discuss a larger scale option. Until then, I passed the decision-making to Caroline, who executed it to perfection.

We still asked Andra that meals be eaten Arcadian style—the highest ranking starting first, then all the way down to the Omega—and she hadn't objected. But the dining area and the Yard had been tailored to the Lukosan style, extra seating for the humans, more common spaces, and Bennett even planned designated adventures to entertain the pups, adolescents, and humans of the Lukosan pack.

At the end of Lukosan's stay, Nash and Caroline would evaluate how it went, and we could decide what to do for the future.

The idea of connecting with other *virlukos* packs is something Eden first brought to my attention the first time she'd met the *micca*. With Nash bringing up similar ideas, I thought that maybe this could work. Maybe that was my legacy—to start to bridge the packs. And watching Eden now, graceful while she moved from Arcadian to Lukosan to human to pup with unexpected seamlessness, I knew it would.

And it had all been Nash's idea. It made me think he could be officially promoted to Delta soon, an outward symbol of how much he'd changed for good. This pack-bonding idea was just the start of the amazing things I knew my brother could accomplish.

This time next year, maybe we could have a gathering of wolves to celebrate *Joulo* in Arcadia, a celebration of different packs.

"What are you thinking about?" Eden's voice broke through my excitement.

"Nothing." I met her curious gaze, lip curled slightly. "What?"

She swirled her finger at me, circling my face. "You had that–that look you get when you're happily pensive."

"Is it too much to be thoughtfully happy?" I raised an eyebrow, eliciting a groan from my mate. "Would you rather I be seriously stupid?"

"Forget it. I just wanted to know what was going on in that brain of yours." Eden smoothed her hair back. "I haven't had time for much conversation with you since all of this started."

I gave her hand a squeeze, guiding her to a seat. "Say the word, and I'm there. Would you like time for a seriously stupid conversation with me or a happily pensive one? Or I'd even offer happily stupid if that would make you happy."

A grin lit her face and she rolled her eyes at me. "I'll take any of it if it means time with you."

I reached for her hands, running my thumb over her fourth finger. I paused, noting the bare skin where her ring had been. "Did something happen to your ring?"

How silly of me to care so much when I'd thought it an ostentatious human tradition only a month or so ago. But seeing her without it sent a jolt of tension down my spine. Hadn't Eden mentioned Andra tried to remove it at breakfast the other morning? Had Andra successfully stolen it?

Eden frowned. "I must've forgotten to put it back on. I took it off for safe keeping, but..." She felt in the pocket of her robe. "It was here in my pocket."

I caught sight of Archer and Andra, and waved them over. They sat next to us.

"What's up?" Andra's eyebrows wrinkled, and she glanced between me and Eden. "Everything okay?" Her heart quickened, and while it raised suspicion, perhaps she could see the alarm written all over Eden.

"Are you sure you put the ring in my pocket?" Eden asked, fruitlessly searching her pocket.

Some sort of shadow passed between Andra and Archer, an unspoken, dark thing. My suspicion rose higher.

Andra tilted her head. "You watched me put it in your pocket. It's not there?"

I shook my head, not wanting to pass my concerns to Eden with her already worried about losing the ring. "We'll make a new one." I hated the words since it had been a grand gesture, but the ring was at least replaceable.

"No, but that one is special." Eden covered her face in her hands.

Andra rubbed a hand on her back like a loving big sister would. "Hey, how about I look for it? And in the meantime, I can get Rory to make you a new one with an Arcadian tree. You and Silas can have rings from the same branch."

Eden sighed. "Yeah, that's fine, I guess. I can't believe I lost it. I'm such a mess."

"Not a mess," I countered. "This isn't your fault."

"He speaks the truth." Archer dipped his chin. "I can start looking for it, but only after a steaming bowl of Silas's famous oats."

"Ellie's famous oats," Eden and I corrected simultaneously.

"Gross. Get a cave." Andra mussed my hair.

I forced a chuckle, trying not to peer too much into how relaxed Andra seemed to be about losing Eden's ring. Had she stolen it? In

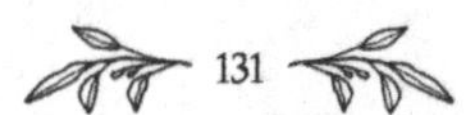

the time since we'd left Lukosan, had she not grown past that childish longing for the past version of me? I thought she'd let go of her infatuation, but maybe her feelings lingered.

I watched Andra closely while we ate and noticed her furtive glances to Eden like she tried to read her thoughts.

"So, what did y'all get up to yesterday?" I leaned forward on my forearms.

There. I caught another meaningful look pass between Andra and Archer, something quiet and dangerous.

"Not much." Archer cleared his throat. "I've been exploring, chatting with people in the pack, and catching up with old acquaintances from our pup years."

Andra rolled her eyes with a half smile, but her heart rate told me something still bothered her. Guilt, maybe?

"What about you?" I asked.

Andra met my gaze, and a flash of wariness crossed her features. She recognized the challenge in my tone, and could probably see it in my eyes. I wasn't trying to hide it from her. I needed her to understand whose land she stood on and whose family she talked to.

Mine.

"I was with Nash in the morning." Andra shifted. "And then I ate lunch and hung out with Archer."

My face scrunched. "Have you seen Nash today? I figured he'd be here."

Don't worry. Everything is fine. Nash hasn't left.

No matter how much I tried to comfort myself with platitudes, I always feared when Nash wasn't where I expected him to be. Maybe he would leave again.

"Andra, didn't you say you saw him last night with Archer?" Eden frowned.

"I–I did." She bit her lip. "Briefly. I'm assuming he's still sleeping. He patrolled Mt. Leconte for most of the day yesterday."

"Why does Kane have him patrolling the Great Mountain?" I craned my neck to catch a glimpse of the Guardian Branch leader. "The fires have been put out, and those trails aren't great during the winter months. Even the Wildcat doesn't travel far in that snow."

Andra tensed. "He's not a pup anymore. He can take care of himself."

The tension thickened like a late-night fog. I held up both hands to placate Andra's temper. Clearly, I'd struck some tender point in the conversation. Was that the reason for the odd glances this morning?

"Nash is capable, and I trust him with my life." I run one hand through my loose waves. *Silva*, it needed a trim. "I worry about him. He has a lot going on."

"You have no idea," Archer huffed under his breath.

"What do you mean?" Eden leaned forward. It struck me again how well she seemed after about a month of illness. That bath had done her wonders.

Archer leaned back, shifting his jaw like he pondered the best words to say. Finally, he shrugged. "He's outspoken for someone who doesn't share much. I mean, he's not very voluntary with his issues. It comes out in pieces when he makes jokes, but it's difficult to tell how much he's hurting unless you're paying close attention."

I mirrored Archer and leaned back in my seat. I hummed, running a hand over Eden's absentmindedly. He had a point. Nash was vocal, but never about anything serious unless the situation was dire.

I cleared my throat, wondering if I needed to go talk to Nash. "Did he say anything last night? Is he..."

I didn't know what I was trying to imply, only that Archer's words made me realize how little I'd really listened to Nash. Sure, I'd heard him, but had I truly understood him?

Archer shrugged. "He appeared a bit spent from the day, that's all."

After more casual conversation returned, I stood and placed a kiss on Eden's temple.

She angled her chin up at me, squinting in the morning sun. "Leaving already?"

I offered a watery smile. "I have a few things to check on. I'm going to send Asa to Guardian's Glade in half an hour or so. Will you be there? I want him to look over your symptoms again. You seem so much better this morning."

Eden nodded. "I feel better. Better than I have in a long time."

I caught her hand in mine, pulling it to my lips where her ring should've been. "Thank Lycaon for that. I'll see you soon, okay? Call for me if you start feeling ill again."

I waited for her to agree before waving at the Lukosans and taking my leave.

I made my way to the far edge of the Residential Quarter. Most of my people were dining or out starting on their first tasks of the day, so I passed only birds and squirrels on my way. At the last den on the last row at the very edge of the border of Arcadia, I hesitated.

Should I let him sleep?

I inhaled and knocked on the door. I waited, but there was no reply.

I knocked again. My heart rate climbed in speed.

Setting manners aside, I wrenched open the door. Nash's room was sparsely decorated with a messy bed, a small table with a mug, and a wardrobe with its door ajar. I half-heartedly straightened the bed, noticing the empty mug and the air around it smelling of *kulas*. Strange for an Arcadian to be drinking it not on a holiday or at a feast, but maybe his Lukosan habits didn't die as quickly as mine.

I moved to shut the wardrobe, but the sharp scent of iron froze my steps.

I found the rag without difficulty, kicked under the bed frame. The blood was unmistakable, not much but enough for concern. Had Nash fallen yesterday on his patrol of Mt. Leconte? Why hadn't he reported his injury to Kane?

I stuffed the rag in my robe pocket. I needed to see Asa anyway, but I hoped that's where my brother would be.

22
NASH

"YOU CAN MOVE IT WITHOUT PAIN, YES?" Asa manually flexed each of my fingers, pressing into the muscles a little uncomfortably.

"I don't think anything is broken if that's what you mean. All of my ligaments are still attached as far as I know." I shifted in my seat at his prodding. "Although this isn't a trot in the woods with you pressing like that."

Asa returned my hand to me and moved to the water he'd warmed when I'd come in. "And you say it left you alone?"

I told him most of the truth. I hated lying, but it was crucial I keep some things hidden, at least for now. Andra and Archer knew, and for now, that would be enough. I would have to tell the truth someday, but I didn't want to ruin this for Silas. The anniversary of his first full year as King of Arcadia, *Joulo*, and his upcoming wedding. I didn't want it to be my fault, too, stealing the joy and life from those monumental celebrations.

So I told Asa that I'd been on patrol when I found evidence of the Hunt. It wasn't a secret that they were around; up until now, we just didn't know where. So the story version of myself stalked the Wendigo, and had it cornered at one of the overlooks. It tried to talk its way out with its silvertongue, but ended up cutting my paw with its claw when it rushed past.

I could tell the wizened healer didn't quite believe me, but he didn't call me out.

"Physically, the Wendigo left me alone. Well, aside from my paw. But the strangest thing happened. I had a vision, like a flash of my memory returning from last year."

Asa froze, his hands around a bowl of warm plantain water. "What is it that you remember?"

I swallowed, needing to choose my words carefully. "I get these flashes—the trees around this valley, firelight, and pain. So much pain. And I saw *Atagahi*, but I can't..."

My breaths increased, and I curled in on myself, trying to minimize the awareness. Everything ached. The pain of grief and guilt far outweighed the twinge of the cut on my palm. The thought of *Atagahi* and its healing waters sent me wondering if we could've brought my father there to be healed. Could I have saved him?

I rocked where I sat, trying to block out the sounds of his screaming in my memories.

"Lycaon, I'm sorry," I choked, holding a shaking hand over my lips where I could still taste the memory of blood.

Heavy hands found my shoulders, putting pressure where I didn't know I'd needed it. "Breaths like the wind, *je lyco*," Asa murmured. "Long, deep gusts."

Slowly, with the pressure from his hands and steady breathing, I calmed my racing heart. Time passed like pine sap in the winter, but each moment brought my Spirit back in alignment with my body. Eventually, Asa pulled my hands away from my face.

"Now, let me clean this hand up." Asa brought the bowl of warm plantain water to the cot, dipping the cloth into the liquid. Gently he dabbed at my wound, the mix stinging and causing the edges of the wound to itch.

"Do you think its magic will affect me any more than it already has?" I watched his hands while he dabbed the remaining blood and dirt I'd missed in my haste last night.

"Time will tell." He placed the bowl to the side and picked up a strip of cloth. "You'll keep me updated, yes?"

I nodded and he wrapped my hand, tying a knot so it would stay in place. "Thank you."

Asa smiled at me in a grandfatherly way and patted my shoulder. "Now, get something to eat, please."

I pushed to my feet as someone entered the room behind me. A chill rippled down my spine when I caught the scent of Silas and something else.

I turned, and my heart dropped to my stomach. He held out a rag spotted with soil and blood. He'd gone through my things, what little I possessed. In the past, it might have bothered me, but if I were in his place and my flighty brother hadn't been seen in a full day, I'd be searching his things too. I had nothing to hide except the truth, and I'd always been a terrible liar.

"What happened?" he asked, tossing the rag on a pile of other soiled cloth from Asa's patients.

I glanced at Asa, who excused himself and disappeared. I waited until I could no longer hear his heart beating, not meeting my brother's gaze. "I slipped near one of the overlooks on my way home last night. The snow and ice are pretty slick up there."

"Why does Kane have you patrolling the Great Mountain? This far in the season, the hikers should mostly be gone. The Wildcat has things under control. We need you closer to home."

I rolled my eyes. "You created this job for me in the first place. I was only following my orders."

Silas sighed. "You could've been hurt. Nash, you have to be more careful."

"I know how to walk, Silas. You don't have to mother me."

"I'm not–" Silas exhaled. "I'm sorry. I talked to Andra and Archer this morning, and they said you looked a bit worse for wear. And I thought... I thought you'd left me again."

I watched him now, and I wondered if he could finally see how broken I was. He at least expected me to abandon him at such a special time in his life. But I couldn't blame him for seeing me that way.

I shook my head. "I won't leave until you send me away."

He scoffed. "As if that would ever happen. What would Father say?'

I flinched too much for him not to notice.

"You okay?" He stepped closer, and I stepped to the side.

"Yeah, it's been a full year since..."

Silas's breath caught.

"I guess you won't have your mourning paint anymore." I tried to smile, but it felt more like a grimace.

He dipped his chin, thoughts far off from where we stood. "Yeah. Better for the wedding."

"You survived your first year as king." I patted his shoulder. "Congrats."

Silas met my gaze, his green eyes all watery. "Are you sure you're okay? Because I'm here for you if you want to talk. I'll clear our schedules, and we can go for another swim."

"Really, Si, I'm fine. I haven't eaten since yesterday morning." I

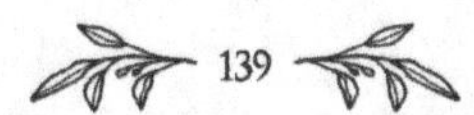

swallowed down my fear and guilt and shame and everything else that threatened to pour from my lips. The fact that he cared enough to check on me made it so much more difficult. "I heard you made Mother's oatmeal. Is there any left for the Omega?"

Silas shifted. "About that, I wanted–"

"I don't want to miss out if Lilah dumps the leftovers for the bears." I moved around him, ducking out the door. I paused, turning my head to catch him in my periphery. "Thanks for making breakfast and for checking on me."

And with that, I quickly brushed through the trees. I passed Asa, who headed back to intercept Silas. The closer I got to the Kitchen, the more my nerves frayed.

Closer.

Closer.

And yet, farther away.

I glanced back, afraid to see Silas trailing me again, but there was no sign of him. And I collided with a warm body. I spun, catching Eden from falling into the ferns. "I am so sorry." I steadied her and took two steps back, putting sufficient space between us. My arms and legs tingled with the adrenaline from touching her—touching anyone I loved for that matter. What if I hurt them like I did my own father? Clearly, no one was safe. What if something had broken in me that day? I could barely live with myself, but if I knowingly hurt my family, my life would be over. It was the reason I'd put space between Silas and I, and the reason I'd continue to do so with the entire pack until the moment he and Eden said their vows.

Then I'd disappear so I couldn't hurt anyone else.

"Oh, it's not your fault. I should've said something." Eden smiled.

And I noticed she walked alone, fully upright and glowing with color and life.

"You're standing." I scanned her from top to bottom, searching for a trick. Last I'd see her, she'd been practically bedridden. "You look great. I—How did you—"

She grinned. "I can't believe I made the crown prince of Arcadia speechless. No quips or snide remarks?"

I shook my head. "I'm amazed to see you so well. How are you feeling?"

She shrugged. "Much better. I feel human again, like I can take in a full breath." She tucked a stray curl behind her ear, fresh with life. "It's amazing what a hot bath can do. Andra helped me this morning, and I've felt like a new person. Or like my old self but stronger somehow."

The thought of Andra made my heart ache. "How is she?"

Eden pursed her lips. "I think you should talk to her."

"Talk about what?" My heart hammered in my chest, and I found myself grateful that Eden would never be able to detect it.

She glared at me from behind her eyelashes. "I think you know. She's clearly into you, and you're clearly into her. Why haven't you done something about it?"

My heart reached previously unknown speeds. Eden wouldn't lie to me.

I scoffed. "You must be mistaken. Are we talking about the same woman? The one that was in love with my brother—your fiancé—up until, perhaps, four or five weeks ago?"

Eden rolled her eyes. "Yes! I think the entire time she's been in love with you, and she's too afraid to say it. She was in love with the idea of Silas, but I truly believe she loves you for who you are."

Shaking my head, I cleared my throat. "No. If there was anything there before, it's long since dead. I've fallen too far for that."

I'd never seen Eden mad before, but this was pretty close. She groaned, frustration lining her face. "If this is about you being the

Omega in Arcadia, I'm tired of it. Either I'll convince Silas to return your titles or convince you to marry the Alpha of Lukosan. But you shouldn't be living like this."

"Except I should, Eden. You don't get it," I snapped and immediately regretted it.

She moved a pace back from me. "What don't I get?"

I stared at her feet, the path, the ferns, anything but meeting her gaze. "I'm not good. I don't deserve good things."

"Nash, that's a lie, and you know it. Iain wouldn't—"

"Iain is dead, Eden. When are you going to realize that?" I glared at her, fire ripping through my veins.

Her shoulders fell. "Nash, what's gotten into you?"

My jaw ticked. "Nothing new. You're just finally seeing me for who I am: the spare brother who lost everything a long time ago."

Without waiting for an answer, I turned my back on her, stalking to the Kitchen. She called out my name twice, but I couldn't bear to look at her or go back. I couldn't apologize for my tone or my words. I had nothing to say anymore. I had nothing good in me.

All I had to do was make it to *Joulo*, to the end of their wedding ceremony. And then I could let them live in peace again without a murderer in their midst.

23

EDEN

I RUBBED MY FOREHEAD as Nash disappeared around a bend in the path. Something had shifted. Nash claimed that I finally saw his true self, but something didn't feel right about that. In the many therapy sessions my parents had put me through while trying to eradicate my delusions, as they called them, I did end up learning some useful advice.

Humans often tell themselves things they believe to be true, things that *feel* true, but aren't. People could lie to themselves so often that they start to believe the lies. So while my parents thought I'd lied to myself so much that I started to believe werewolves existed, I realized it was more nuanced than that.

I often believed I wasn't worthy of someone caring or compassionate because my parents didn't have much to spare for me. But just because I was treated a certain way didn't mean that's what I deserved.

Which is why Nash's words unsettled me. He said over and over again that he was the Omega and unworthy and not good. Like Archer said at breakfast, Nash hid behind his jokes, some bordering on self-deprecation. Sure, most of them were poking fun, but some of them he actually believed deep down in his Spirit, even though they were lies.

I resumed my walk to Guardian's Glade, mulling over the best way to start encouraging Nash to maybe get him to believe some of the good things about himself. He always protected his family, he could liven any dreary mood, and I was confident he'd never met a stranger.

As I reached the turn off the main path, I passed a few wolves returning from a patrol. It surprised me to realize that I recognized two of them, even in their wolf forms. They were the two that had gone with Kane to support me in my stand against Nyx—Alden and Ramona.

I bowed my head when they passed, and their ears dropped back in a sign of submission. I prided myself on how much I'd learned while I'd been sick. It wasn't much, but I'd pestered Nash to explain certain expressions and reactions from wolves. I'd seen things on nature documentaries, but nothing came close to watching things unfold between pack members.

Things were looking up. Maybe I would make a decent queen, and I certainly felt so much better this morning.

At the double door to Guardian's Glade, I noticed Silas's robe on his hook.

He must be out for a run.

He'd mentioned business to attend to, and I wondered if it had been a ruse to get some alone time. I hoped not, but I saw how my illness weighed on him. The dark circles under his eyes took on a bruised quality this past week. I wondered if it would ever fully leave him, the worry and fear even while my strength returned.

I slipped inside, noticing Asa waiting for me. "Sorry to keep you waiting." I offered an apologetic smile.

He returned the expression, the corners of his eyes crinkling from years of mirth. "No need for apologies, *je kunin.* I'm glad to see my favorite patient is on her feet. How do you feel?"

"Like a brand new person." I shrugged. "I don't know what changed. I had a bath this morning, and I feel miraculously better. Must've been something in the water."

Asa laughed, a wheezy sort of sound escaping his lips. "Or perhaps, your body has finally done its duty and fought off whatever ailment attacked you for so long."

The door behind me opened, and I turned to find Bennett striding toward me. "Thank Lycaon you're here!" The dark skin of his arms shimmered. "The Tailors found this while washing up."

The water on his arms made sense now. He held out his fist and unclenched his fingers to reveal my wedding band.

A sound escaped me, and I threw my arms around Bennett. He stumbled back. "Thank you, thank you, thank you!"

I steadied myself, catching Bennett masking the bewilderment from my hug. Perhaps I should've been more professional and courtly, but it crushed me that I'd lost my ring so soon. To have it returned to me flooded me with relief.

I took the ring from him, slipping it on the fourth finger of my left hand. "I can't believe I lost it. I'm never taking this thing off again."

Bennett bowed and left us. I turned back to Asa, admiring the smooth wood of the ring once again.

"Back to our conversation." Asa cleared his throat. "As a Healer, I want you to continue your teas and herbs for at least a few more days. That way we can be sure you are fully recovered."

I placed a hand on his arm. "Thank you, Asa. For everything you do here in Arcadia."

Without warning, the throne room swam in my vision. I clutched Asa's sleeve, trying to bring the branches above back into focus. No matter how much I blinked, nothing cleared.

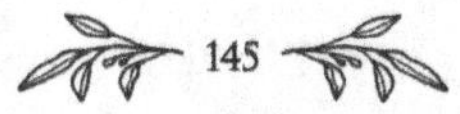

"*Je kunin?*" Asa braced my arms with his. "What is it?"

"I don't–I can't quite bring anything into focus. And I–" I tried to breathe in, but I choked on the attempt. I coughed again and again. Cursed illness. I thought I was getting better. Something dark appeared in my periphery, most likely spots from coughing so hard.

Asa inhaled sharply, tightening his grip on my arm. "*Je kunin.*" He sounded so concerned, scared even. I wondered how bad I must look for the Head Healer to be afraid.

There was no getting better or magical bath cure for me. It seemed like this illness would never leave, not truly.

"*Je kunin.*" Asa's voice shook.

I squeezed my eyes shut, but my head swam even more. "I need to lie down."

Asa helped me to my bed and poured me a glass of water. I glanced up at him, noticing the tremor in his hands and wondered if he thought this would kill me.

"Asa, what's wrong with me?" I breathed. I knew he didn't have an answer for me. The past month puzzled him as much as the rest of us.

He passed me the water, glancing at my hand when I accepted it. "Everything will be fine, Eden. I have to sort some things out. I will return when I have, um, sorted things. Rest up. I'll send someone to come sit with you, but in the meantime, get some rest." He cast a nervous glance to the side door, almost worried someone would come in to snatch me. The shaking had not stopped in his hands. He cleared his throat again, staring at my hands. "Rest."

And he left, robes billowing behind him.

24

CAROLINE

"I'M TELLING YOU, it doesn't make sense that she's healed." Leander paced around the fire of the Sage Brush. He didn't have vision, but the Seer certainly had the Sight. He never hesitated on his endless circle around the blue flames.

"You think it's suspicious, too?" Ransom leaned over the manuscript Aubrey read from earlier, looking for new answers. "It feels like a trick. The Raven Mocker is toying with us."

"We don't know that it's a Mocker. We don't have proof yet." Markus, head in my lap, tossed a rock in the air, catching it and tossing it up again while I played with his sandy-colored hair.

"No," I said with a shrug. "But we have a way of finding out."

Leander stopped pacing and turned to me. "You and Ransom should go watch over her tonight. Tell her it's a precaution to make sure the illness has truly left her. Once she falls asleep, Ransom will step into her dreams. Then we will know."

Aubrey groaned from her place next to Ransom. "But Caroline and

I spoke with the catamount. He told us that they had her already. Isn't that proof enough?"

"I think we should tell Silas." Markus offered.

"Not yet," the three Seers said in unison.

Markus began to argue his point, but a strange sound caught my attention. I tried to focus, tried to parse out if it was an animal or a person. They were moving fast. "Everybody, shush," I hissed.

The room grew quiet, and the footfalls grew louder.

"Someone's coming." I turned to Markus.

Leander cocked his head. "It's Asa."

No less than two seconds passed before the Head Healer lumbered into the main room of the Sage Brush. He stumbled to a stop, paws pushing in the dirt, and I wondered how long it had been since he ran like that.

His breaths were labored, and his tongue lolled to the side. Aubrey pulled a bowl from the shelves and poured water for Asa to drink. We waited in tense silence while he regained his composure.

Leander was the first to speak. "You have vital information."

Asa straightened, water dripping from his white muzzle. "*There is a Raven Mocker attached to the queen. I saw it with my own eyes.*"

Ransom cursed from the corner. Markus inhaled sharply next to me.

"Because you are the only one who can see it aside from Eden herself," Leander offered.

Asa inclined his head.

"It's what we feared." Leander moved to the shelf, running his hands along the spines of a few books before pulling one out. "Ransom, you know what to do."

With a flurry of movement, the Seers went to work, and I moved to stand next to Asa. "Are you all right?"

He bowed his head, ears pinning back for a moment. *"Thank you for your concern, je lyce. I doubt I will ever recover from such a blow. Never in my life have I had a patient with a Mocker. I am pained to know I can do nothing to help my queen."*

"She's not gone yet." I placed a hand under his jaw, meeting his gaze. "We already have a plan to put into action. We won't roll over that easily."

Ransom and I walked out with Asa back to Guardian's Glade. Asa left for his quarters, to do what he could in the face of this danger.

Inside the throne room, the temperature seemed cooler than before. The late morning sun had been blotted out by clouds, and a harsh wind rippled through the foliage. I knocked at Silas and Eden's door and waited. When no one responded, I let Ransom and me in.

Eden lay in the large bed alone, pale and fragile compared to an hour ago when she'd been vibrant and lively again.

"What now?" I asked Ransom, still watching Eden's chest rise and fall with shallow breaths.

Ransom set his bag on the table, pulling out the book Leander gave to him, along with some herbs and a jar of murky liquid. "It will take a while. We'll have to wait for Eden to enter a dream before starting the ritual."

"How long can that take?"

His silence drew my attention. He braced himself on the desk, shoulders tense and straight. "Minutes, hours, days... Some people rarely enter dreams, but if Eden is ill as she obviously is, it won't be long. Take a seat."

I obeyed, sitting in Silas's chair.

We waited for two hours before Silas returned holding his robe, sweaty from wherever he'd run off to. His eyes found Ransom, Ransom's things, me, and finally Eden asleep in bed. "What's going on? Why did no one call for me?" He moved to her side, tossing his neglected robe to the floor. With such gentle care, Silas felt her forehead with the back of his hand. "What's happened? Why is she burning up like this? Where's Asa?"

"*Je kunan*, please. Calm down." Ransom held his hands up.

Silas snapped his head to the Seer with a look of hatred in his eyes that I'd never seen before. "Don't tell me to calm down. *Silva*, is she breathing?" He turned back to Eden, practically petting her loose curls.

"Silas." I stood, facing him on the opposite side of the bed. "Look at me."

For a moment, he watched Eden, eyes flitting back and forth over her face looking for any signs of harm. Finally, he tore his eyes away and met my gaze. Tears threatened to spill over. "Caroline, what do I do?" he breathed, shaking his head. "I can't control it. I can't protect her."

I squeezed his shoulder. "We already have a plan, but I need you to sit down and talk to me, okay?"

He nodded, moving stiffly to his chair behind me. Once settled, he kept his eyes on Eden much like he had the past month when he'd had free time in his schedule.

"Si, we think there's a chance..." I glanced at Ransom who shook his head.

Not telling the truth yet.

I cleared my throat. "We think there's a chance we can discover a reason for her illness if Ransom can get in her dreams."

Silas's head snaps up. "Why do you need to crawl into her mind? Is there no other way?"

"You know there isn't." Ransom sighed. "This is the logical next step. We have Asa's permission."

Silas crumpled. "I want to be here."

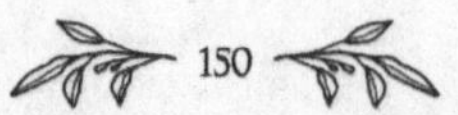

"No," I stated as firmly as I could. "I'm sorry, Silas, but you're going to be a distraction. And we need as little of that as possible if we want Eden to enter dream sleep."

"I can help."

Ransom moved toward him. "You've been an immense help taking care of her so far, but if you want her to be well again and to live all her days in Arcadia happy and free, you need to let us do our jobs."

Silas searched for anything, any reason he could stay, but he failed. His shoulders dropped, and he assented. "I'm going to the Falls for a swim to cool down, and I'll be back. I'll wait in Guardian's Glade if you need me."

Grabbing his robe and taking one last look at Eden, he left.

"And now, we wait." Ransom exhaled, leaning back against the desk.

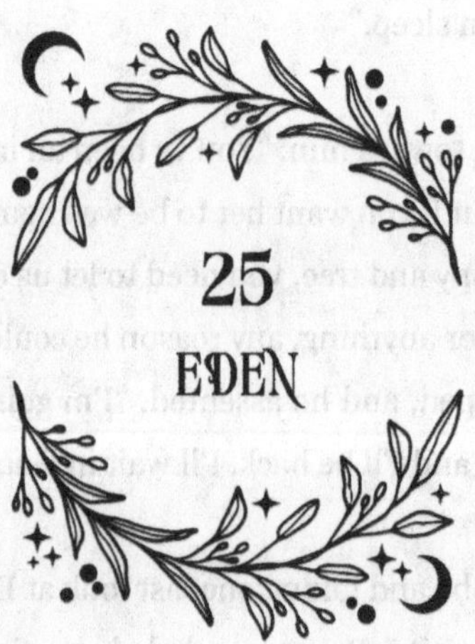

25

EDEN

IT WAS NIGHTTIME IN GUARDIAN'S GLADE, the lanterns lit and glowing with warmth. It felt like springtime despite winter's chill outside of Arcadia. But I was alone in the Glade, the two thrones empty and threatening.

How could I rule when I was so weak?

I lay down in the aisle, noticing small purple flowers for the first time. Had I walked over them this whole time? Had I trampled their beauty without noticing?

I turned my head to the side, peering at the dainty cups facing the sky, like tulips the size of a single grain of rice. A shadow fell over my face, and I glanced up, expecting Silas or Caroline, maybe even Nash. Instead, I was met with darkness.

A form—the shape of a woman—towered over me, a strange mask hiding her face. Her robe fluttered behind her in the wind. But where my robe was one solid piece, hers had been shredded into countless strips so that they tossed violently behind her.

I saw her profile silhouetted by the light of the moon. She was regal and terrible. Something heavy hung over her, and I wondered oddly if the heaviness was my fault.

I almost spoke when she shrieked with fury. Storm clouds gathered with impossible speed and blotted out the moon. I was in the dark, and the birdlike woman pointed at me, one long fingernail hooked and shaking.

"Do not fear me."

"Who are you?" I swallowed, my mouth and throat as dry as a desert.

"Death." She withdrew her shaking finger. "It will not hurt."

Her mangled robes separated from her body one at a time, swirling into a tornado of fabric and leaving the woman's bones. And I realized that what I thought had been her hair was actually ebony feathers.

I tried to scream, but no sound answered. The torrent of fabric whipped around my face like a veil. My hand clenched around a black dahlia, and a crown of twisted willow settled on my head.

Sadness, tragedy, pain.

I was dying.

I was becoming Death.

Ghastly, grim, and ancient.

Antlers loomed above me, an empty skull with flames for eyes peered down at me. And I realized I stared into the face of a Wendigo.

"Oh, it's you." My lips did not move, but my voice dropped into the night.

"Wolf Queen, where are you?"

"Guardian's Glade, in Arcadia."

"No." The word hung limp in the space between our breaths. "You're in the Between."

"The Between. Of course. That's why the stars are gone." I gazed at

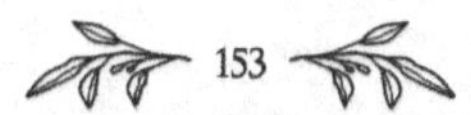

the sky, the storm clouds rolling away to reveal a starless sky. Through the veil of fabric from the bird lady, I could see the moon, alone in the dark like me.

"Wake up, Wolf Queen." The Wendigo's jaw opened, unhinging until it gaped at an obtuse angle. "Wake up."

A flash of light blinded me. My head throbbed, and I felt sick to my stomach. When my eyes adjusted to the light, I found myself still in Guardian's Glade, but snow blanketed the room, unblemished by tracks. Both thrones sat empty, snow piling over the seat and arms.

"AHK!"

I whipped around to find a raven, dark feathers contrasted against the pure snow. It perched on something strange, an odd branch maybe.

I stepped toward it and froze.

It wasn't a branch.

It was an antler.

The antler of a dead Wendigo, its lanky skeleton half buried in the snow.

"AHK!" The raven hurtled toward me.

I covered my eyes with my palms, but the bird dug its talons into my scalp, pulling my hair up. A few more ravens circled me, pulling at my hair, my skin, my fingers.

I tried to draw air into my lungs, but I couldn't breathe.

Why couldn't I breathe?

26
CAROLINE

ETERNITY SEEMED TO PASS, and I busied myself straightening and dusting the neglected books and scrolls. Afterwards, I sat down in the chair with a sigh. Ransom didn't deign me with a response.

A short while later, Ransom stiffened and quickly gathered his things.

"What can I–"

"Shush!" Ransom interrupted me.

I glanced at Eden, who appeared the same, only now her eyes moved rapidly behind her lids. I wondered what it must be like to walk through someone's dreams and how disturbing it might be if Ransom were the kind of person to wield that power in cruelty.

But I knew Ransom. He didn't find any joy in this. The firm set of his jaw told me as much as he burned a bundle of herbs and swigged the murky liquid. He murmured in the Ancient Tongue under his breath, a sort of prayer.

"Quick." Ransom moved the chair close to Eden's side and dropped into it. "Watch my eyes. If you start to see white, put the bottle in my hand. I must keep drinking unless I pull myself out of the dream voluntarily."

"But how will I know?" I held the bottle and watched Ransom's chest start to heave.

"Watch my eyes." He caught his breath between sentences. "You'll know the difference."

He placed his wrist in Eden's hand, grasping her own, and instantly stilled.

"Ransom?" I whispered.

No response.

I searched his eyes only to find darkness. It reminded me so much of what Silas had done with the nightshade. My hands started to sweat while I watched Ransom for any sign of struggle or illness.

And now I wait.

For an aching moment, I wondered if Leander wasn't better suited for this kind of thing. Even Aubrey would know best, but I knew almost nothing about Seer rituals and ways. I watched Eden and wondered if she'd survive all of this. Could there be a way to stop the Mocker from spiriting her away from this Realm? Could we stop it before it brought her to the Other?

I ducked to peer into Ransom's eyes, the tiniest of white starting to show. I waited for another heartbeat and two and three to be sure before I placed the bottle in his hand. Mechanically, he put it to his lips and drank. The inky black of his eyes expanded until the whites were invisible again.

I exhaled slowly, pacing back and forth in front of the bed. Minutes passed, and I gave Ransom the bottle twice more. I peered into Guardian's Glade, but we were alone.

Sputtering behind me sent my heart through the tree branches above. Ransom had fallen out of his chair, one knee on the ground to brace himself. I moved to help him, but he held his palm out, struggling to breathe.

He coughed so loud, I feared Silas would come running from wherever he waited. I poured Ransom some water and he downed it all, still coughing after he passed me the mug. I filled it again and he stood finally, sipping at the water this time.

The whites of his eyes barely showed, and his eyes hadn't yet returned to normal. I placed a hand on his forehead. His skin burned mine.

"What can I do?" I whispered, glancing at Eden. She lay the same way she had before, so still and quiet.

"Help me sit." Ransom grasped my arm, and I guided him to his seat once more.

"What happened? Did I do something wrong?" I stopped the bottle and placed it on the desk with Ransom's other things.

"No. I was forced out." Ransom breathed heavily like he'd been drowning. I wondered if that was the effects of the liquid or fear from the dream. "There was a willow, Kalona's willow. I think it's the same one you and Aubrey saw. The Raven Mocker knows you've seen it. She knows we're onto her. And Kalona doesn't want us to win."

"Kalona, like the legend? What does she want?" I asked, replacing his things in his bag until the room appeared as it had before, only tidier.

Ransom shook his head. "I couldn't tell. Eden wasn't helpful. She was hesitant. Or maybe it was some trick of Kalona's. Maybe I appeared in a frightening way. It's difficult to say what form a person will take from dream to dream. It was nighttime in Guardian's Glade. The stars were gone. I saw the willow tree, but Kalona kicked me out before I could see much more."

"Once you're able, we need to go to the tree." I straightened my shoulders expecting pushback.

Ransom deflated. "I know. I don't see any other option."

I threw the strap of Ransom's bag over my shoulder. "Ready when you are."

After sending Bennett to find Silas and collecting Aubrey, Markus, and Leander, Ransom and I caught everyone up. They'd sat down with Asa to ensure he understood our position and plan. Now, Aubrey and I led the group to the edge of the river, following it until it dumped us out at the bend where the willow stood.

Aubrey's intake of breath was my first hint of a problem.

"*Kanin arhan, rakas?*" Ransom hushed.

"It's all gone," I whispered, heart sinking.

The bottles, bones, and railroad spikes had disappeared. The branches swung loose in the breeze, unladen by Kalona's collected trash. The pile of bones beneath the tree had been uncovered and built like a fence around the tree.

"Holy *silva*," Markus murmured.

On the old willow, the skull mask of a Wendigo was fixed. Underneath it, scratch marks marred the bark.

Ransom started forward, and I followed. He held his hand out, helping me over the short fence of bones. A few paces from the tree, he stopped, and I peered around him at the inscription.

"*Lo nemicci slava,*" Ransom muttered, venom on his tongue.

"What did he say?" Markus called.

I turned around, scanning the treeline for anything, any hint of the Hunt. Tracks must've been covered outside of the bone circle, but

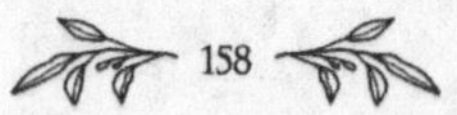

inside, the grass was swept clean like winter had never touched it. But where had they gone? Had they taken the hag stones and bottles and railroad spikes with them? Or had they found some other tree to tie Kalona's presence to?

Ransom cleared his throat again. "For the Enemy's Honor."

27

EDEN

I SOMEHOW ESCAPED THE RAVENS clawing at my skin.

After the amount of pain, I expected to bleed or have scratches all over, but my skin was mercifully unmarked. I wouldn't have been able to explain that to Silas when I saw him.

The visitation from the Wendigo disturbed me. He told me to wake up, only I couldn't be dreaming, not when everything felt so *right*. The illness was a dream. This was reality.

Taking my time in the darkening evening, I strolled through the Heart of Arcadia, the old ruins calling to me like a lullaby in the night. The runes, once gouged in deep, sharp marks, had worn away from time and handling to a soft memory.

As I stepped onto the main platform of the ruins, *kuslar* fluttered out of the undergrowth. Their faint blue shimmered in the clearing around the ruins, the trees, and the stones circling the Heart of Arcadia. A glimmer of gold pulled my gaze, and I caught sight of *micca* stepping into view. Some of them had small instruments, clearly handmade and well-loved. One began to play a tune on a whistle, the high notes trilling a melody on the gentle breeze. The other musicians joined in, and out of the woodwork, brighter blues began to emerge.

An aching grew in my chest when I recognized two of them. In their human forms, Iain and Elder Macon approached the ruins and bowed when they stopped.

"You made it." Iain smiled, his hair woven in a braid in a way I'd only seen on Nash in person. "Will you join me for a dance?"

I glanced down at my robes, but I hadn't remembered changing into my ceremonial dress. I hadn't known it was finished, but perhaps the Tailors surprised me and I'd forgotten.

I held Iain's hand, and he guided me into the clearing. Tendrils of starlight swirled around our knees.

"I'm afraid I don't know the steps, *je kunan*." I glanced sidelong at the other dancers—wolves in human form, *kuslar*, *micca*, and other creatures I'd yet to meet—and wondered if they would laugh at my ineptitude.

Iain's chuckle warmed me to my core, and I wondered if this was what having a good father felt like. "*Je lyce*, you already know this dance. You join us every night. Do you not remember?"

Before I could form a reply or even begin to understand his words, my feet moved, and the dance began. Soon I lost my train of thought, and I danced and twirled and bowed and switched partners until I lost Iain in the haint-blue light of the clearing.

In truth, it was difficult to see much of the Spirits. They moved so fluidly, like smoke on a lake, that I struggled to make out distinct lines. They were but vapors in this existence, only semi-corporeal while the *micca* spun their melody magic.

And I wondered why it was that I'd been chosen to dance with spirits. Perhaps I bridged two realms, my body in Arcadia and my mind in the Other. What a gift it would be if I could dance like this forever.

As I finished the thought, the music stopped, and the *kuslar* and Spirits flickered out one by one like street lights in the dawn. I found Elder Macon across the clearing, reaching for me before his Spirit snuffed out.

"Iain!" I shouted, not caring that animals or enemies might hear me. I spun around, but he found me first.

His hands found my shoulders, cold seeping through my thin sleeves. "Eden, do not return to this place. Go home. Leave now, and find Silas. The ravens have trapped him. He's—"

His steel eyes blinked, and I was left standing alone, facing the path to the river.

The river.

I would find Silas at the river where he always found me.

Throwing caution to the wind, I raced through the trees, down the soft, mossy path. The gurgling sound of the river grew louder with each step. I hurried my pace, heart thrumming.

A new sound stopped me in my path.

Silas screamed.

"No," I whispered. It had been difficult to breathe before, but it was near impossible now.

I have to save him.

I ran. My feet slipped in the dirt, caught on sharp stones and shifting tree roots, until I stumbled to a halt at the bank. I climbed onto our boulder, the exact place where he kissed me for the first time. I expected to find him waiting for me, but where was he?

"Please," he sobbed into the dark.

"Silas?" I turned, scanning the bank and the trees behind me, but in the strange lighting and the growing fog, I couldn't find him.

"Eden!" he shouted. "Eden, run!"

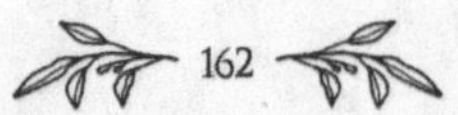

His voice was thick with tears, and I wondered what tormented him. If I could get to him, I could show him we were safe. No danger threatened us. Nyx was gone, and I was better.

"She wants your soul," he cried and yelled in pain.

Where is he?

"She's draining you. She's trying to–"

I heard it now, the splash of water like a whip. I scrambled back to the bank and jogged the edge of the river until I found him. In the blue light of dawn and the glow of strange orbs floating down the river, I caught sight of his bare arms outstretched. He was bound between posts that hadn't been there before. Mossy hands clawed at his torso from below the water.

Without a second thought or any lingering fear of the inky water, I plunged into the deep. My dress clung to my body, and I regretted that he had to see me in it before our wedding.

"You're going to be okay," I murmured, reaching for his left wrist. I began to pull at the knots while hands tugged at Silas.

I kicked at them, clumsy in the attempt.

"Eden." Silas lifted his head, his eyes a solid black. "I'm sorry. I'm so sorry."

He repeated the apology over and over while I undid the first knot and then the second. Each one unraveled faster in succession, until his left arm was free. He wrapped me in one arm, crying into my shoulder and repeating the same two words over and over.

"It's okay, Si. You're okay." I held his head in one hand, eyes scanning our surroundings for any sign of danger or this mysterious woman who wanted my soul. "Let's get you free, yeah?"

I untangled myself from Silas and began working on his right wrist.

"I can't see." He laughed in a sort of disbelieving way. "All I want to do is see you one last time."

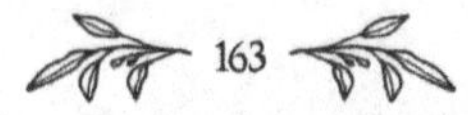

"You'll see me today and every other day for the rest of our lives," I whispered, pulling the first knot free.

"For the rest of your life," he cried, curling into himself again.

It was so unlike Silas to despair. He'd often been exhausted, but still kept a decently positive outlook. But this was something new.

The second and third knots loosened, and finally his hand slipped free. The moment the bonds fell away, Silas scrambled past me like a feral creature to dry ground.

"Silas." I shook my head, stepping high to untangle myself from my dress. "Wait for me."

"I'm sorry. I'm so sorry." He fell to the bank, holding a hand out to stop me.

"Si–" The mossy hands yanked me back, and this time, I heard hissing as they dragged me under the water.

I could hear music, something haunting in the dark. It lulled me into a peaceful place, somewhere I could stay forever. Like dancing with Spirits, like Silas's arms, this water cradled me and carried me adrift to somewhere I would call home.

Forever.

28
SILAS

I SHOOK MY COAT, sending water droplets in all directions. Swimming in the icy waters always helped to reset my mental state. My thoughts cleared enough for me to see that Eden wasn't in immediate danger. She was asleep in our bed, being watched and cared for.

Exhaling all the stress, I pulled on my robes and fastened the buttons. I chose the long way back to Guardian's Glade from Feru Falls, meandering westward, cutting across the Boneyard, where a few people sparred. I found my way into the Aisle of Kings, treading softly until I arrived at the grave of my parents.

Taking a seat, I cleared my throat. "I wish you were here to give me advice. I've run out of ideas or things to try to help Eden heal. I know you didn't make a mistake bringing us together, but Father, do I bring her back to her people? Would they be able to help her better than I can? How can I rule well if I can't even care for my mate?"

The silence weighed on me. There were ways to evoke the dead and pull them to corporeal form, but it was rare magic and difficult except at certain times of the year when the planes of the Realms were thin. I wished I could talk to them. I could drink nightshade again, but would it matter? Deep down, I already knew my options ran thin.

I rubbed my eyes in the late afternoon sun. "I miss you both. I miss you so much that my chest aches. Life isn't the same without you here with me. You should've been there for my mating ceremony and for the Passing of the Elders. You should've been there for my first litter of pups and all the days in between. How am I supposed to move through life without you?"

A dark-eyed junco trilled in the branches somewhere above me, a sign of resilience. I smiled to myself. It could've been a coincidence, but I took it as a sign. "I love you both."

I dusted my hands on my robes. With one last bow to their stones, I made my way eastward, toward the Yard. I gazed up at the trees, noticing a few more crows than usual. They were noisy, but beneath their chatter, I heard the quick panting of a wolf rushing toward me.

I turned in time to dodge Bennett when he skidded to a stop. "What's wrong?"

His tongue lolled, ears tucking down like his tail. *"You need to return to your room. It's Eden."*

I didn't wait for him to finish the second sentence before I was sprinting through the Yard, shoving past my people milling about and chatting with Lukosans. I'd deal with their questions later about why their king moved with such purpose.

I busted through the double doors of Guardian's Glade and heard shouting. I pushed the door open and stumbled to a stop before an empty bed.

The shouting ceased when I turned to Caroline. Her hand covered her lips like she'd done the day our father died.

"No." I shook my head. "Where is she?"

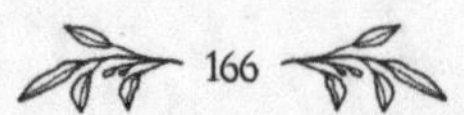

Ransom cleared his throat. "We just returned from–"

"Returned?" I nearly roared, almost ripping out of my skin. "You left her here alone?"

"Silas–" Markus started, but I whirled on him.

I pointed a finger at him. "That's *je kunan* to you, Elder or no. Where's my mate?"

"*She went this way.*" Leander, in wolf form, whined from behind the side door.

I barreled through the group and right past Leander. I knew where Eden would be, where she would always be.

The similarities to that day with Nyx weren't lost on me. Nettle-brained Seers and their snake-like ways. I could've killed someone right then and there from how much anger flooded my system.

My vision throbbed alongside my heart while I slid around the bend in the path. Leander moved right behind me at a comfortable trot and the others followed somewhere behind. The trees thinned, and I launched myself past their barrier to the spot where Eden and I had first kissed.

The joy of that moment flickered out when I saw a form in the water.

"Eden!" A sound slipped out of me that I didn't recognize, and I ran straight into the water, wading to the place where her body floated.

Hands of *ugals* brushed me when I swam past, slippery and unsettling. I'd banish all of them tomorrow if they were responsible for this. But when I reached her, I could hear her slow, steady heart.

She's alive.

I slid both arms underneath her, lifting her out of the river. Dozens of *ugals* surfaced beneath her, and I realized they'd been holding her up.

"Thank you," I choked, holding her chilled body close to mine.

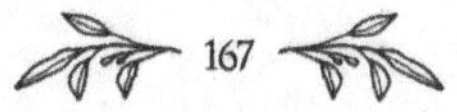

"Thank you. Thank you."

"*Vislava, je kunan,*" one gurgled before they all disappeared beneath the surface into the current.

Leander paced the bank, ears and tail raised while Caroline, Markus, and Ransom stopped at the water's edge. I marched past them to the first patch of soft earth I could find before I set Eden down.

"*Something is watching from the eastern bank,*" Leander growled.

I couldn't make myself tear my eyes away from Eden's face. Her lips were blue-tinted, skin so pale. I held her close to me, rocking us side to side.

"Silas, what do we do?" Caroline asked.

Her words barely registered. I felt them standing nearby, but I didn't care. Nothing mattered to me besides Eden.

"Eden, I'm sorry. I'm so sorry," I cried into her shoulder.

I wouldn't leave her side—not unless I knew she'd be right there next to me, waiting. I murmured those words of apology over and over until they didn't sound real anymore. I would never stop apologizing. I hadn't been enough to keep her safe and healthy. How could I forgive myself?

"Silas?" Eden's voice sounded hoarse, but from sleep or swallowing water, I didn't know.

I pulled back enough to search her bleary eyes. "*Je rakas, sen sun rikas. Ja doleo, je rakas. Ja doleo. Ja doleo.*"

I held her close again, even tighter than before. She held onto me like her life depended on it.

"Please don't leave me," she whispered, almost frantic.

"Never. *Niveime.* I promise." I kissed her temple, wondering what she'd been dreaming of before. What led her to the river?

29

CAROLINE

After carrying Eden all the way back to their room and getting her a fresh and dry robe, Silas led us into Guardian's Glade, leaving Leander to watch Eden while she drifted back to sleep, despite her wet hair.

The tension rippled from his shoulders, and I knew we were in for it.

"What in Lycaon's name did you think you were doing?" he snapped. "You asked me to trust you, to wait for you to find me so you could do whatever it is that you Seers think is best. *Ja vole vaara ussen. Nislava innu rakas au municci. Ja roka kanin sen sun, sur surin roka.*"

Silas didn't often explode. He always knew how to manage his frustrations well, but once he tipped to the wild side of himself, the Ancient Tongue flooded him. I knew we deserved some of the insults he spat at us, but he didn't understand the full picture. And it was our fault for keeping that a secret from him.

"Silas–" I started.

He rounded on me now, eyes blazing and wild. "I don't want to hear what you have to say right now. I can barely look at you, *je nemicci.*"

My enemy.

I bit my lip, trying to fight the inevitable tears. "You'll understand if you would listen to me."

He scoffed and spouted off more insults before shoving past us. He slammed his bedroom door behind him.

Markus sighed. "Well, that was–"

"Entirely called for." Ransom scratched his neck. "We need to tell him."

"Not today." I shook my head. "He won't hear anything we have to say today."

Leander, in human form, slipped out of the room and into Guardian's Glade. "That went well. What treachery shall we commit next? Defacing the old ruins?"

Markus chuckled and quickly covered his mouth. "I'm sorry. I didn't…"

I held back giggles. Ransom bit his lip to hide a smirk. We were all hysterical after such a scare. It was inappropriate, considering what we'd learned in the past hour. Silas would slaughter us where we stood if he heard.

I herded the three men out of Guardian's Glade back to the Sage Brush. Now that we knew the truth, we had real information to give Silas, a reason to push past the anger. If he could calm down and listen to our theories, we might have a chance to get through to him. He might never get over what happened, but he had to know the truth of it sooner or later.

30
EDEN

SILAS RAN HIS FREE HAND over my arm, his other bringing a steaming cup of apple cider chai to his lips from my favorite café.

How strange that I'd been in the river with him. And now... but this was a happy night. It would be unwise to dwell on sad things.

"It still makes me laugh that you're drinking cider when you have coffee available." I sipped at my peppermint mocha. I was usually a black coffee kind of girl, but the seasonal drinks trapped me every time, especially around Christmas.

It had been so long since I had a good latte, but this was my favorite place to get one. They were right off the main square where all the fun Christmas action happened. They built a temporary ice skating rink, strung lights across the square, and street performers always played the best Christmas classics.

Across from me at our table, Silas smirked at me. It felt a bit strange to have him here in the openness of the city, the streetlights casting a warm yellow glow over his skin. Several yards away, the city's

Christmas tree glittered, its large, red ornaments reflecting the lights and gentle snowfall. Silas's Christmas gift to me was to take me back to civilization for a night. Bundled up, I could be anyone, and no one would expect to see the missing girl from the forest sipping on a hot drink and listening to buskers singing their rendition of "I'll Be Home For Christmas."

Strangely, Silas was still in his court robes, and no one seemed to care. No one stopped to ask if he was an actor or a caroler. They must have assumed he was the ghost of Christmas present, taking me to see what impact I had on the world.

"Thank you for all of this," I hummed.

"Anything for the Queen of Arcadia." He grinned something feral, his eyes glimmering black in the night. I shifted away from him, and immediately his eyes changed. "What's wrong?"

"Nothing. I'm seeing things, that's all." I rubbed the bridge of my nose. When I turned, I wasn't surprised to see the bird lady. I'd seen her frequently since we left Lukosan. How had I ever thought she was a Wendigo? Her feathers fluttered in the snowy breeze, and I wondered if she'd approach me with Silas around.

A violinist began to play "O Holy Night," one of my favorite songs of the season. Forgetting the bird lady, I closed my eyes and took a deep breath of the cold air. I jolted when it stabbed at my lungs, making me ache from the inside out. It shouldn't have been so painful to breathe.

"Silas," I choked.

"Listen to them." His eyes flashed to a caroler who stopped to sing with the violinist.

"Behold your King; before Him lowly bend," the soloist sang.

Silas stood, and I feared he would make a scene. He must've thought he was the king they sang about. He *was* the king of Arcadia. But these people didn't know that. And he was about to break the Arcadian rule of secrecy that had kept Arcadia safe for all those centuries.

I pushed out of my chair, stumbling into his path. "Silas, please."

I grasped his dark coat, noticing the fur lining the collar. He looked like the guys that lingered around the Christmas market with their girlfriends and wives. Funny, I hadn't remembered him changing his clothes.

"You're not helping," he growled.

"I'm trying," I whimpered. Why did I feel so defeated?

"Eden." He gazed down at me, eyes wild. "Eden, it's me."

"Silas?"

He shook me hard. "Eden, can you hear me?"

I shook my head, trying to move back, but my legs wouldn't move. "You're scaring me. Please stop. Please—"

He shook me hard once more, and I tumbled backward into a snow drift. It was painfully cold in the forest, and my ceremonial dress was ruined for the second time. The forest trees danced above me in the bitter wind. But the breeze carried voices.

"Take a break. Get some rest."

I tried to speak, but my words failed me.

A second voice said, *"How can I rest? She's dying."*

The first voice spoke again. *"Try to sleep. She'll be better in the morning. Surely you know that by now."*

I thought it *was* morning. I glanced around. The sun on the snow blinded me. But the lights shifted, and I stood on a dark stage, wrapped in scratchy clothing. A Nativity was being put on at a church that I didn't recognize, but I knew it was my grandmother's. It had been years since she passed, but she was here. I could feel it. If I could only find her.

I scanned the crowd only to see faces of wolves, countless names I'd already forgotten, both Arcadians and Lukosans. What a terrible queen I'd proven to be. An *almost* queen.

I'd wanted to be a strong leader, someone who brought hope to others. While I watched the Nativity from the side of the stage, I thought about Mary and Joseph ushering Hope into the world. Would I ever be capable of that? Or was I doomed from the start?

On the stage in costumes, I spotted several of my college classmates, along with some of my coworkers at the parks. Strange that they all gathered together like this regardless of beliefs or age.

I spotted Nash dressed as one of the sheep. Silly, really. Didn't the director get the joke? He was a wolf in sheep's clothing. It was no wonder I started to feel scared around him. Had I believed him a sheep all this time? Or had he always been one of the big bad wolves?

31

ANDRA

"IT HAS TO BE HERE SOMEWHERE. Keep looking," I growled, digging through the same set of dirty robes piled at the Tailor's quarters.

Archer dropped the robes he held. "An, we've dug through all of these baskets. Eden's robe is nowhere in here."

"We can't stop now. What if someone else finds the ring?" I pushed the hair out of my face. "They would be cursed and would die, and it would still be my fault. I can't let that happen, Arch."

"Maybe they washed the robe already?" Archer scratched the back of his neck, casting his gaze around the area. "Do you think they have a clothesline or something? Maybe a special branch?"

I squatted where I stood, gripping my hair in fists. "I can't quit now. I can't."

Archer set a hand on my arm, gently pulling me up and into a hug. "We'll figure something out, yeah? Regroup, ask one of the Tailors about it, and try again."

I nodded into his shoulder.

"Come on." He nudged me toward the path. "Let's grab an early breakfast."

We followed the river up the path to the Kitchen, crossing the rivers over some flat stones. We passed two wolves trotting toward the Yard, chatting animatedly.

"*I can't believe it. She wandered into the river. She would've drowned if it weren't for the ugals.*"

"*Who would've thought they would be her rescuer? I mean, they're not usually so kind to strangers. Where was the king?*"

"*Oh, he's furious. Apparently, he left her in the care of Caroline and Ransom. They left for a short time, but when they returned, she had disappeared.*"

"*Didn't someone say he called them enemies and a dishonor to the pack?*"

My head snapped to Archer, whose face turned pale. I rerouted back across the river and cut through a dense section of forest, Archer hot on my heels. The cursed robes were difficult to run in, but we made do, coming to a jog near the entry of Guardian's Glade.

I stopped in front of the double doors, catching my breath. I couldn't hear what lay inside or smell anything unusual aside from breakfast that we left behind.

Archer opened the doors without a sound. Inside, silence greeted us. It would've seemed normal—an empty clearing and dappled light on the mossy floor, except the throne had been toppled over.

"Are we certain this is a good idea?" I whispered to Archer, stepping back out on the path.

He crossed his arms. "We need to check on them. And you need to tell him the truth."

"Are you crazy?" I threw my hands out. "If he's this furious to start

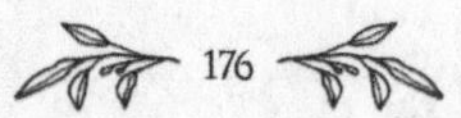

damaging things, he'll kill me. It's my fault. And technically doesn't that count as an act of war to poison another Alpha?"

Archer shrugged. "Technically, Eden is just a member of the pack for now, but yes, I think so."

"And you want me to tell him the truth?"

He patted my shoulder, turning me toward Guardian's Glade again. "You need to do the right thing regardless of the consequences. I thought you learned that already."

I groaned, but stepped down the path. Before I arrived at Silas's door, Archer set the throne upright again, adjusting the branches so they weren't crooked.

I knocked.

"Enter." Inside, Asa sat with a book open on his lap. "Good morning. I'm afraid Silas is off at the moment. Shall I tell him you all have stopped by?"

I glanced at Eden, who'd lost all color in her face from the previous day. I couldn't see her ring finger from where I stood. "What happened? She seemed better yesterday."

Asa hesitated. "She's relapsed. I've never seen anything like it in my time."

I could tell he chose his words carefully. If the stories were true, he could see Kalona whenever she was near.

"Nothing strange has happened?" I raised an eyebrow, hoping Asa would divulge what he knew. Archer placed a hand on my arm as a warning.

Asa closed his book, *Emily Wilde's Encyclopaedia of Faeries*, and stood. "Forgive me, Alpha, but I must ask you to let my patient rest. I will tell Silas you stopped by."

I waved a hand. "Don't mention it. I'll go find him myself. Can I at least say a blessing over Eden?"

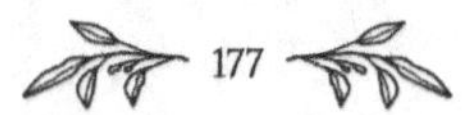

He clearly wanted to say no, but he motioned for me to approach the dying queen. All I needed was confirmation. I couldn't steal the ring with Asa watching, but at least I would know.

I moved to the far side of the bed, picking up her left hand in mine. Her ring gleamed dark on her pale, cold hands. She was so cold.

"Eden, I'm sorry for everything you're going through," I whispered, staring at her ring. "May Lycaon give guidance and a clear path for healing and reconciliation."

I gave her hand a squeeze before walking past Asa and Archer straight through Guardian's Glade. I didn't stop until I reached the stream cutting through Arcadia. I dropped to a boulder, dipping my feet in the frigid waters, and cried.

Archer sat next to me, but said and did nothing. He had a knack for comforting without words. His presence was enough. Who would I be without him?

"Were my actions really so horrible that they deserved such a terrible consequence?" I sniffled. "Is this really all divine retribution for mistaking my feelings?"

"What do you mean?" Archer asked, absentmindedly stacking small stones.

I wiped my nose. "I mean, thinking I loved Silas and doing everything in my power to split him and Eden up, only to realize that I loved the idea of him and the past version of him. When, in reality, the person I truly cared for was right in front of me."

"I'm flattered, sis, but–"

I shoved him into the stream. "Not you, nettle-brain."

He laughed, clambering out of the river. "I want to hear you say it."

I tried to slow my breathing, to stop the tears from slipping away. But it all hurt too much. "I love him, Arch. And it's killing me to watch him suffer like this. To top it all off, I've accidentally cursed his brother's fiancée. So not only will Nash get banished for treason, but Silas will lose his mate and brother. All he's left with is his sister, because when he finds out the truth about what I did, we'll be banished, too. Or worse, dead."

Archer sighed. "I really don't think he'd go that far. Bodily harm, for sure. But death seems a little extreme for Silas, even with an unchecked temper." He grinned. "But are you going to admit to Nash that you love him? I mean, clearly there's nothing to lose if both of you will be kicked out within twenty-four hours."

"Please don't say that." I had to level my breathing yet again. I covered my face with my hands. "It's my fault."

Archer gently pulled my hands away. "It's time to tell Nash and Silas the truth. It's up to you who you'll talk to first, but I'd suggest Nash since you may not get the chance before Silas sends us packing."

I groaned. "Now? When I look like a wet mouse?"

Archer stood before helping me to my feet. "It's endearing. It shows that you're genuine."

My heart thrummed, and I wondered what life would look like after today, after I drew a line in the sand with two people I loved more than anything. It would never be the same.

32
NASH

I LINGERED IN MY ROOM longer than necessary. Kane told me to stay in and get some rest, so I did. But I couldn't take the silence, so I walked to check on Eden. I'd promised to read *Twilight* to her, but I didn't trust myself to be near her, not after knowing the truth of what I did.

I didn't trust myself to be near anyone anymore.

The closer I got to Guardian's Glade, it was evident something had gone awry. People and wolves whispered about Silas and Eden.

"Almost ran right over me." One of the humans from Lukosan shook her head, chatting with Kyla. "It's like he'd seen a ghost."

"What's going on?" I asked, sidling up next to Kyla.

She scrunched her face, her usual stony façade melted away. "Everyone is talking about how Eden almost drowned yesterday."

I held her elbow for support, my knees feeling weak. "What?"

Kyla hooked her arms around my neck and squeezed. I hugged her back in shock. She sighed. "I'm so sorry. I thought you would've known already."

Maybe Silas caught on and knew what I'd done, knew not to trust me. Or maybe Andra or Archer told him before I built the courage. I wouldn't blame them for not wanting to betray Arcadia's king by keeping secrets.

I pulled back, searching Kyla for any hint of tricks, but her eyes were red-rimmed and swollen. The empath that she was, it made sense why this hit so hard. She felt everything so deeply.

"Oh." I turned to find Andra behind me. "Sorry, I didn't mean to interrupt whatever..."

She glanced between me and Kyla and stalked away. I waved a hand and left Kyla to run after Andra.

"Hey," I called, trying to grab her sleeve. "Andra, slow down. What's going on?"

"Nothing." She slowed down enough so that I didn't have to jog to keep up. "I'm happy for you, that's all. It makes sense—you and Kyla. I just wanted to see if you were okay after last night, but you should go back to be with her. She's a much better comforter than I am."

"Andra, stop." I snatched her wrist, pulling her to face me, grabbing her waist with my other hand. "Look at me, please."

She tilted her chin up to look me in the eyes. Red rimmed her eyes, and her skin was puffy underneath. Lycaon bless her for loving my family so much. They would need that kind of care when I was gone.

"Thank you for coming to check on me." I sighed. "I didn't know."

"Didn't..." Andra frowned. "No one told you?"

I shrugged. "Kyla did when I asked. I overheard her talking about Silas with one of the humans in your pack."

Andra shook her head. "Birch trees. But Nash, Caroline said he was furious. Called them a dishonor to the pack and that they were his enemies. He blames the Seers for Eden nearly drowning. Apparently, they were supposed to be watching her when–" She cleared her throat, eyes brimming with tears.

I shook my head. "I wish I'd been there for him, you know, despite everything."

She stood on her toes to wrap her arms around my neck, and I sank into her embrace. I breathed in the scent of her—spicy like sassafras and something woodsy. I wished I could melt into her and disappear for a long time.

"Will you promise me something?" The words spilled out before I could stop myself.

She pulled back to look me in the eyes, but I held her tight. "What is it?"

I leaned my forehead against hers. "If things change, if things are different and I'm, um, free after all of this... Will you–"

"Nash!" I turned to see Kane approaching at a fast pace, eyes glancing between me and the Alpha of Lukosan.

I let go of her, and she straightened her borrowed robes.

"Silas is requesting your presence." Kane cleared his throat. "Immediately. You're on leave until further notice for your family emergency."

He bowed to me and Andra and disappeared among the crowded Yard.

"I'm sorry, I have to go." I sighed, wishing I had more time.

"I promise." Andra smiled. "If things change, I will."

She hadn't known what I was asking, that I hoped she would let me stay with her. But chances are, nothing would change, and I would have to face the consequences of my actions. I gave her hand a squeeze before making my way to Guardian's Glade.

Alden, another one of the Guardians, stood in front of the double doors. When I approached, he stepped aside and allowed me entry.

We'd never had guards at the throne room before. It had never been necessary.

Inside Guardian's Glade, Asa talked in hushed tones with Aubrey. They turned my way when I entered.

"Thank Lycaon you're here." Aubrey held my hands in hers. "He'll listen to you. He isn't making sense anymore."

"What's going on? I heard about–" I didn't want to say drowning, not when she was alive. I didn't want to think about what might have happened had she not made it.

Silas might actually have killed someone in his grief. I wouldn't put it past him. Which is why I stood on treacherous ground.

"Eden said your name a few times in her sleep." Asa's eyebrows furrowed. "Silas says he won't trust anyone but us to watch after her now. He has things to attend to, damage control after last night, but he can't leave her alone."

I pointed to myself. "And he wants me to watch her?"

Aubrey shrugged. "He says you're one of the most trustworthy now. He's also removed your title of Omega and made you a Delta."

My shoulders dropped. "He promoted me?"

She nodded, a small smile on her lips. "Welcome to the Delta fold."

The majority of the pack technically resided in the Omega territory, but only one wolf usually held the title. Then Deltas were the heads of each Branch like Kane and Bennett and Lilah. Ransom and Aubrey were a strange case where they both were Deltas together. And Asa and Elder Markus were between the Deltas and Caroline, the Beta. They acted as Healers of the body and spirit, so they stood between the pack and the main leaders.

To make me a Delta was to bring me officially back into the pack as a member of status.

I cleared my throat. "Are you... are you certain?"

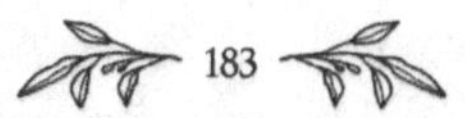

Aubrey rolled her eyes. "Go. Silas needs you."

I held their gaze until I arrived at the door, steeling myself before knocking.

"Enter," Silas called. His voice sounded tired.

Inside, the lanterns were still lit from the evening. I turned them out and posted myself by the wardrobe as close as I dared to either Silas or Eden.

"I heard what happened," I started, unsure of what to say. "Andra told me, and I came as soon as I could. I wish I'd known. I would've been there for you last night."

"I know," he said, not taking his eyes away from Eden who slept peacefully. The silence hung in the air for a minute or two before Silas shook himself out of his daze. "Watch her for me?"

I started to decline. "Silas, I don't—"

"Please." He stood now, grabbing my arms with a strange intensity. "Please. This is more important than patrolling or entertaining Lukosans or flirting with Andra. Please."

I found myself bobbing my head. "All right. I'll watch her. Of course I will. I didn't think I'd be the best choice, given my status."

Silas's eyes shadowed. "Did Aubrey not—"

I held a hand up. "She did. I just don't believe her. I mean, Si, I'm not good, you know? I haven't proven myself to you yet."

"You're still here. That's proof enough." Silas threw his arms over my shoulders, patting me twice before backing up. "I'll be back soon. If you or Eden need anything for whatever reason, Aubrey and Asa can get it for you. Please do not leave her side."

With a dip of his chin, he ducked out of the room, and I was left alone with the most precious thing in my brother's life.

I dropped into the seat Silas vacated. "Eden, what do I do?" I pressed the balls of my palms into my eyes, pushing until I saw stars.

"These hands aren't mine anymore. Whose are they?" I blinked until the room focused again. "I think in another Realm somewhere, my mother and father never died. The forest didn't burn, I never lost my memory, and I'm someone I'd be proud to be. But here, I'm paying for sins I didn't remember... or at least not until a few days ago."

I pulled my knees to my chest, resting my chin on them. "When my siblings and I were born, Elder Macon said I'd leave an immortal legacy. We weren't born equally, the three of us. Silas received leadership and courage and loyalty. Caroline received intelligence and ferocity and wisdom. And me?" I glanced over at Eden. "I received cowardice and regret and, ironically, a demented sense of humor.

"Luckily, that humor deflected most of the questions until now. Most people thought I was flighty or didn't have a lot of drive. They didn't know my soul had been twisted. How could they? And you know, I think I started disappearing because I couldn't figure out who I was. I think I left for the greater forests to find myself. And I discovered something violent and wicked."

Tears flowed freely now, and I brushed them away. "When there weren't any other options or any other voices saying otherwise, what was I left to believe? Why would anyone love this feral beast in me? And I thought for a moment, like you said, maybe Andra and I could—" I choked, but recovered. "Things won't change. I won't be free of this. So she and I can never... Because I've come to realize that forests hold secrets, and I've held onto the darkest one for too long. I have to tell you because you might be the only one who understands me, who understands how difficult it is to live within the balance of human and wolf, of monster and creature."

I hit my knees to beg her forgiveness for my betrayal. It was worse than anything I'd ever confessed aloud. But I had to tell someone. Someone needed to hear how I'd been forced to relive my worst moment, heartbeat by excruciating heartbeat.

"A year and two days ago, my father went for a patrol in the woods. It was rare for him to do so since he had Guardians for that. But I'd written to him, saying I was coming home. And somewhere in the *Washita* mountains, I must have run into someone or something connected to the Hunt, because the first memory I've been granted is walking by that demon. He was so sure of himself, so confident he'd get in his master's good graces once he'd murdered the King of Arcadia with his own son's directions. Because I led him right to my father. I knew his scent, and he knew mine. So of course my father ran to me, his wayward son."

I took in measured breaths, trying to speak around the tears clogging my throat. "Nyx had me wrapped around his claws in his head, like an extension of him. I felt the waves of hatred and violence flooding through my veins. I couldn't stop it, couldn't hold back. So I fought my father exactly how he'd taught me, tooth and claw. And I fought like my new father, Nyx, taught me—to the death. There wasn't another option.

"And the shock on my father's face... I think it almost hurts worse than knowing I killed him." I sniffled, furiously wiping away tears. "Eden, I'm the one who clawed him, broke him, stabbed him, ripped him apart, until he was barely alive. I'm the one, not Nyx. I deserve the same kind of death that Nyx met that day by the river. I deserve to never rest peacefully and never return to this Realm once I'm gone. Because I didn't just lose my father that day. He lost a son. Nyx made me his right hand. And it will haunt me until my last breath."

I wept. My shoulders shook from the force, and I couldn't draw a full breath. I wondered for the hundredth time why the Wendigo chose to show me now. Surely it would've been more beneficial to expose me at Lukosan, causing chaos amidst chaos. Or maybe my presence there threw them off guard.

I wondered if the creatures of the Hunt knew me by name, if they knew my preferences and my gait. I wondered if they would know me by scent alone. How long had I spent in their company? How many vicious acts had I committed at their sides that I couldn't remember?

"Nash?"

I froze, holding my breath.

The bed shifted when Eden sat up. "Nash, what's wrong?"

Without hesitating or looking back, I ran.

33

CAROLINE

I'D FALLEN ASLEEP IN MARKUS'S OLD ROOM that sat vacant now that he inhabited the Elder's study. It still smelled like him. Aubrey and Ransom invited me to breakfast in their room before Aubrey was summoned to Guardian's Glade.

In the silence of his wife's absence, Ransom and I sat, sipping at tea halfheartedly.

"How's the wedding planning coming along?" he asked, shifting on the bench.

I nodded. "As good as it can. I think Eden's ceremonial dress is finished, and I need to finalize day-of plans and check in with Lilah about the evening meal."

He breathed out of his nose, which I knew to be his way of laughing. "I meant your wedding, Caroline."

My face grew hot. "Right, well, I haven't had a ton of time to plan that yet. It'll be sometime in *Starra*, but I don't have other details besides that."

"Do you have someone doing the ceremony?" He sipped his tea.

I hadn't considered it yet, but it was customary for either the father or the Elder to conduct the ceremony. It could be neither in my case. But why did Ransom care?

"Why, you want to do the ceremony?" I asked, setting my tea aside.

After choking on his sip, Ransom also put his tea aside. "Lycaon, no. I would hate that. But Leander would be an excellent choice. He's well-spoken and helped train Elder Markus when Elder Macon had things to tend to."

"That could work. Only—"

I was interrupted by cursing when Aubrey led Andra through their front door.

"What is it with you Seers and the dark?" Andra rubbed her shoulder, where I could only assume she'd hit it on something.

"What a surprise." I stood, bowing my head. "What brings you to the Sage Brush?"

Andra's hazel eyes darted to Ransom, taking in the tea and the small fire. She moved her gaze over the benches and quaint decorations of two young Seers. Finally, she met my gaze, something hidden in the shadows within her.

"It's Nash."

"And you didn't go after him?" I kept an even pace, not too fast to alert people like Silas had last night but fast enough to make proper haste.

My brother was nothing if not a flight risk.

"He didn't look like himself." Andra half-jogged to keep up, being several inches shorter than me. "I didn't know what to do, but I worried..."

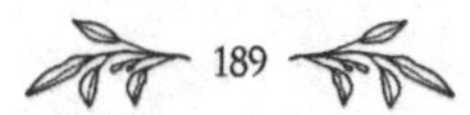

"You worried you might chase him away." I inclined my head. "Hopefully he hasn't gone too far."

"He headed west, not north or east," Aubrey chimed in. "So not across the river boundary or through the falls."

I stopped in the middle of the path, Andra and Aubrey skidding to a halt on either side of me. I composed myself before speaking. "I need to talk to him alone."

"But—"

"You must—"

I held up a hand. "I need to talk to him alone because if either of you is there, he won't confide openly. The only thing I can hope for is honesty, so I need you to stay out of it until I need you."

Andra started to protest, but Aubrey stepped forward. "We understand."

With a bow of her head, Aubrey grabbed Andra by the elbow and led her away to Guardian's Glade.

After fortifying myself, I moved toward the Aisle of Kings, confident that I knew exactly where my brother would be. I arrived to find my grown brother looking like a young boy. In a way, he was—a small child aching for his father's arms to wrap around him and tell him it would all be okay. Weren't we all? Losing a parent was never easy, but losing both and a year of your life would take a toll on anyone.

"*Onni, sen vole je vene?*" I lingered a few steps away, treating this how my father always treated Nash when he returned from a hiatus. A wild animal returned in his place.

"Go away, Caroline. I don't need you." I heard the tears in his voice, but he kept his face turned away.

I squatted where I stood. "If you want to talk about it, I'm here for you. I'm always here for you, you know that."

"I don't know anything anymore." Despair laced his words.

"Surely you know family even if nothing else in the world makes sense."

"I'm not family, Caroline. Not anymore."

"Nash." I stood, moving a step closer.

"Stay away from me." Nash scrambled away, turning to face me now. "I mean it."

I held my hands up. "Okay. I'm stepping away." I watched him, noting his red-rimmed eyes and wild heart rate. "What's going on?"

He shook his head, turning his eyes away.

"Nash, I need you to talk to me. You're my brother. I want what's best for you."

He let out a sardonic laugh. "You'd change your mind if I said."

"What are you talking about?"

He shook his head, his hair falling in his face. "I can't. Not now. Not yet. I promised myself I wouldn't be the reason... I can't be."

"The reason for what, Nash? You're not making sense."

"Nothing about me makes sense anymore." He ran his fingers through his hair, gripping it tightly. "I can't do this anymore. I can't."

"Nash—"

He crouched low, hands shifting to claws and back to fingers. The cry that broke from him sounded feral. I'd never been scared of Nash before.

"Nash, you need help. Asa can—"

"No one can help me, Caroline. Don't you see?" He cried now, his chest heaving with sobs. "I did this to myself. I brought misery to our kingdom. I am to blame. I am dirt and death and decay. I am blood and betrayal. I am *nothing*."

He repeated the last words a few more times before dissolving into tears.

"Nash, please," I begged. "Come to the Sage Brush with me. You

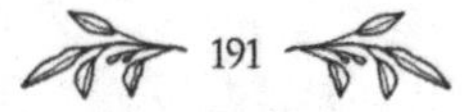

can sleep this off in Markus's old room, and we can have a conversation over some *kulas*. Maybe you can tell me what's been going on that I've missed."

"I'd rather die."

His biting words startled me more than they should have. It could've been the way he spat them out or the strange way the trees bent his cries, but I didn't feel safe alone in his presence.

"Nash, come on," I pleaded.

"I mean it," he hissed, climbing to his feet. "I would rather die than bring more harm to you or Silas or Eden. I can't do this anymore."

I threw my arms up. "Can't do what, be a brother?"

"Yes!" He held both hands out to me. "I resign from being your brother. In fact, you should've fired me a year ago."

I rolled my eyes. "You're being a child."

"Really rich from you, princess." He crossed his arms. "You think you have all this parental sway with me since Mother and Father are gone, and I'm the irresponsible Omega. Well guess what? Neither of them could control me anyway."

The truth of his words stung.

He pointed at me. "And another thing, I can see in your eyes how little you think of me. But you're the one in the wrong here. Because I'm doing what's best for our family, our pack. I'm the one protecting you all, and you don't even know it. You can't even see past your own muzzles, and frankly that's embarrassing for you, given how condescending you like to be to non-Historians."

I scoffed. "Oh, grow up, Nash! Just because you didn't get a job with higher responsibility doesn't mean you can throw me under the bridge for enjoying order and knowledge."

"You mean being a know-it-all? I didn't know that was a job here."

"How very Omega of you to say so. Shows that Silas made the wrong choice in making you a Delta. I should've had you banished instead."

He squeezed his head like it might explode. "That's what I've been trying to do this whole time! Banishing me is the kindest thing you could do."

I folded my arms. "And what's the worst thing, forcing you to stick with your family, your blood?"

"My blood is tainted. I deserve to be cast aside," he snapped. "No one wants the sick, the broken. Why do you think Andra's mother disappeared? She knew she was the weak link and wanted to make it easier for her family. So she left. Let me leave, Caroline. And you can have your precious order."

"And what, you win?"

"This is not about winning!"

"Then what is it about, Nash? Because I'm beginning to think you have no better reasons to leave than that you don't love us anymore."

"I killed him!" he barked.

My brain didn't catch up with the words fast enough to form a response before Nash launched into words that made me tremble.

"A year ago, I killed him. I ripped his left foot from his body, gouged a hole into his side, scratched up his arms trying to make him lie still. I fought like he taught me, and I fought well. And I won, Caroline. I won. I survived. This flighty Omega killed the King of Arcadia. And the Hunt worships me for it. So yes, in a way, I do win. But don't think for a second that victory is enjoyed by those who grieve."

I stepped back, swallowing hard. "What are you saying?"

He covered his face in his hands, pushing his hair back like our father used to. "Are you deaf? I killed Iain, King of Arcadia, an innocent man who cared for countless creatures. I killed him while Nyx watched. I stopped being your brother that day. I became the Son of Nyx, and if I stay here longer, I'm afraid of what I'll do."

I couldn't find words. I couldn't speak. I couldn't breathe.

Breathe. You have to breathe.

"Nash, this isn't true. The rumors are just creatures being nasty. They don't know–"

"Oh, they know." The way he said it sent chills down my spine. "They know the truth more than I do."

I shook my head, willing any of this to make sense. "Y-you'd never hurt us. You still–"

"I'm not your brother anymore, Caroline." His eyes appeared like the still surface of a frozen pond—frosty and ice cold. "I am your enemy."

"No. I refuse to accept that."

His chest heaved with his breaths. "It would be in your best interest to leave. Now."

"Nash–"

"Go away!" he roared, rattling my eardrums as fur melted to his skin, his face twisting in agony while the beast inside him assumed control.

And I ran.

34
SILAS

I STOOD WITH KANE at the eastern border of Arcadia on the *Suya* side of the river where the ice clung in sheets to the stones, water rippling beneath its surface. The air smelled like snow, and I needed to work out with Kane details on enhanced secrecy now that we'd doubled our numbers with the Lukosans. And with the Hunt causing problems and Eden's illness, I wanted to be sure we were safe.

In addition, there were more hikers and travelers to help in the winter, stuck without food or warmth from accidents or plain stupidity. The Guardians had saved many from death already, but there would always be more mistakes and more disasters to help clear up.

"I'm thinking we should concentrate our patrol efforts on this side of the valley." Kane gazed deeper back into the snow-laden forest. *"There's more of an opportunity for surprise here. But for our true duty, we keep one or two roaming the mountains per day, rotating to keep sharp for potential people in need."*

I could see my breath clouding around my whiskers. *"I like the *plan, but what are your precautions if–"*

"*Silas!*" a panicked voice interrupted.

Kane and I turned to find Elder Markus running full speed toward us, launching over the river and skidding to a stop in the snow. He panted and steadied himself.

"*It's Nash. It was him this whole time.*"

"*What's going on?*" I cut a glance at Kane, whose face faded to a ghostly pallor.

"*Nash killed your father. He's threatened Caroline, but she's okay. I think he's headed north for the falls.*"

I stood, frozen in my place for a heartbeat.

Nash. The truth fully settled in, and an ache sliced through me stronger than I'd ever felt.

And my world rent in two.

It can't be.

The world passed in a blur while we ran, undergrowth hissing. We tore through the Yard for a second time in less than a day. With Markus in the lead and Kane beside me, we hooked right, following the path to the falls.

Markus halted at the Gateway. "*I don't smell him.*"

"*Did he scale the bluff?*" Kane asked, eyeing the wall of stone surrounding this side of the valley.

Markus started listing theories, but I put my nose to the ground. Nothing.

"*...but they were in the Aisle of Kings before. Maybe he's still there. Or maybe–*"

I shot off, leaving the two behind me. I ran faster with the rage

fueling each pounding step. I knew exactly where he would be. He waited for me because he knew what was coming for him.

An eastern wind picked up, pushing me forward.

Maybe Markus was wrong. Maybe Caroline misunderstood.

I halted again at the Boneyard, this wretched place. Almost three months ago, I'd wrestled Nash to prove myself, frustrated and confused and still grieving our father.

I caught sight of him now, watching me with his head low. His hackles raised in his dark fur, looking so like Nyx when he let out a soft growl. There was no fighting the accusations. His body language said it all. Nash's ears were alert, and he showed no shame for the treachery he'd committed.

I'm going to kill him.

"Traitor!" I roared.

He said nothing, only watched. Markus and Kane moved to stand beside me.

"Say it to me like you said it to Caroline."

Nash raised his head. *"I killed my father."*

"You killed my *father. You're no son of his. You're no son of Arcadia,"* I growled, circling him now like prey. I'd pin him down. I'd grab him by the throat. And I'd show him no mercy.

"You're right." He tucked his tail between his legs. *"I'm not."*

"What's stopping me from killing you here?" I barked. *"You committed treason. You committed murder."*

"Do it." He snarled. *"It would be a mercy for what I've done. Don't think for a second that I revel in this information when I've only come to the realization myself."*

"You would blame it on memory loss, wouldn't you?" I snapped. *"This whole time it's been an act, hasn't it? You've known."*

"No. I swear to you, I didn't know. But when I walked the Alum

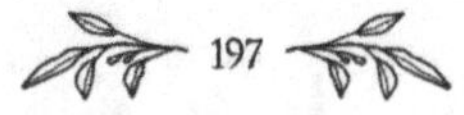

Cave Path—"

I froze. *"You went to pay the beast respects."*

"I went to find answers, Silas."

"That's je kunan to you."

His tail swished. *"I went to find answers, to see why the micca kept their distance and why the kuslar damned me to a dark fate. What had I done to deserve it? Except I do deserve it. I'm deserving of every bit of your anger and rage and pain. And I welcome it. It's a fair penance for what I did. And apologies will never be enough."*

Across the Boneyard on the other side of Nash, Caroline emerged, followed by Andra and Archer and the other Seers. My heart sank. I didn't need them to bear witness to this. It would be gruesome, a bloody stain on Arcadia's history.

But this has happened before, and I was warned.

I saw Elder Macon's image of my paw print in my mind, and I wondered if the blood filling the print was Nash's or my own. He'd warned me of the dangers of history's capability of repetition and patterns. I didn't believe him. I didn't want to believe him.

If only he were here now to give me wise counsel.

"Run," I growled. *"You will never find peace here again. From the far south to the far north of these mountains, everyone will smell the blood you spilled, taste the treason on their tongues."*

"Please, Silas. Death is pre—"

"You will respect me in my kingdom," I barked.

"Je kunan." He lowered his head, flattening his ears. *"Please, death is kinder."*

"You don't get my kindness anymore." I snarled. *"Kindness is reserved for the honorable."*

I glanced at the people I'd sworn to protect, the people I loved. They didn't deserve this. I'd never seen Caroline more frightened, not even the day our father died. Markus moved to put his body between her and Nash. Ransom moved to stand next to Aubrey.

But one look at Andra, and I knew.

She knew.

How long, I couldn't say, but she'd known before this moment the truth behind what Nash had done.

"*You knew?*" I hissed.

Andra shifted her weight, glancing at Archer.

"*You both knew?*" I roared.

I snapped my head to Nash. "*Get out.*"

Nash's ears pinned back.

"*Get out!*" I rushed at him.

Nash did what he'd never done before when facing me in a fight: he ran. He scrambled up the north bank with me hot on his heels. I chased him until he disappeared through the cleft in the stone wall leading to the outside world.

I howled long and low.

Will I ever be whole again?

"*Je kunan?*" Kane approached me, caution in his tone.

I stalked back to Guardian's Glade, one deliberate step at a time. I felt their presence behind me, giving me space but not enough to breathe.

Somewhere a raven called, and something shifted in me. Ravens were omens, but the worst had already occurred. I'd been betrayed by my own brother, my best friend. No pain or heartache could compare to that, could it?

I phased at my bedroom door, entering only to find Eden deep asleep, murmuring about dancing.

"Silas, I'm sorry. It's probably for the best." This time, it was Caroline. She reached for my hand, but I pulled it from her reach.

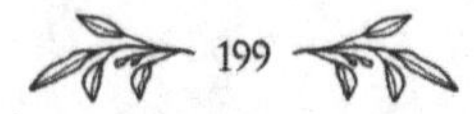

Everyone watched me from the open door.

I raged. I tore books from the shelves, knocked over the stand of crowns, and even sent one of the lanterns crashing to the ground. I watched it until its light fizzled out. I screamed until my throat was raw from the effort.

I threw the mugs and the water jug to the floor, sending the tray with it. I kicked the chair over and sent Eden's sketching things flying. I paused, chest heaving with the effort to pull air into my lungs.

I spared a glance at Eden, whose face wrinkled in sleep, but she hadn't budged. I didn't know whether to be grateful or even angrier.

"Get out!" I shouted, rounding on them. I pushed them out of my room into Guardian's Glade. "*Alla esen. Vanni, nu vene, alla esen.* Leave me in peace!"

They scrambled, and I watched them scatter like squirrels or birds in the face of danger.

Let them run.

As the doors of the throne room swung shut, I dropped to my knees. All the adrenaline seeped out of me like heat in the winter. I diminished second by second. I was nothing. And I would be nothing forever.

Nothing mattered anymore. Not *Joulo*, not the wedding, not our relationship with Lukosan, not even Eden's illness.

Meaningless.

Everything is meaningless.

35

CAROLINE

I N THE WAKE OF DISASTER, it's not the kings or the queens or the heads of houses that do the work. They stand on their stages and their podiums or sit on their thrones speaking falsehoods and empty platitudes.

In the wake of disaster, it's those under the rulers who get things done. It's those with power but out of the limelight who make hard decisions and bring life back into normalcy.

Despite my grief, despite my fears, despite my stomach-clenching pain, it was my job to manage the issue, assess the damage, and fix it.

But how could I ever bring peace and order back to Arcadia?

How would *I* ever feel right again, let alone the whole kingdom?

Markus had stayed the night in the Sage Brush, staying with Leander and giving me space, despite checking in on me every hour or so. He'd brought me tea and held me while I cried until I sobbed myself back to sleep.

Even now, when his work beckoned, he sat across from me,

watching me push eggs around my plate.

"You need to eat."

"It's like eating ash."

He took my hand. "I know it hurts now, but it'll get better."

I shook my head. Nothing could heal this kind of wound.

My eyes stared at nothing, a hazy view of the world while I struggled to focus on anything. "You don't get it, Markus. My brother murdered my father, your king. Do you not understand the gravity of that?"

"I know, but these things pass. Even terrible things like betrayal."

I finally met his eyes. "I don't need you to fix it, Markus."

He shook his head. "I'm not trying to, but–"

I held a hand up. "No. I need you to listen. Don't offer advice or try to solve this. Don't be cheerful or even positive."

He moved back. "There's no wisdom sitting in your sorrow for the rest of your life."

"There's also no healing if you don't process the pain," I snapped back.

I couldn't believe that he pushed back on this. I only wanted him to hear me, to listen and sit with me. This wasn't an issue needing solving. It was an event that would forever mar my life. How did he not understand that?

I pushed to my feet too fast and sent the chair toppling back. "I need some air."

Markus stumbled to his feet. "Wait, Caroline."

I whirled on him, placing a hand on his chest. "I need air alone." I grabbed my hastily packed bag on the way out.

"There's air in here!" Markus called. "Caroline!"

He didn't follow. I didn't know if I should be glad he obeyed my wishes or hurt that he didn't chase after me, never mind the oxymoron I'd become.

I pushed any thoughts of Markus aside, trying to sift through my list of things to get done.

Check in with Lilah to ensure that she had everything she needed to feed the Lukosans.

Chat with Kane about new precautions with the Hunt and now Nash added to the mix.

What a valuable asset he must be to the Hunt.

I shook the thought away and listed other things I needed to do.

Finalize Eden's ceremonial dress and get her to try it on once more.

Check on Eden.

Check on Andra and Archer.

Since the incident at the Boneyard, they were suspicious. They'd known about Nash, and they chose to keep it to themselves.

I resolved to put that at the top of my list.

I crossed through the Yard—unusually silent for mid-morning—and made my way to the temporary housing for the Lukosans. It surprised me to catch a flash of violet among the human garb of the Lukosans.

"Aubrey?"

She turned around to face me, face gaunt like she hadn't slept. "Caroline."

She moved, revealing Andra and Archer sitting behind her. Archer waved once, lips in a flat line. I eyed Andra, whose borrowed robes were rumpled. She watched me, a bruised color under her eyes.

"You look like bear scat." I propped my hands on my hips.

"Right back at you, Beta." She exhaled, running her hands over her face. "I didn't sleep at all."

I plopped down on the log where Archer sat, dropping my bag at my feet. "I cried most of the night. I almost can't believe it. But his eyes yesterday…"

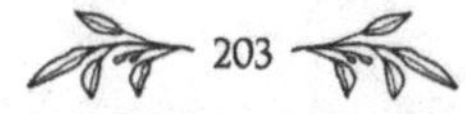

Andra shifted in her seat. "Wherever he is, I hope he's okay."

I watched her for a moment. It didn't take long to realize we stood on two sides of the same river. "You're worried about him, about a traitor?"

Andra's shoulders dropped. "He didn't know. He told us, but we couldn't betray him by telling you. He–"

"Holy *silva*, you intentionally hid it?" I stood, bumping into Aubrey who clamped her hands around my arms.

"Please hear them," Aubrey hummed. "Listen to the whole thing start to finish, and then make your judgments."

It felt like another betrayal despite it being the wisest and most respectful thing to do. But I didn't feel like being wise or respectful. Eventually, my responsible side overruled my inner hurt. I dropped back on the log, and Archer gave my shoulder an awkward pat.

Crossing my arms, I cleared my throat. "Talk."

Andra pushed her hair out of her eyes, resting her hands on the back of her neck. "I'm not sure where to begin other than the day my mother died."

I perked up. "What does Amelia's death have to do with this?"

"Nothing." Andra shrugged. "Or everything? I think it put things into perspective for me that I hadn't considered maybe ever. I thought about heirs for the first time, a legacy. I had to be responsible without someone to tell me what the most responsible thing to do was. I had to lead a pack without someone to guide me. I had to navigate my grief without an outlet. I found my own ways of coping, but in the end, I felt hollow. And I heard that Silas was engaged. And I sent a messenger. And he died under my care. He died so soon after I became Alpha. That kind of responsibility weighs on a girl." She swallowed, shaking her head. "I started thinking about Silas and Nash and you and all our crazy adventures that one summer. I missed y'all. And I didn't want that dynamic to change. And with a human thrown in the mix, who knows what would've happened.

"And I invited you all to stay." She shuffled her feet in the grass. "I'm sure they talked your tail off about all the nettle-brained things I did to Eden. I was cruel, more irresponsible, and childish than I have been since I was a pup. I wanted control, and I wanted things to stay the same because I was so hurt by my mother's passing. I held onto anything I could to stop the world from moving, but in the end, it moved on without me."

I raised my hand, trying not to interrupt. She shook her head, pointing at me.

"What does this have to do with my brother?" I couldn't say his name. Not yet.

"I'm getting there, I promise," she assured. "While they were in Lukosan, Silas wanted to propose. So he asked me to get a ring made for him. While out walking, I was thinking of my mother, thinking of how she died surrounded by ravens. And I thought about how beautiful and haunting it would be to die with the sound of an unkindness of ravens squawking in your ears. And I found a tree with a bunch of them. I should've known."

She shook her head, hands on either side of her face. Archer reached across and gave her knee a squeeze. My stomach sank when I connected the dots. I turned and met Aubrey's hollow gaze.

Andra breathed out slowly. "I've replayed it over and over in my head. How did I not feel it? But I snapped off a branch of a Mocker tree, and that's what they made Eden's ring out of. Caroline, I swear I didn't know. I wouldn't have done it if I had known."

She held my hands, grasping them like I was her lifeline. Her eyes glistened with tears.

"I mean, I witnessed it with my own eyes, you know?" She wiped

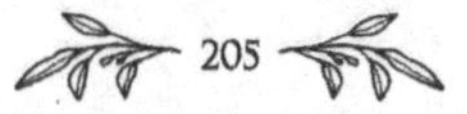

away rogue tears with the back of her robe sleeve. "So I tested my theory before saying anything because I knew it was a serious assumption to make. But it worked. And I would've solved it had Bennett not taken the robe away before I could steal the ring back. I would've been banished for theft or deviousness or whatever if it meant helping Eden, but I don't think I can figure out a way to convince her. She wouldn't hear it from me."

"You knew this whole time she'd attracted a Raven Mocker?" I pulled my hands away from hers.

She nodded. "I should've told someone, but would you have believed me if I claimed that I needed the engagement ring because it was from one of Kalona's trees? I wouldn't after the stunts I pulled last month."

She had a point. And I hated that it made sense, however twisted her reasoning.

"So Archer and I were going to the Aisle of Kings since no one usually goes there at night so we could come up with a way to get the ring. This was before the bath incident, but we heard screaming. We went to explore, wondering if it was a Spirit, but we found Nash bleeding and covered in dirt. Caroline, he didn't know. I swear he didn't, not until that night."

Andra paused for a minute or two, shoulders shaking while she drew in slow, deliberate breaths. It gave me a moment to piece together what she said about Kalona. Perhaps if we gave her back the ring, she'd leave Eden alone. Eden would be healthy again, and we could make a new ring from a tree that didn't belong to the master of the Hunt.

Andra hummed, calming her breathing so she could speak again. "We coaxed him into telling us what happened. He'd been injured. He told us he went to the place off the Alum Cave Trail where Nyx's cairn used to stand."

I straightened, sticking my hand in my pocket to feel the stone I carried with me everywhere from Nyx's cairn.

"A Wendigo met him there. It gave him the memory of that day back in gruesome detail."

"But it could lie," I offered, a gleam of hope busting through the cracks.

Archer shook his head. "And what does it gain from that? Maybe a little chaos, but Wendigos are noncommittal creatures. Why would they lie about that?"

"The point is," Andra went on, "Nash didn't know. He was a wreck when we found him. I was so scared for him, and I'm embarrassed to say, a little scared *of* him, too. He told us the whole thing, and we listened. He didn't want to ruin the wedding or *Joulo*. He wanted to leave quietly after all of it and after telling you and Silas the truth. But he didn't get the chance. He broke down yesterday, and I guess it's getting to his head that he's somehow Nyx's son or something. And he wasn't even in control of his body back then. Nyx had possession of everything. So how can we blame him for being used by someone else?"

Silence filled the space for a beat. I cleared my throat to voice the question that had been bugging me. "How does that correlate? Why pick Nash?"

"Glad you asked, Beta." Archer bumped my shoulder with his. "This was my theory. Something must have woken Nyx in the first place. What if the current of the River shifted when Iain saved Eden all those years ago? She was supposed to die or something, and Iain rescued her. Then Silas happens to run into her in the forest one day? A rather specific coincidence." Archer scoffed. "So Iain, of course, chooses Eden to be Silas's mate, because the current changed that day. But what changed the current?"

"The way Eden explained it, she fell into the river." Andra leaned

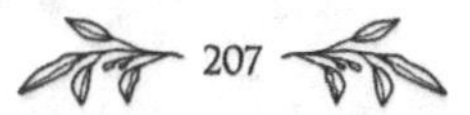

forward, tears mostly gone now. "But what pushed her into the river?"

I stared at both of them, back and forth. I even glanced back at Aubrey, but she betrayed nothing. Finally, she shrugged. "What pushed her into the river?"

"Glad you asked, again." Archer rubbed his hands together. "Here we have two theories. Either an earthquake like the one from *Lo Sain e lo Feru* shook the mountain enough to wake Nyx up and knock Eden down, or the Nunnehi knocked Eden down and woke Nyx up. Or technically, both of those theories could be the same theory if the Nunnehi caused the earthquake."

"The Nunnehi?" I scoffed. "Really? You think the invisible ancestors of the *micca* and supposed warriors of fate knocked her into the river? Just to be Silas's mate?"

Andra shrugged. "For all of us. They see the current differently than we do. They're weaving it in a way we won't see until years down the line. So think about it. This whole time, there's a fate woven into each action mimicking Lycaon and Nyx's story, bringing Eden to Arcadia, guiding me to one of Kalona's trees, and possibly crafting something with Nash that's bigger than we could understand."

I pinched the bridge of my nose. "So if the Nunnehi have it handled, what do we do about it?"

Andra and Archer shared a look like only siblings can.

"We need your help," Andra started.

"We need you to get the ring off of Eden's finger." Archer brandished his left hand. "That way, we can give it back to Kalona."

I groaned. "But how do we find Kalona? Ransom already tried to get into Eden's dreams to find her location around here."

Andra smiled, but it didn't quite reach her eyes. "Nash."

"Let me get this straight." I held both hands out. "You're suggesting we follow a banished murderer to the den of the Hunt so we know where to go once we steal the engagement ring of the future Queen of Arcadia to set the current of the River to rights?"

Archer pursed his lips. "That pretty much sums it up."

"And you believe this will work?" I glanced back at Aubrey, who'd been quiet the whole time. She knew her answer before I'd even sat down.

"It's the only way forward. We may save two lives while we're at it." She shrugged.

"I can't believe I'm saying this..." I sighed. "But I'm in. Where do we start?"

Andra stood. "We follow Nash."

Archer held a hand out to help me up. "Easy as breathing, right?"

36

EDEN

I COULDN'T BREATHE.

I dreamt I was falling fast.

But not like most people, where they jerk awake.

I fell...

And fell...

And fell...

I wondered if I'd ever touch the ground. And I realized I wasn't falling, but swimming in something cold and slick.

No, swimming wasn't right.

Sliding.

"Last one to the bottom is the runt of the litter!" Nash hollered, flying past me on his side. His tail thwacked the icy side of the hill and sent snow flying as he sledded far ahead of me.

"No fair!" I laughed. "You're heavier than me!"

We were in the neighborhood where I'd grown up. The neighbor behind our house had acres of land that we had access to during the winter months for endless sledding. Strange they weren't concerned about massive wolves on their property.

Three more wolves flew past me, one running and the other two sledding on their stomachs. I'd never seen such buffoonery from such serious wolves before. Ransom, Leander, and Markus skidded to stops at the end, roughhousing with Nash until I stopped about three or four paces away.

I would never beat them in sledding even if I tried, and not even with a head start.

"*Go for it!*" Markus barked up the hill, tail wagging behind him.

I pulled myself to my feet, breathing hard, and turned to watch the girls. With a running head start, Caroline and Audrey slipped down the hill. Andra was hot on their tails, a zipping pace on her stomach, tail wagging back and forth.

"Look out." Ransom ushered Leander to the side.

I stumbled backward into Silas. I had little time to register his presence before Andra crashed straight into Nash, followed by Caroline and Audrey. They squirmed in the dog pile, untangling limbs and tails.

Silas wrapped his arms around me, a warm embrace in the chilly, winter air. "I'm so happy."

I kissed his chin.

He tucked his chin on the top of my head. "You, this, my family. It's been a long time since life felt easy for any of us, and I'm so happy we could be together."

I glanced down at his arms around me and held back a cry. Thin, dark arms caged me in, spindly fingers with sharp claws interlaced like a lock. The chin on my head started to hurt, pain shooting down my spine. I raised my eyes to meet the gaze of a Wendigo, the scent of rotting flesh encompassing me.

"What's wrong?" Silas asked but from so far away. "Don't you

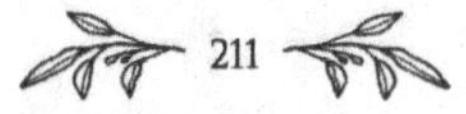

recognize me?"

I stumbled back a step, glancing to where the sledding party had climbed up the hill to sled again.

As bodies slipped down the packed snow, they were no longer shapes and faces I recognized. A sleek, black mountain lion slid gracefully past where we stood, hopping to his feet without pausing. A large, lumbering gray thing slipped down the slope, laughter like tumbling rocks escaping his cracked lips. Behind him, a lanky creature with reddish, slimy skin zipped down the bank, her voice calling like the rain. Ugals slid around other creatures similar to ones I'd seen on the hokey paranormal websites I used to peruse. Whistling jack, a wampus cat, the white screamers, tommyknockers, and the ghost dog that looked an awful lot like Nyx.

The creatures and cryptids rushed down the slope, snow drifts exploding while they scrambled for purchase at the bottom of the hill with claws and teeth.

But worst of all, striding down the hill with terrifying grace, Kalona watched me with her beady, bird-like eyes. Every inch of her had been chiseled from bone, sharp and protruding like her skeleton wanted free of the skin and feathers.

"You," I breathed. I realized the strange group far outnumbered me, and I'd take two steps before claws punctured my skin or my throat was torn clean out.

How had I not recognized they weren't my friends but my enemies?

"How lovely for you to join us, *pilukos*," Kalona crooned. "You seem surprised to see me. I thought you'd gotten used to my presence by now."

"It was you I've been seeing all this time." My heart thrashed in my chest as the group slowly closed in around me. "Leaving Lukosan, I thought–"

"You thought I was a paranoid hallucination after your close calls with the Wendigos." Kalona laughed, and it sounded like screeching bird squawks. "As if I would ever be so dimwitted as a Wendigo."

The Wendigo to my right shifted in the snow, a rattling sound coming from behind the skull. I wondered if Kalona had always been so cruel.

"Tell me, mortal. How does it feel when I steal each breath? How will it feel when I free your heart from its cage forever? How will your people feel when I devour each of your unlived days?"

Make it stop.

Make it stop.

It's just a dream.

I shut my eyes, willing myself to wake, but Kalona's screeching laughter sliced through any hopes I had of awakening from the nightmare.

37
NASH

G *ET OUT!*

My brother's words chased me into the shadows of the forest.

The biting cold seeped through my paws and fur, chilling me to the bone. It didn't help that I'd plunged straight through Feru Falls to escape as fast as possible.

My paws had taken me up the Great Mountain to the lodges. In the cloudy afternoon light, fat snowflakes fell in waves, dancing like the *kuslar* along the riverbanks. I curled up under a spruce tree at the Cliff Tops overlook, shivering in the single-digit temperature, and tried to process what my life had become.

Silas didn't give me a chance to explain. Not that I really deserved one, but he had to know I would never have hurt my father had I been in my right mind.

The air clouded when I exhaled, little drops of condensation clinging to my whiskers and freezing almost instantly.

I curled in on myself, tucking my nose into my tail. The world rolled out before me like a blanket, folding and crumpling and fading with age. It wasn't some perfect, white landscape below, but something freckled with conifers and covered in the skeletons and corpses of deciduous trees. The black scars and felled trees jutting across the landscape were the only evidence of the wildfires that raged in November.

"What am I going to do?" I huffed, more condensation freezing to my whiskers.

I couldn't return—not now and maybe never. The place I called home and could always return to had been lost to me. I'd become a lone wolf like I'd wanted so many years ago.

I thought about my decisions, wondering if I could've handled it better, if I could've held it in for a little while longer, and maybe...

But I'd done everything for my family. After the discovery and return of memory, I kept my distance, minded myself like a child, and did my best to keep everyone safe from my hands and history.

I would continue to do so. I'd keep myself far from Arcadia and Lukosan, manage whatever broken thing resided inside of me, and would keep those I loved safe from me and my history. And that meant doing my best to take down the Hunt from the inside out.

The idea alone spiked my adrenaline.

I was already dead to Silas, to Caroline, and soon enough I'd be dead to all of Arcadia and Lukosan. It wouldn't matter if I went out, teeth bared. It only mattered that they would be safe.

Silas and Eden would rule as King and Queen of Arcadia.

Maybe, in death, I would be forgiven.

And the Hunt would end with me.

I stood, shaking the snow from my fur. I had a loose plan, now I only needed to find the shadow where the Hunt lived. I'd figure out what to do once I arrived.

"Hey, stranger."

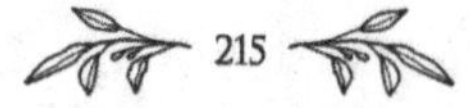

I jumped. I hadn't heard anyone approaching, hadn't heard the pounding heartbeat or the shaky breaths. Andra approached downwind of me, so I never smelled the gentle memory of autumn clinging to her fur.

"*Get away from me.*" I stiffened, hackles raising.

"*You know, you keep saying that.*" Andra's tail swished when she stepped farther toward me. "*And I keep not listening.*"

"*People have died just being close to me, Andra. I can't—*" I whined, taking a step back toward the ledge.

She'd cornered me. I'd allowed myself to be cornered. How stupid of me.

"*One person died because someone cruel used you. It wasn't your fault.*" Andra's tail flicked when she glanced between me and the cliff's edge behind. "*Please step away before you get yourself killed. I'd blame myself if something happened to you.*"

I growled but stepped away from the edge.

"*Isn't that better?*" Andra dropped to a sitting position. "*Now, can we talk?*"

"*There's nothing to say.*"

"*There's a lot to say, Nash. I promised you—*"

"*You promised me under pressure.*" I collapsed in the snow, afraid I wouldn't be able to stop myself from running. I was too good at it. "*I relieve you from your promise.*"

"*I didn't even get to tell you what I was promising you.*" Andra's tail wagged. How could she find amusement in this? Where was the joke or the joy or whatever it was that kept her so positive? I couldn't see it.

"*Go on.*" She sniffed. "*Ask me.*"

I huffed. "*What were you going to promise me?*"

She licked her lips, whiskers freezing ever so slightly. "*I promise you, Nash—prince and Delta of Arcadia—that when things change, whenever you're downcast and whenever you need it the most, I'll be there. I'll be by your side on your darkest days and the brightest ones, too, in whatever capacity suits you best. Sister, friend…"*

"*Mate?*" I breathed hard, trying to steady myself. Was I falling? Was I dreaming? Had Silas killed me in the Boneyard and this was my Spirit's dying dream to lull me into eternity?

Andra's ears perked up. "*If you wish.*"

I licked my lips, turning to gaze over the mountains. "*I'll think about it.*"

It was the best I could do when I didn't want to say no. But I couldn't put Andra at risk like that. She was too important.

"*Do you have any plans this afternoon?*" She stood, shaking the snow off her fur. "*I'm considering going on a hunt for the Hunt.*"

I shot to my feet. "*No.*"

I swore she raised an eyebrow. "*You're a Delta. You can't tell me what to do.*"

"*I'm not a Delta,*" I growled. "*I'm a lone wolf, my own Alpha.*"

Andra glanced back and three wolves stepped out of the shadows. I cursed myself for my inattention. Andra was too good at distracting me.

"*It doesn't look like you're alone to me.*" Andra straightened to her full height, so regal in the drifting snow.

My eyes moved over Archer, Aubrey, and Caroline. A wave of nausea engulfed me, and I shook my head. "*Y'all shouldn't be here.*"

"*We know the truth, Nash.*" Archer moved to stand next to his sister. "*We'll stand by you until everyone else does, too. Including yourself.*"

Aubrey nudged Caroline, who warily stepped toward me. She dropped a small stone between us, a stain on the snow, before backing away.

"*What is this?*" I sniffed at it. It smelled like blood.

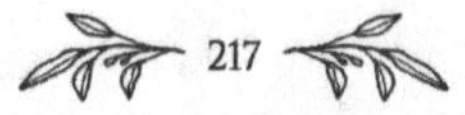

"I stole it from Nyx's cairn." Caroline stood to her full height. *"I think it might help you weasel your way into the Hunt if you bring like a gift. Maybe gifting something of his that Arcadia stole would prove your loyalty to the Hunt. Maybe it would convince them you were safe and on their side."*

I whimpered, stepping back, careful not to get too close to the ledge. *"Why do you still have this? It shouldn't– I don't–"*

"Take it." Aubrey's ears flattened before straightening again. *"You need it to earn their trust."*

"And then we take them down." Archer pawed the snow.

Andra stepped forward, nudging the stone toward me. *"Together."*

I wanted to protest, to send them all away, but it sparked something in me that had been unlit for quite some time. It sparked the desire for a pack of my own, a place I would always belong despite my nomadic tendencies and desire for spontaneity.

These people belonged to their own places, families, and homes, but for a temporary pack, it would do.

Andra must have seen the shift in me. She moved back when I picked up the stone, the foul taste of iron lingering on my tongue.

Andra sniffed the air, the snow increasing. *"Well, where to?"*

38

SILAS

EDEN WOKE THE NEXT MORNING to the remnants of my fury. She found me, asleep on the ground at the foot of the bed, and coaxed me under the covers where I wept.

And I dreamt of something dark and wicked.

I don't remember much other than the images of my father's body and Nash's bloody teeth and face. I woke us both with my screams.

In the light of the coldest afternoon, I curled myself around Eden, whispering apologies and trying to make sense of the world again. I thought I'd grieved before, thought I'd stabilized after losing my father. Nothing could have prepared me for this kind of pain. I trusted Nash, I let him back in the pack, promoted him, and tried to always be kind like our father taught us. What had I done wrong?

"Si?" Eden's muffled whisper pulled me out of my reverie.

I hummed a response.

"Will you promise me something?" She shifted until she faced me, eyes filled with such timidity it worried me.

"Anything, *je rakas*." I tangled my fingers with hers, kissing her knuckles where her engagement ring rested.

"When I'm gone, will you bury me with your family?"

"Hey, don't talk like that." I gave her hand a squeeze. "We have a long time before that happens. Ages."

She chewed on the inside of her cheek. "Even then, you'll have to do something. And I thought that maybe you could bury me with your parents, if that's allowed. That way, whenever you're sad or angry or lonely, you only have to go to one place to be with all of us." She brushed my hair out of my eyes. "And you can introduce Caroline and Markus's pups to me. And tell me all the ridiculous prophecies that Ransom and Aubrey and Leander give you. And you can update me on whether they bring back red wolves to the Great Smokies."

It pained me to hear her speak of our lives like I'd live mine without her. "Why are you talking about this?"

Eden swallowed. "You and I both know, don't we?"

The silence after her words suffocated me.

"We both know there's no getting better for me." She cleared her throat, words choking her. "At least promise me that you'll have a spot where you can come talk to me wherever I end up."

"You'll be in the Other Realm," I breathed. "They—they have to accept you. You're one of us now."

Tears slid down my cheek and dripped into my ear. I hated this conversation, but I hated more how much it killed me that she might not be there during *Sarva*. What happened if her Spirit never returned?

"Hey, it's okay," she assured. "It'll be all right, Si. You'll be fine, I promise."

So many promises. But a promise is only a promise if it's kept.

"Eden," I breathed. "Please don't leave me."

"If I ever have the choice, I'll always choose to stay." She smiled at me.

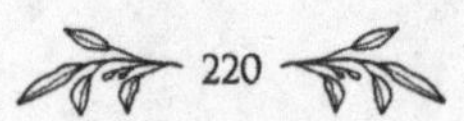

I couldn't take it anymore. Not now.

I pulled her to me, legs tangling with hers, and I cried into her shoulder, her hair, her neck. I apologized so many times I lost count, because in the end, wasn't this my fault? Didn't I bring her to Arcadia in the first place? I put her in danger, and I brought her to another place with even more danger. And somewhere in all of that, wasn't I to blame for this pain, this cursed disease?

I don't know how long I slept. I remember waking in the afternoon, both Eden and I eating some lunch, and going back to bed.

Time passed in a slippery way, like a fish through open hands. I wasn't sure who I would be if I stopped trying to hold on. Would time swallow me whole? Would I fade into nothingness?

"Si?" Eden's voice woke me from my restless nightmares.

I groaned in response, pulling the blanket over my head.

"Hey." She shook my shoulder. "Wake up."

I peered out from the relative safety of the blanket. Eden sat up, brushing her hair over one shoulder, the once springing curls losing their definition after that golden day of hers.

"What is it?" My voice was hoarse. I wondered if I had been screaming again. I glanced around, noticing the lit lanterns and dim surroundings. "Is it nighttime again?"

Eden squinted at the foliage. "I think it's getting there."

"What's going on?" I rubbed the sleep out of my eyes, stretched, and yawned.

Eden passed me a hastily written message.

A, C, A, and A gone after Hunt on own volition. - R

I fought the urge to crumple the note in my hand. I hated that I knew who the letters represented. I hated that it made me so angry. I hated that I didn't blame them for their reaction. But most of all, I hated that I'd been hiding from this instead of leading my people through it. What kind of king had I become?

"Who brought this?" I waved the note in the air.

"Leander. About three minutes ago." Eden picked at her nails. "I had to read it a few times before I understood what it meant. Are they going after Nash to save him or..."

I ran a hand through my hair. "I don't know."

"They're going to get themselves killed."

I blinked.

"You have to stop them."

I hated that she was right. Apparently, I hated a lot of things this morning.

"You read the note." I tossed it in her lap. "They went on their own volition. I doubt they'd listen to their king if I asked them to come back. It's probably why no one told me."

"Silas," Eden said, sounding incredulous.

"Why should I care?"

"You're their king," Eden scoffed. "He's your brother."

"He murdered my father and put you in danger. I can't forgive that."

"So you're going to let history repeat itself?"

I finally glanced up at her. "What did you say?"

She rolled her eyes. "You're sitting here doing nothing when you're their king! They expect you to stand up for them, to stand by their side when they face the dark. And you're hiding."

"No, what did you say after that?"

"You're going to let history repeat itself?" She furrowed her eyebrows.

"History," I hissed, pushing to my feet.

Scouring the near-empty shelves and the floors from my grief-filled rampage, I finally found the book that I'd so carelessly flung to the ground in my anger. I gingerly brushed it off, dropping back on the

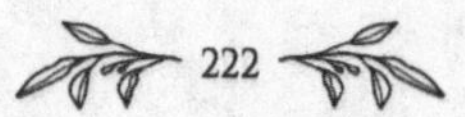

bed with the book in my lap.

"What is it? What did I say?" Eden peered over my shoulder.

"*Lo Sain e lo Feru*," I muttered.

"The Legend. Why?" She held onto my arm.

"Lycaon meets Nyx at the river, there's a great fog and an earthquake and then the next king, right? Well, some speculate that the Nunnehi were involved."

"The what?" Eden coughed, and I waited for her to get a drink of water before continuing.

"The Nunnehi. They're the ancestors of the *micca*. There are still some around, though it's rare to see one. They're invisible."

"Invisible?" Eden sounded skeptical.

"Unless they want to be seen. Remind you of anyone?" I raised an eyebrow at her.

"Yeah, the little guys. Go on," she prompted.

I pointed at the Legend in the book where it spoke of the sound of metal and stone. "There was a sound that echoed across the valley, something metal and stone. What if that was the Nunnehi? What if, this whole time, the Nunnehi have been orchestrating all of our history?"

"Lycaon and Nyx?"

I closed the book. "And you and Nash and the Hunt. All of it."

My brain thrummed with ideas, swirling so fast like water over the edge of Feru Falls. I couldn't keep up. I pushed to my feet and paced, stumbling over the things I'd slung to the ground.

"I'm not following, Silas," Eden croaked, coughing again.

"The Nunnehi are written about in Cherokee myths, but they're widely believed. They operated alongside the *micca* to assist lost children, injured travelers, or even the sick. They would take them into their homes, eat with them, and send them on their way back home. The Nunnehi are mostly friendly, but they don't like conflict or being discovered. They're tricky."

"Sounds like Irish faeries," Eden grumbled.

"My point is, they will fight if necessary. Say if a power-hungry *virlukos* upsets the balance of the valley? What if the Nunnehi struck a deal with the two brothers? They put Nyx to sleep, and Lycaon would live but only in Spirit."

"What does this have to do with Nash?"

"It has everything to do with Nash." I offered her a tremulous smile. "And you, *pilukos*."

Eden shifted back. "Me?"

I started picking things up and putting them back in their places while I talked. "My mother always said that day by the Little River was different. She never said why. But maybe she'd connected things I hadn't. Or maybe the Nunnehi showed themselves to her. She always had a knack with the Spirits.

"What if—that day you saw us for the first time—the Nunnehi purposefully woke Nyx? It would've taken time for him to gather strength, rebuild, and find the Hunt again. There was an earthquake the day Lycaon faced Nyx. So what if the earthquake is what made you fall?"

"It was a river. I slipped." Eden shrugged. "I mean, maybe, but why would the Nunnehi wake Nyx?"

I shook my head. I picked up the lantern I'd thrown and righted it. "I don't know. They operate on a level with the Spirits, so they don't always let us in on their plans. But they must've known something. Maybe it was something about you and your fate. Or maybe it was about me or Nash or Caroline. My point is, if we want to stop history from repeating itself, Nash can never become Nyx."

"You've lost me again." Eden brushed her hair out of her face and started to weave it into a braid.

I hung the extra robes in front of the wardrobe. "He still did what he did, and I can't change that. But maybe the Nunnehi guided his fate. Perhaps they guided him to Nyx that day when he first lost his memory. Maybe they were the ones that cut him off from Nyx's possession. Maybe this whole time, they've been shaping the current of the River."

"So we're powerless to stop it?" Eden tied off the end of her hair.

"Not entirely." I picked up the tray and the upended water pitcher. "We make our own choices, so it's possible someone chose something the Nunnehi didn't expect. Maybe this is rerouting a poor decision, or it could be intentional. Either way, this has them written all over it because it doesn't make sense for Nash to do what he did on his own.

"Different creatures kept calling Nash the Son of Nyx. What if that's just a title for whoever takes over next? So he's not Nyx's blood son, but sort of spiritually. If Nash assumes Nyx's role, history repeats itself. But if we stop him from taking Nyx's position–"

"We stop history from repeating," Eden cut in. "We save Nash."

"And stop the Hunt."

"And possibly fulfill destiny." Eden furrowed her brow. "But how do we do that? You banished him. Isn't that permanent?"

I waved the air. "I'll figure that out when I get there. But if I'm right—and I really hope I am—Nash can be redeemed."

Eden beckoned me over. I sat on the edge of the bed, adrenaline still pumping through my veins, that I wanted to bust out and run wherever the wind guided me. Instead, Eden pulled me close and kissed me gently. I leaned into her. I never wanted to leave her.

She pulled back with a laugh. "Go! You have work to do."

I groaned. "You'll be okay here by yourself?"

She sighed. "I'll be better when I know Nash is where he belongs."

I pressed my lips to her forehead before getting to my feet. "I'll make sure there's someone to take care of you. Maybe Asa or Leander."

"How do you say good luck in the Ancient Tongue?" Eden chewed the inside of her lip.

"*Dumahn slava.*" I chuckled. "*Au bene.* I need all the luck I can get."

"I love you, silly king." She smiled, a sorrow deep in her eyes.

"*Je rakassen, pilukos.*" I kissed her knuckles one last time.

39

NASH

I T ALL HAPPENED SO FAST, I barely had time to process.

First, I led my mini pack through the mist with the stone in my mouth, and then the line disappeared, and I was alone. Again.

Some temporary pack leader I was, losing my family the moment things became confusing.

I could smell the Hunt, knew the strange, rotting scent that accompanied many of the group. We'd followed their scent trail farther up the ridgeline well past the lodges of the Great Mountain toward Mount Guyot in a haze of cloud. The humans called it smoke, the Real People called it blue smoke, but we called it the Veil.

After losing my people in the Veil, I kept trekking uphill. No way was I about to set down this stone to howl for them. I would never give away my position like that, announcing my arrival. The Hunt might not be against me entering the group, but they wouldn't like my companions.

Ducks called overhead, and I started seeing fringed phacelia blanketing the floor without a hint of snow. Suddenly, a figure appeared in front of me, sending me skidding back a few feet.

She stood below my eyesight, around three or four feet tall, her dark dress falling to her feet, sleeves tied at her wrists. Her long dark hair had been braided and pulled to the side. But what struck me the most was the way her eyes glowed, like a bit of sun caught in her irises.

I recognized the Nunnehi at once, realizing that Andra and Archer might have been right about everything. They told me their theory of Nunnehi changing the course of the River of time, piece by piece. It seemed plausible at the time, but it shocked me to have one appear in the dark like a slippery shadow.

"*Sunsen vene?*" she asked. "*Densun vaara.*"

Strange that she seemed hesitant for me to continue following the scent trail. Was this not in their plan?

"*I know they're dangerous.*" I bowed my head to the Nunnehi woman, still clutching the small stone in my mouth. "*But that's why I'm here. I have to set things right.*"

She tilted her head. "*Sun nuvole municci esen?*"

I tucked my tail. "*I didn't think I was pack material, but maybe someday.*"

"*Hon nuvole municci ehon. Sensun vene usslava hon kunin?*"

I huffed. "*I'm about to face the Hunt and you're asking me about my love life?*"

Was it destiny that I would have a pack of my own? Was it fate that I might be able to start a life with Andra?

The Nunnehi woman giggled, beckoning me to follow her. I hesitated, but followed. If they guided the River by changing fate, I didn't want to get caught on the wrong side.

The Nunnehi people were notorious for leading people off the paths and into their cave cities for weeks at a time, returning the stolen people at their leisure but well-fed and well-rested. I didn't have time to wait, but I wasn't sure what I was doing. Maybe she had answers for me.

She turned, snatching my wounded paw. *"Nu rikas lo veime."*

With a firm press of her thumb into the wound, my mind burst into a bright light. Memories filled my head where previously there'd been a void. I could walk between them like a hall of doors waiting to be opened. And one door opened on its own.

Like a dream, I observed the Nunnehi girl approaching Kalona—the Raven Mocker and mother of ravens—on the shores of the fabled lake of healing. *Atagahi* had been hidden from the world, a secret for those who needed it most. So why were the Hunt here?

"All we want is unity between packs," the Nunnehi woman reasoned. "Since Lukosan and Arcadia split so many years ago, we have tried to bridge the gap. Nyx was our first chance, and he ruined it by killing his father. Nash is our second chance, and you're interfering."

"Too late now," Kalona snapped. "You woke us when you woke Nyx, and I can't rest until the item that belonged to me is returned. Then and only then will I leave this place. It's unbalanced."

"Your ideas of true balance are small and weak. Balance isn't measured with an eye for an eye and a life for a life."

"Your opinion means little here." Kalona's feathers ruffled. "We intend to correct history where you so rudely intervened. Nash will assume Nyx's place in the Hunt and balance will be restored leaving the world at peace again."

"Your peace is false." The Nunnehi cursed Kalona before the scene disappeared.

I stood back in the snowless forest, facing the same Nunnehi woman. She disappeared with a giggle, the sound of flutes fading in the space she left.

40

SILAS

A

FTER ENSURING LEANDER could check on Eden, I left my robe on the hook at Guardian's Glade and set off to Feru Falls.

I struggled to find their scent trail in the snow, but it was easy to pick up Aubrey. She always smelled of sage and other herbs in either human or wolf form. After that, it was easy.

Nash must've hooked east and taken the Trillium Gap trail, which meant he went for the Great Mountain. Aubrey and the others followed him up the snowy path. I found indentations, former prints now obscured by new layers of snow, and I wondered how long ago they'd left Arcadia. I'd slept almost a full day, and in the dying light, it grew harder and harder to see signs of any animal passing.

I relied on my nose, and it brought me to the Cliff Tops Overlook. My breath clouded in front of me, freezing to my whiskers. They were all up here, following the scent trail Nash left. I wondered where it led them.

The clouds covered the stars, and the dark that surrounded me had a presence. I shook off the thought and carried on, following Aubrey's scent trail again. While I snaked around trees, heading up and down game trails and slinked through thick snow, I wondered what I'd find when I arrived.

Would I come face-to-face with the Nunnehi or the Hunt? Would I be too late? The thought of arriving to my family's mangled bodies urged me to a new speed.

I'd only seen a Nunnehi once before. I had little knowledge aside from legends. All of the stories mentioned music, drums, dancing, and song. But the world had gone quiet, like the calm right before a storm.

The scent trail grew stronger by the step, and I knew I would find them before long. I started paying more attention to my surroundings and the creatures I encountered. Slowly, it dawned on me where the Hunt was. I wondered if they had come to the realization and picked up their pace or if none of them had been to *Atagahi*.

I ran, kicking up snow behind me.

It all made sense now, the story that the Nunnehi had woven for all these years. The Spirits together told this story, and of course, it would bring me to *Atagahi*.

I'd been there once many years ago as a young pup on an outing with my father. We'd found an injured bushwhacking hiker alone in the wilderness. I helped pull the hiker's body onto my father's back, and he carried the hiker away from the city. I asked him where we were going, but he said nothing. I heard ducks flying above, odd for midday in late spring. And then, the Veil surrounded us, so dense that I had to listen for my father's heartbeat and the weak heart of the hiker to find the way.

We'd spilled out on the shores of a blue lake surrounded by forests with beds of fringed phacelia. Ducks flew overhead, and birds sang and my eyes took in as much as possible. Creatures of all kinds, Spirit-filled and Plain, good and evil, large and small, drank from the lake's cerulean waters. I'd never seen anything like it.

My father slid the hiker off his back and pulled his body into the lake's water. The hiker mumbled something, rubbing his eyes like he'd woken from deep sleep and blinked. He turned this way and that, and asked if he'd gone to Heaven.

That's when the Nunnehi man appeared. He'd explained the hiker would have to stay with the Nunnehi until he passed. Any human to bathe in *Atagahi's* waters would swear service to the Spirits in whatever capacity until old age carried them from this world to the next. Later, I'd asked my father why he didn't have to stay with the Spirits since he'd been in the water. He explained that *virlukos* are half Spirit constantly, whichever side isn't presently visible. So we were already part of that Realm, whereas humans weren't.

I stumbled on the game trail that Aubrey had followed and thought of Eden. Would she accept the fate of staying with the Nunnehi if it meant she could live? Would she rather pass on than live apart from me but always nearby? Could she come and visit if she were a part of the Nunnehi? Could she still marry me if she were changed?

The trees were much more difficult to make out, and I realized I was in the thick of the Veil obscuring *Atagahi*. A heartbeat sounded close. I turned to face the creature, a low growl rumbling through me.

Caroline ducked under the snow-laden branches, bumping right into me with a yelp. "*Si?*" She shook her fur. "*What are you doing here?*"

"*Coming after you. I—*"

"*I lost the others.*" Her ears perked up and her eyes flitted from tree to tree in our small visibility.

"*What do you mean?*" I joined her, scanning our dim surroundings.

"*We had a straight line set up, and I guess once the Veil settled, we broke formation without knowing. I didn't want to howl in case of the Hunt. But now, I don't know where they are. And the scent trails are disorienting."*

I bent low, sniffing the trees and stones ahead. Dozens of scents covered each other, layering until they all blended into one.

"Scenting is useless." I swished my tail and debated what to do. *"When Father and I visited that one time, we kept walking uphill. So as long as we're headed up the incline, we'll eventually arrive or come close enough to hear the ducks."*

"Ducks?" Caroline questioned.

"Trust me on this. Come on, keep your nose to my tail." I started up the incline, ensuring she stayed right behind me.

I prayed that the rest of them were safe somewhere at *Atagahi's* shores.

"Si? What's that noise?" Caroline whined.

I paused, holding my breath. My heart thudded in time with Caroline's when a scuffling sound echoed down from somewhere above us.

Someone yelped. A cacophony of snarling and snapping ensued.

Someone fought, and someone lost.

41

NASH

I PUSHED PAST THE SPOT where the Nunnehi woman had stood and crested the mountain. The path spilled me out at the shores of a blue lake, ducks swimming through the crystal-clear waters that reflected a cloudless, starry sky. Across the lake, I made out the dark party of beings, strange shapes, and sizes compiling their numbers.

A raven cawed above me, flying directly across the lake to the Hunt. I realized there would be no turning back when the catamount ran toward me on the shore.

I started making my way toward him, each step made with effort.

The catamount met me halfway around the lake, hackles raised. *"Son of Nyx, what are you doing here?"*

I reminded myself to stay calm. They all knew me. This would be like the times I pretended to be human at the dance clubs. I'd bluff my way through conversations and charm my way into people's hearts... and free meals. And no one would ever know.

"I have a gift for our Master. One that has taken me a while to

find." I tilted my head and curled my lip up to show him. "*I wanted to bring it to her personally.*"

His muscles relaxed the slightest bit. "She will be most eager to see you."

I followed a half a pace behind the catamount, holding my head high.

Breathe. Just breathe.

"Dearest, what brings you to *Atagahi* so soon?" Kalona said, standing from her throne of bones. "The human is not dead yet."

I held it together despite the callous words about Eden.

"*I have a gift for my Master.*" I bowed low at her feet before placing the stone and taking two steps back, choosing my next words carefully. "*A piece of my father's cairn, stolen and now returned.*"

Kalona bent to retrieve the stone, inspecting it. "Nyx would be proud you've taken so well to restoring his Spirit, but there are many more stones to find. I find that most sons would envy power over legacy, but your choice bodes well for you. Walk with me."

I fell into step beside her, continuing in the same direction I started when we left the others behind.

Kalona fixed me with her sharp gaze. "When will you tell me your decision?"

I swallowed. "*My decision?*"

"Will you choose the Hunt over Arcadia? You asked for more time so long ago now. There are things in motion that need to be settled. You know there must be a balance. The pesky Nunnehi do, too, though they have a strange idea of the concept."

I couldn't keep Kalona's gaze, so I glanced across the lake. I caught sight of the Nunnehi woman standing in the shadows with my family, my pack. Andra, Archer, and Aubrey huddled in the shadow of the Nunnehi woman. I wondered where Caroline could be but dismissed the thought. She always had a plan.

I needed to improvise, to give myself more time or at least my family enough time to escape without being seen.

"*Why don't I decide now?*" I stopped walking, and Kalona turned to face me, eyes narrowed and guarded. "*I came all this way to give you a gift, so I should make my decision plain before everyone, too.*"

"Excellent. They will be most pleased. The waiting has been difficult for them. They are not as patient as I am which is why I had to move them to *Atagahi*. You understand."

The Hunt had never intended to linger. In fact, they wanted to leave. Had my decision kept them here? That would be another reason that this was all my fault.

"*I understand.*" I glanced back at the Nunnehi woman, noticing Archer was missing. Where had he gone?

As we approached, all the creatures—the Wendigos, the gegahs, the catamount, the sluaghs, and everything in between—all gathered around the throne when Kalona sat in her throne.

"The Son of Nyx has made his decision," she called, each muttering voice or quacking duck quieting with her command. She nodded for me to speak.

I licked my lips. "*After much consideration these past weeks, much deliberation and processing, I've decided that the best interest for all of you and for me is...*" I paused to breathe. "*For me to stay in Arcadia.*"

Murmurs rumbled through the crowd until Kalona lifted a taloned hand. She composed herself. "You mean to say, you've decided to leave the *virlukos* unbalanced."

I blinked. "*I didn't–*"

"There are too many on the brighter side of the Veil. Either you come with us, or there is no longer balance in this valley. What will you do to right the wrong?"

It took me a moment too long to draw together what she meant: that somehow the number of lawful Spirits outnumbered the chaotic Spirits, that she believed murder would right the wrongs of the death of Nyx and other members of the Hunt.

I moved back, but the catamount sank its teeth into my haunches. I yelped, snarling while the sluaghs pulled at my fur from above.

"Will you choose to die instead?" Kalona asked from her throne, leg crossed, chin propped on her hand. "Balance can be restored by many Spirits."

The catamount ripped into my flesh with claws and teeth, pulling strips of fur with each blow. I considered it might end this way, but now that it was happening, I wasn't sure I'd prepared to die. I only hoped that Andra would be able to find a piece of me to bury so that my Spirit could come back at *Sarva*.

Too many things happened at once to register.

The pain blinded me.

The pressure released from behind.

And Kalona screamed.

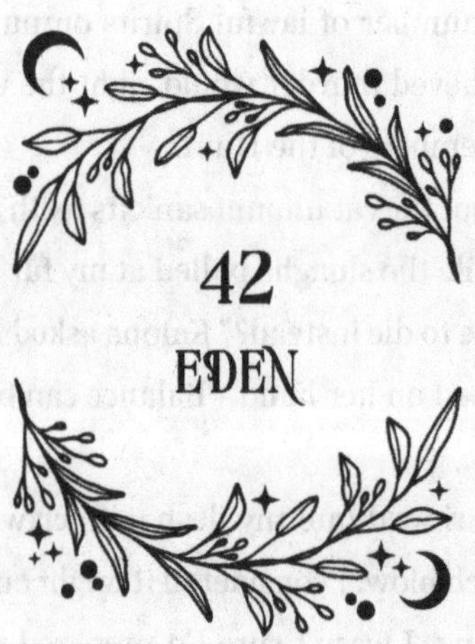

42
EDEN

FURY RIPPED THROUGH MY BODY, and I shifted, my skin half melting with the wolf pelt wrapped around me until only my human legs and hands remained. The rest of me was some shape similar to a wolf.

I commanded legions. I was on a battlefield, wrapped in armor only the deadliest wolves could penetrate. I was unstoppable.

And I was lonely.

Where had my pack gone? It had been a while since I had felt their presence. The twisted crown of honeysuckle reminded me of them, but I couldn't remember why. There was someplace I was supposed to be, a ceremony or a feast or something that they expected me to be at. No, I was the reason for the feast, right?

A wolf held a paw to my head, trying to draw the memory out. Were we supposed to dance? Was that where I promised to meet Iain and Elder Macon to pick our dances back up?

And a promise is only a promise if you keep it.

No, I was meant to go on a walk with a Wendigo. He promised to tell me his secrets and show me the ways of his people. Or was it the Nunnehi I'd been promised I would meet? She was supposed to play her flutes for me, and I was going to dance for her people at *Atagahi*.

But *Atagahi* was in ruins. I could feel the pull and the ache of the Spirits that called it home. It pained me. I began to tremble, and the earth shook in condemnation of the damage being rendered to those peaceful shores.

I cried, an ache settling that I didn't understand. I was needed at a funeral, though I didn't know whose. So why was I wearing this silly honeysuckle crown?

With some effort, I pulled it off of my head, noticing my wolf skin was now gone. In its place, I was clothed in a shimmering blue dress that swished at my ankles. I left the crown on the battlefield and meandered into the trees.

This was where I needed to be. I belonged here.

Kuslar and *micca* and Nunnehi and wolf Spirits emerged from the dark, all glowing in shades of blue. I bowed to each of them when I passed, and I realized my skin had begun to glow, too. Or was that a trick of the light?

Careful not to fall in, I sat on a mossy log that acted like a bridge over a river. The waters below rushed past, their inky black looking deeper than the ocean. I dangled my feet over the water, wondering if it would feel cold or warm to swim.

I launched myself into their depths, cold to the bone. I spun around in the current, submerged in a dark only the stars knew. I vaguely remembered this from my past, but how long ago? Or was this moment the past, too?

I opened my eyes underwater, and to my surprise, I glowed a dull blue. What a strange attribute for a human to have. It must've been some *virlukos* thing Silas forgot to mention.

Silas. He waited for me. But where?

And why did that make me so sad?

I opened my mouth to speak, but I choked on the pitch-black liquid.

I couldn't breathe.

Why was that becoming a theme in my days? Why was it that I struggled to breathe? Or maybe that was normal when human girls became werewolf queens and started to glow haint blue.

Maybe this was the way things worked.

Maybe I had no choice.

Maybe this was it.

43
CAROLINE

S ILAS AND I SCRAMBLED up the last part of the bank, tumbling out next to a brawl. Archer had the catamount by the throat, squeezing it with all of his might. Nash lay limp in the grass, dazed and surrounded by enemies.

Kalona stood, and everyone froze except for Archer. She moved to stand directly in front of Nash. "Explain yourself, Son of Nyx. What is this treachery, an ambush?"

Nash attempted to phase, but settled back in his wolf form, whimpering, "*No, I swear.*"

Kalona pushed a bare foot into his head, rolling him back down. "You dare lie to me? I've been nothing but kind and accepting of you into our ranks. And you betray me."

"*Please,*" he whined.

The earth began to shake, causing a cacophony of sound. Archer dropped the catamount and tackled Kalona. Chaos broke out among all parties, and all the creatures jumped on Archer who ripped at Kalona with all he had. Silas ran into the fray along with Aubrey and Andra who spilled out of the forest across the lake, and I sprinted to Nash.

"*Caroline,*" he cried, attempting to phase again and failing.

"*No time.*" I glanced at the catamount that started to move slowly. "*Water.*"

I grabbed Nash by the scruff, pulling with all of my effort, and he whined with the movement. He pushed as much as he could, and in the end, we made it. He slipped into *Atagahi's* water.

I watched the flesh reattach, the fur replaced like new, and the cuts and scrapes and puncture wounds healed like nothing had happened. In a matter of moments, Nash had fully recovered.

"*Duck.*" He straightened.

I turned, expecting to see ducks like Silas had said, but Nash launched over me, burying his teeth in the throat of the catamount, putting more pressure until the cat stopped moving.

Nash joined me, muzzle bloodied, and we started toward the tangle of bodies when Kalona screeched. It stopped everyone in their tracks.

Archer had phased, his body limp and Kalona's talons holding him up. She hadn't escaped unscathed, her feathers a mess, a gash across her chest and one down her arm. Somewhere amidst the crowd, Andra growled.

"Since you won't restore the balance, Son of Nyx, I will." With force, she threw Archer's body at her feet. "Soon, I will end your queen's misery, reclaim what is mine, and take my children away."

With a rush of wings and an unsteady flight, she disappeared into the trees, the Hunt thundering after her. Andra phased, sobs escaping her like thunder as she raced to her brother's limp body, and my breath left my lungs.

44
ANDRA

LYCAON, NO. PLEASE.

River, save him.

I slid to a stop next to my brother's bloodied body and cradled his head in my arms. His body had wounds all over, the most serious being the crimson tear through his torso where his ribcage appeared damaged. The rest of him had been mangled in the brawl.

He didn't have long.

"Hey, Arch. Can you hear me? We're going to fix you up, brand new," I whispered. "Let's move you to the lake, okay?"

"Can't see," Archer rasped. "Did we win?"

"That isn't funny, Arch." I shook my head. "Tell me where it hurts the most."

He blinked. "It doesn't."

I let out a choked sob. If I could get him to the lake, he could be fine. He'd be healed, but how much time did he have?

I looped my arms under his and started to pull Archer. His limbs hung limp. I paused and wiped my nose. "I'm sorry. We have to get you to the water."

"Where's Nash?" he wheezed.

I craned my neck for him, trying to force my hands not to shake. Nash pushed past Caroline, rubbing his muzzle on Archer's scratched neck. It smeared the catamount's blood across Archer's skin. *"I'm here."*

Archer shifted his head with a grimace. "Tell her that you love her."

I met Nash's gaze, his eyes wide and face a pale shade of gray. I couldn't do this now, not with Archer bleeding out.

"What do you mean, Arch?" Nash sniffled against Archer's sweaty hair.

Archer swallowed, then coughed up blood. "Tell her that you've always loved her. Tell her you don't want to waste time anymore. Clearly, life is too short to wait to love."

"Arch, I–"

"Promise me?"

I put a hand over my mouth, trying to keep it together. I couldn't fall apart, not now.

Nash glanced to the water a dozen paces away and back at Archer. *"I promise, buddy. But now we have to get you to the lake."*

"I'm in the lake, aren't I?" Archer smiled, blood coating his tongue. His breath rattled now, a wheezy, slick sound. "I didn't realize how warm it would be. This is the best way to end a day."

And his heart stopped beating.

A gasp escaped my lips, my body trembling where I knelt. A cry left my lips, and Nash pressed his body to mine. He phased, arms around me instantly. "I'm here, Andra. I'm here. I've got you."

I screamed.

I raged.

I ached.

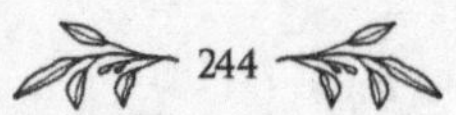

I broke through Nash's arms and flung myself on his body. "Please. Lycaon, please. Come back, Arch. Please come back."

Nash wrapped his arms around my torso and pulled me away.

"No!" I shouted, reaching for Archer.

Aubrey and Silas carried Archer's body to the lake. I beat at Nash's chest, nails digging into the skin around his neck, and I tried to escape his arms so I could reach my brother. But Nash was too strong and I, too weak.

In the waters of *Atagahi*, Archer's wounds healed. His bones reset, his skin reattached, his blood washed away, his face a peaceful calm. But there was no returning his Spirit. And there would be no returning mine.

45

NASH

ARCHER GAVE HIS LIFE FOR A MURDERER, and I didn't have time to thank him.

The events at the lake passed in a blur, but I'd never be rid of the image of his ribs crushed and mouth full of blood.

The Nunnehi woman stayed with us while Silas and I carried Archer's body all the way back to Arcadia, leading the way of our funeral procession down the mountain and through the valley. The Nunnehi walked confidently right over the boundary of Arcadia, not missing a step across the river where Andra and I had just been goofing off a few days ago.

Before I knew.

Before our lives changed.

Before she promised.

I hadn't said it out loud, but I accepted her promise. And I wanted to give her one in return.

Guardians met us at the river and offered to carry Archer's body from there. Andra clung to one of Archer's cold hands, never leaving his side. Each member of our party stepped across the boundary in the dim hours of the morning, filing after the Nunnehi and the Guardians. Everyone except for Silas.

I knew this was coming, but I still hadn't decided what I'd say yet. Silas had come to my aid when he had every reason to leave me alone to die. He still came when I needed him most, and I didn't deserve that.

I cleared my throat. "Before you say anything, I don't blame you for your decision. Or for hating me. I hate myself, and I—"

"Shut up." Silas shook his head. "Don't speak."

I closed my eyes, waiting for the fury I deserved, the hatred I'd seen in his eyes in the Boneyard. I waited for the words I'd spoken over myself since the Wendigo cast the blood spell on me and released those first memories.

It's my fault our father and Archer are dead. I deserve the same fate.

This aching moment stretched around me. I wanted to push it off, to wait a little longer and pretend like I was still the nettle-brained Omega that ran away for a while. But I also wanted to get this over with, to face my damnation with as much bravery and dignity as I had left. But there wasn't much to spare.

"You and I have been through so much together." Silas swallowed. "We used to be best friends, you and me. And when Mother passed—" He shook his head again, crossing his arms to hide his hands. "When Mother passed, I didn't just lose her. I lost my whole family. Father caved in on himself, Caroline froze over like Feru Falls, and you... you left me."

"Si." My voice scratched out in a whisper.

My brother bit down on his lip, but I could tell he was trembling. "And you—" His voice gave out and a growl escaped his clenched teeth.

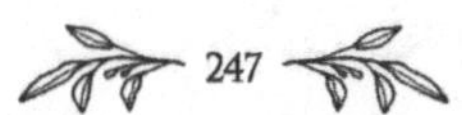

"I tried to hate you. I wanted to make sure you suffered the pain I felt. You ruined my life that day, and you changed all of Arcadia with your actions. And I realized that in all of this, you suffered the most and no one knew. I never knew. I..." He took measured breaths. "I'm so sorry, Nash."

"What?" I croaked, the air around my words clouding from the chill. My heart hammered in my chest, and I repeated his words again in my head.

I'm so sorry.

"Why—" I choked and realized I was sobbing. "Why are you apologizing? I'm the one who—the one..."

"No." Silas shook his head. "It wasn't your fault. They used you and kept the truth from you. That's not your identity. It's not on you."

"But he's dead."

"And we're all dying." Silas threw his hands in the air, tears clogging his voice. "The Nunnehi do what they want and the River keeps moving. That's life." He took three steps forward, and I flinched, aware that he had every right to kill me for treason or just out of spite. But his arms wrapped around my shoulders, his head leaning against me. "You're my brother, Nash. And that will never change."

I held onto him like his nearness kept me alive. Maybe it did. I never felt whole away from Arcadia, away from my family. And when I faced the prospect of banishment, I didn't know where I would go or who I could turn to.

Now, I had a brother again.

"If you ever need to leave for a while, you'll always have a place to call home here." Silas patted me twice on the back before giving me some space. He exhaled. "Now, come on. I'm spent, and I want to check on Eden. Plus, Andra needs you more than ever."

Glancing up at the stars beginning to peek out from behind the snow clouds, I released all the tension I'd held in for the past few days. I followed my brother across the border of Arcadia, a different son than the one that crossed that border yesterday.

And I wouldn't waste the chance I'd been given.

46
SILAS

AS SOON AS I ENTERED GUARDIAN'S GLADE, bodies surrounded me until I couldn't breathe. The peace I'd felt after my talk with Nash vanished.

"She's worse." Ransom handed me a damp cloth. "We've done all we could to keep her comfortable."

"She won't take any of the tinctures or remedies I bring her." Asa passed me a bottle. "This is a mix of chamomile, passionflower, and valerian. If you can get her to take it, she may be able to calm down."

"She's been asking for you." Leander gently nudged me forward.

I grabbed Nash by the sleeve, pulling him with me while Leander ushered us into my bedroom. Inside, the air tasted stale, and I could smell the illness around us.

"*Silva*, she's–" I swallowed, turning to Nash.

His face mirrored my feelings, wide with shock. I moved to the side of the bed, using the cloth Ransom gave me to dab away the sweat on her face. Eden had shrunken in on herself, small and fragile and drowning in blankets.

"Eden, it's me," I murmured. "Can you hear me?"

I watched her face for any sign of pain or even awareness. She still breathed and her heart still beat, so we had two things going for us.

I can't do this now.

I wished I could breathe for a moment. Between Archer's death, Nash and I's reconciliation, and now Eden being so ill... I didn't know how much more I could handle. Her breaths hitched in sharp gasps, like there was a hole in her windpipe and air wasn't getting all the way into her lungs. It sounded so similar to Archer just before he died.

"Okay," I started, glancing around the room. "Here's what we're going to do. I'll—We'll—*silva.*"

I couldn't get my thoughts to fall in line. Nash rummaged through the bookshelf and returned with a shiny black book in hand. The cover had two pale hands holding a bright red apple. Nash threw it open, flipping to somewhere about a quarter through the book.

"I've been reading to her," Nash explained. "Not consistently, but she really likes this book. Maybe it'll help calm her if we get some of Asa's tincture in her and I read?"

I nodded, appreciating that he was making decisions so I didn't have to. I couldn't think.

Nash cleared his throat. "Another legend claims that we descended from wolves, and that the wolves are our brothers still. It's against tribal law to kill them. Then there are stories about the cold ones."

I dipped the tip of my smallest finger in the mixture Asa gave me and ran the liquid along Eden's bottom lip. She wheezed.

"There are stories of the cold ones as old as the wolf legends, and some much more recent. According to legend, my own great-grandfather knew some of them. He was the one who made the treaty that kept them off our land."

"Come on, Eden. Come on," I whispered.

I brushed her hair out of her face, dabbing at the sweat again. I prayed for a change, for her eyes to flutter open, for her breaths to even out—anything was better than this shallow-breathed existence. I was conscious of people watching in the doorway.

Why won't someone do something?

Nash stumbled over a few words, cleared his throat, and continued. "You see, the cold ones are the natural enemies of the wolf. Well, not the wolf, really. But the wolves that turn into men, like our ancestors. You would call them werewolves."

"Nash, I don't think it's helping," I hissed.

Nash closed the book and dropped it on the bed. "We need to get her out of this room. It's too stuffy in here."

I scooped her up in my arms, and it amazed me how frail she seemed to me now. Her presence had always been vibrant and glowing, but with her like this, it almost seemed like a light had gone out.

Nash held the side door open, and I carried Eden to the clearing, where I'd set up her bath, a clean stretch of sky above us where the clouds had bled away into stars. The curtains still hung in the trees like Spirits dancing between the branches. Gently, I set Eden in the clearing, wrapping her blanket around her and resting her head in my lap.

"I don't understand what's happening." I held her tight, rocking slightly. "I can't lose anyone else, Nash. Not like this. It's not supposed to happen like this."

"I'm going for help." Nash raced through the trees.

Lycaon, help her.

"Please," I cried, hating how helpless it felt to care for someone.

Control had always been my downfall, the thing I craved the most. But not some power-hungry control freak. I wished I had the power to make Eden well again, to make each day of her existence happier than the one before. To bring peace to my family, to my valley, to the world.

Somewhere along the way, I'd spun out of control, and I fought to find it again. If I found the right herb or knew the right human illnesses, maybe I could save her.

Nash returned with Asa, Ransom, and Leander.

"Please, help her." I turned to them, seeking assistance of any sort. Their faces were grave in the darkness before dawn.

Asa, skin pale, cleared his throat. "*Je kunan*, Kalona is here."

I couldn't see her. I knew I wouldn't be able to in the mortal realm away from *Atagahi*, but I still tried.

"Si." Nash knelt next to me, scanning the trees. "What do we do?"

I turned to Ransom who gazed up at the stars. "What is it? What do you see?"

"The Raven's Sparks," Ransom said, a wistful sound in his voice.

"What?" Nash asked.

"It's something I told Caroline would happen." Leander sniffed. "Markus knows. Here they come."

The rest of my family moved around the bend in the path, slipping through the trees until they stood around me, following Ransom's gaze to the falling stars. Andra stared at Eden.

"Markus," Caroline murmured. "The stars."

He gazed up in awe. "Entry into the kinship of sorrow."

I vibrated with anger, still holding Eden in my arms. "Someone, please, tell me what to do."

Everyone refocused their attention to Eden when Andra jumped forward, grabbing Eden's left hand in hers. As soon as I saw what she did, I fought back, careful to not injure Eden.

"Andra, stop!" I growled. "Not this again, please."

Nash pushed my hands away from Andra, and I gaped at him.

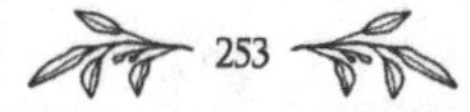

"Andra!" Markus started.

But she was too quick, too fueled by grief. She jumped back from us, brandishing the ring high in the air.

"You want it?" she yelled, voice swallowed by the dark. "Come and take back what's yours, Kalona."

A shrill screech sounded from across the clearing as a raven swooped down and snatched the ring from Andra's outstretched palm. It perched on a nearby yew tree branch, momentarily shapeshifting into the half-woman, half-beast creature that we'd faced at *Atagahi*. For a second, a cruel glint shone in her beady eyes, but in a flash, she was gone.

Eden coughed in my lap, eyes fluttering open. She gasped for air. I cradled her, pulling her hair back from her face.

"Breathe," I whispered. "Breathe. Look at the stars, Eden."

She blinked, still gasping, but her eyes moved with the shifting of the meteors lighting up the sky above us. I had about a dozen questions—Had the ring been keeping Eden ill this whole time?—but the most important thing for that moment was that my mate could breathe again.

Eden shifted her eyes to me, and I smiled. Her eyebrows furrowed. "What is it?"

I ran a hand down her cheek. "I love those soft, bear cub eyes."

She sniffed in a sort of laugh. "Bear cub?"

"Nash told me not to tell you." I glanced up to where he held Andra's hand several feet away.

They talked in hushed voices, Andra sniffling and Nash comforting. In a way, I was grateful that a good thing blossomed out of all this pain and suffering. I'd witnessed firsthand how love could bind up broken things, and maybe it would be the healing balm to the wounds we'd all sustained.

"I feel like I've missed out on something," Eden murmured, following my gaze.

I kissed her forehead, squeezing her tight. "I have a lot to catch you up on, *pilukos*."

47

EDEN

I WOKE FROM A DREAMLESS SLEEP, something I now saw as a mercy. Almost seven days had passed since Archer died. Once I'd eaten and drank my fill of *kulas*, Silas finally allowed me to gather a group in Guardian's Glade to fill in the missing gaps. Between accounts from Silas, Nash, Andra, Caroline, Markus, Aubrey, Ransom, Leander and Asa, I was able to piece together a few things.

The Nunnehi were indeed shaping the River of time, tweaking things here and there in their invisible ways. They'd been the ones to wake Nyx in the first place, introduce me and my soon-to-be husband, and set Nash on the river he had to cross for things to fall as they should. The Nunnehi wanted unity and to stop history from repeating itself, and they knew Nash had the right character to correct the mistakes of the past. Only Nyx interfered and their plans derailed until Nash returned home.

I desperately wanted to find *Atagahi*, but Silas refused to even entertain the idea in fear that I might be stuck there forever. I thought one day I may be able to convince him, but only time would tell.

I learned of Archer's death at *Atagahi*, a brave sacrifice to save Nash from the ruthlessness of the Hunt. Nash explained that from what little he gathered, the Hunt served some purpose in its twisted way. Perhaps there was some balancing of fate after all.

Asa had been treating me with everything he had in his arsenal of herbs, so much so, we'd severely depleted his stock. I promised I'd go out with him in the spring to forage for anything he needed. He beamed, but I think he was just glad to see me upright.

Andra apologized again for what happened in Lukosan, but specifically her inattention to detail and fear of being out of control. It was something I thought she and Silas had in common, which was another reason they'd probably have killed each other had they tried to connect all those years ago. But I was the most grateful that Andra had the strength in the end to pry that ring from my finger. She saved me, and it more than made up for the difficulties I faced in Lukosan.

Despite the chaos of the Hunt and Kalona and my illness, Caroline had managed to keep the wedding on track and check in with the Tailors. They'd finished my ceremony dress, and just in time, too.

The days that followed the night the Raven's Sparks fell, Silas kept a close eye on everyone. They seemed relieved when he had to be pulled away to the Tailors to get his ceremony robe adjusted and refinished because it gave them a little space to breathe. Especially me, since breathing was the thing I'd missed most the past weeks.

But this morning, I'd awoken alone on account of wanting to follow the time-honored human tradition of not seeing the betrothed the day of the wedding. It turned out to be a lot more difficult in a small valley kingdom, nestled at the roots of Mt. LeConte. It was doubly difficult that the wedding would take place in the late evening, so I'd been confined to my room where Nash finished reading *Twilight* to me.

"'Look, I said I love you more than everything else in the world combined. Isn't that enough?'" Nash's voice for Bella was pretty awful, but his Edward was even worse. "'Yes, it is enough. Enough for forever.'" Nash cleared his throat. "'And he leaned down and pressed his cold lips once more to my throat... the end.'"

I offered soft applause in the light of the lanterns.

Nash closed the book. "You know, I think I prefer Eddie over old Jakey-poo. Never thought I'd side with a vampire over a werewolf, but old dogs can change."

I threw my pillow at him, which he promptly chucked right back in my face.

He stood and stretched. "I'd better get changed. Big dinner plans."

I rolled my eyes. "Uh-huh, and when is your hot date arriving?"

He smirked. "I'm keeping my options open, but if you're talking about a certain feisty Alpha, I think we have a date with the dance floor."

Nash left, and I had a few minutes to myself before Caroline came to help me into my ceremonial dress, cinching in the waist and fastening the sleeves. Aubrey adorned my face, painting a solid black line across the eyes, marking the royal family along with dots to line my face. She added a line to my chin with five lines growing from the left side.

The apple tree.

Love.

Good health.

On my forehead, Aubrey painted a diamond with a line straight through it.

The cherry tree.

New beginnings.

Mortality.

And finally, both women helped me braid my hair into a crown, weaving bits of honeysuckle into the plait. They led me behind Guardian's Glade to the River, making me close my eyes.

I waited for what felt like forever to open them.

"E! You look beautiful!" It was Nash's voice.

"Are you decent?" I frowned, wondering if there was a reason my eyes had to be closed.

"Perhaps not morally, but I'm wearing my ceremonial robes if that's what you're asking."

I opened one eye to find Nash dressed in his white ceremonial robe with his hair tied back in a braid. He looked the part of a prince more than ever before. But his hands were full, carrying a bouquet of flowers, full of Solomon's Seal, bloodroot, and lily of the valley. Perfect for a magical wedding.

"For me?" I accepted the bouquet. "You shouldn't have."

"Nervous yet?" He grinned. "It's not every day you have a second wedding ceremony."

"The first didn't count." I rolled my eyes, but he fixed me with a look of amusement. "It didn't count, did it?"

Nash laughed, and I was tempted to hit him with my bouquet. Lucky for him, it was too beautiful to ruin.

"Is there anything I should know about Silas? Any last-minute secrets?" I raised an eyebrow.

Nash hummed, clearly having to dig deep. "When it rains in the summer, he likes to lie in the middle of the river, claiming it grounds him. And when we have to cut a tree down when it's sickly, he cries. And he always puts on the right sleeve of his robe first."

I dissolved into laughter. "Not what I meant, but I'll take it. Any strange wolf customs I should know about?"

"You mean aside from the ghost dad that chose you to be the first human queen of a werewolf kingdom in one of the oldest mountain

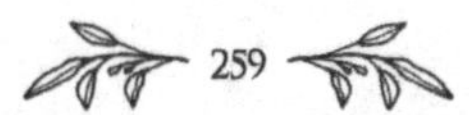

ranges in the world?" He scratched his head. "Nope. I believe that covers it. Shall we?"

He offered me his arm, and I took it. We walked the path that looped south toward the Great Mountain. I still hadn't been since I'd come to Arcadia. I'd have to get someone to go with me and show me the secrets that lie hidden from humans.

But it was clear now why Caroline and Audrey led me out here blind. The lily of the valley glowed tonight, a soft yellow tinge lining the path that snaked through the trees.

"Nash?"

He hummed in response.

"Do you think I can do this?"

"Wouldn't be by your side if I didn't believe in you, E." He squeezed my hand with his arm. "You're going to be amazing. A change up, but just what this pack needs."

"Promise you won't leave us without saying goodbye?" I don't know what made me say the words, only something in the air smelled like change.

Nash didn't immediately answer, a sure sign that his answer would be serious and well thought out. When he did answer, the humor had melted away into melancholy. "I promise to never leave without saying goodbye if I get the chance. Does that suit you, *je kunin*?"

"It'll do."

We settled in silence until we arrived at the Yard, a faint glow shimmering from the clearing.

"I'm scared," I whispered.

Nash scoffed. "Yeah, I can tell. Your heart is beating one hundred and fourteen beats per minute."

I groaned, and Nash pulled me to a stop.

"Hey. Look at me, this night is only about you and Silas. Forget

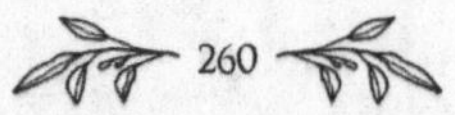

everything else. Focus on the fact that you're alive, and you're marrying the man you love. Trees could catch on fire, a Wendigo could crash the dance floor, and the *kulas* may all be gone by dawn. But nothing can change those two things. Yeah?"

I nodded and pulled him into a hug. "I love you, too, Nash."

He squeezed me a little tighter before releasing me. "No tears. I'm going to insult humans each step until we get there."

"What?" I giggled.

"Humans wear ridiculous outfits to bed. Humans believe birds aren't real. Humans wear silly shoes. Humans think cats are funny. Humans spend most of their time looking at their screens. Humans tear down natural wild areas to build sterile nature areas. Humans hide from the rain. Humans think bears are the scariest thing in the forest."

"Out of time," I whispered, holding back laughter.

Someone had fashioned a curtain out of ferns so that I could only get glimpses of people waiting in the Yard. All of Arcadia and Lukosan sat behind that curtain, all there to watch me marry the man I loved.

"Go get him, Princess." He squeezed my hand, guiding me through the fern curtain.

The crowd caught my attention first, mostly a sea of white ceremonial robes dotted with Lukosans in borrowed robes. I spotted a few Lukosans in the crowd I recognized, like Claire and Jacob, giving them a small wave before turning my full attention toward the man who stood in front of the throne.

The first thing I noticed is that Silas trimmed his hair. He resembled the man I'd first met upon arriving in Arcadia, polished and kingly— an incredibly handsome wolf king, his head adorned with a wreath of cherry blossoms. His face had the royal line across his eyes, as well as his symbol of the spruce tree and the cherry tree like mine, dots connecting them all, no more yew tree for mourning.

Bright white robes draped over Silas like water, a far cry from the snug green pants and crewneck he'd worn the night of our first wedding. When I stopped within arm's reach, I noticed that all of the stitching had been replaced with silver thread, leafy patterns stretching over his shoulders. He looked ethereal. I wondered for the first time in a while if I was dreaming this whole thing because he was too perfect.

Nash passed me off to Silas.

"Hi." He tried to fight the grin forming on his lips.

"Hi." I held his hand in mine, and we faced Elder Markus, clad in his charcoal ceremonial robe, painted with the Elder tree symbol and dots lining his face.

Markus cleared his throat. "Arcadian law states that we offer a moment of silence to give space to anyone who would object to the decision of King Iain, may his Spirit find peace among trees."

The crowd murmured the honor phrase and quickly grew silent, only the sound of crickets in the night air.

Markus cleared his throat. "Tonight marks a moment in history, one that will never be forgotten in the annals of Arcadia: the first union between a human and a *virlukos*. Though many have had their share of doubts, not a single Spirit could say that Eden isn't strong, competent, and kind. And most of all, she loves our people, our kingdom, and our king."

"Hear, hear!" Nash called out from the front row.

Chuckles rippled over the crowd, and Silas squeezed my hands. We'd done this before, stood holding hands and professed our love. But something about this moment felt sacred, never touched before and never to be touched again. I'd never grown up wanting to make history, but awe overwhelmed me.

Markus clasped his hands together. "So with the blending of two cultures into one, do you have the rings?"

I froze, glancing between Silas and Markus.

Silas cleared his throat, muttering under his breath, "We don't have—"

A murmur crossed the crowd, and I turned to find Andra standing in a white ceremonial robe, holding up a carved box with a wolf paw print carved on the top.

"This is a gift for the King and Queen of Arcadia." She managed a smile. "A gift from Lukosan made from Arcadian trees."

That elicited low chuckles from the crowd, a good sign that they could joke about something that almost claimed my life.

Silas accepted the small box, opening it to reveal two carved wooden bands, three swirls intertwined in the center, the thinner one meant for me and the other for Silas.

"To replace the one I screwed up. And they've already been passed around and blessed by everyone present today." She bowed her head. "I hope you like them."

"They're beautiful, Andra." I beamed, pulling her in for a hug. "Thank you."

I handed her my bouquet, and she stepped back down to stand next to Nash. Silas pulled out my ring and I pulled out his.

"If you will share your love with your witnesses." Markus grinned, taking a glance at the Book of Traditions that the Elders kept.

Silas cleared his throat. "We've known for a long time we'd be here today, didn't we? That something in *Shaconage* conspired to bring us together starting all those years ago with a girl and a wolf and a river." He ran his thumb over my hand. "Eden, you are blood of my blood, bone of my bone. I give you my heart, I give you my body, and I give you my Spirit, until we pass into the Other." He swallowed, meeting my eyes when he slipped the ring on my finger. It was, of course, the perfect fit, no doubt some sort of Seer magic.

I cleared my throat. "If someone asked me three months and one day ago if I expected to marry a wolf king, I would've laughed. If someone asked me if I expected to be a queen, I would've called them delusional. And yet, here I stand, in awe to be considered for such an honor and loved so deeply." I reached up, tucking one of Silas's stray curls back under his crown of cherry blossoms. "Silas, I think my Spirit was meant to find yours, with or without divine intervention. And if I can stay with you until the end, that will be enough."

I slid the ring on the fourth finger of his left hand. Admiring the ring, Silas clenched and unclenched his hand.

"Nash," Markus said, motioning for him, "if you'll join me."

I caught Nash giving Andra's hand a squeeze before he stood next to Markus.

"Hello, again," he whispered, giving me a conspiratorial grin. He appeared so much like Iain in the evening lantern light. In a way, he was still here with us, in the pieces of himself that he'd passed to his children. I wonder if they saw it that way.

"If you will hold out your hands." Nash separated two pieces of cloth, similar to the ones from Lukosan, which still sat in the wardrobe waiting to be fashioned into a memento. One piece, the royal silver, represented Silas. The other piece, a pure white from the trimmings of my dress, represented me.

"With your acceptance of this step into the future and agreeing to bind yourself to Silas, King of Arcadia, it is customary to show an outward expression of this in a handfasting ceremony. Consider these hands you're holding."

I moved my gaze from our hands to Silas's face. He smiled. This wasn't our first rodeo, but this one felt even more joy-filled and set apart.

Thank Lycaon he's mine.

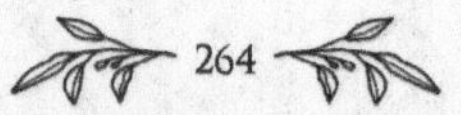

Nash placed one hand on top of ours and one on the bottom. "With these hands, you will shape the future, crafting a life that no one else can craft. With these hands, you will feed each other, nurture each other, and hold each other for many days to come. And with these hands, you will hold tradition and welcome strangers."

Nash paused, moving his gaze over to our Lukosan friends before he unfurled the first piece of fabric that represented Silas. He draped it over my arms like before, tucking one end under my thumb and wrapped the other end around my other hand, slipping it between Silas and I's hands. "The first strand represents you, Silas." Nash unfurled the second piece of fabric, a piece of the ceremonial dress I wore, and draped it over Silas's arms and tucked it between our hands. "The second strand represents you, Eden. Your life and legacy begin today, a course destined by the River for you to find each other. With your hearts and hands now bound, our community would like to speak blessings over you. May the River always run alongside you."

"May health be your daily companion," Asa spoke.

"May the breeze cool your hot days, and the sun warm the frost," Kane added.

Caroline cleared her throat. "May your blankets always be warm—"

"And your room always welcoming," Markus finished.

Jacob spoke up from the crowd. "May the path be gentle on your feet and paws."

Silas chuckled, giving my hand a squeeze.

Andra smiled. "May friendship and love be yours, wherever the wind takes you."

"May your vision be clear and your dreams reachable." Leander bowed his head to us.

About a dozen other people spoke up from the crowd of witnesses, speaking blessings over our union. And seeing the Lukosans and

Arcadians together warmed me to the tip of my toes.

"May your lanterns light the path ahead."

"May the rain wash away your sorrows."

"May you live as long as you want and never want as long as you live."

"May you find peace among trees."

"May the wind be always at your back."

"May the raven never grace your doorstep."

My heart lurched at the thought, but Nash put a hand over our hands, drawing my attention. "And what Lycaon blesses, let no *virlukos* or human or creature of Earth pull apart. Your new life begins right here in this moment."

Silas beamed, his face light like the sun. With a confidence different from before, we pulled the ends of the strands until a square knot formed. Silas brandished the tied knot, and the crowd behind us cheered.

Nash stepped down, pulling Andra into a hug while Markus resumed his place. "Following this, Silas wanted to say a few words."

Silas gave my hand a squeeze before stepping forward without me. I moved to stand next to Markus, making sure my ceremonial dress was out of the way.

"Lucky timing brought Eden and me to Lukosan in early November alongside my brother, Nash." He bowed his head to Nash. "There, we reconnected with our longtime friends—practically family. Despite a few bumps in our journey, I am grateful that Andra, the Alpha of Lukosan, could be present today with her pack. And I would be remiss if I didn't say a few words about her loyal Beta, Archer."

He paused, and sniffles floated around the crowd. Many knew Archer well, and quite a few came to love him in his short stay in Arcadia. When we'd done the funeral for him, Andra asked that he be kept in Arcadia, among family. The grief hung over the valley like a shroud, bringing everyone's pain into sharp clarity. Nash hadn't left Andra's side apart from sleeping, but even then, he set up a tent near hers. I could tell, gazing out at this mixed group assembled for a wedding, that while their hearts celebrated, they also felt deep pain.

Silas cleared his throat, emotion choking his words. "Archer is more than a friend. He's a brother. He was loyal to death, giving his life for our brother. And I'm grateful that his Spirit will walk these paths, climb these hills, and rest in this valley." He paused again, sniffling and adjusting the strands of hair that fell into his face with the slight breeze. "It's never easy losing someone you love, especially when the path of their River ends so abruptly. Which is all the more reason to celebrate the people we love while their River still runs alongside our own." He turned to smile at me. "And I'm grateful you're all here to celebrate us. It means the world."

I joined him, and several in the crowd clapped while others howled.

Markus approached Silas, holding a large wooden chalice filled with *kulas*. "And now, if you will join me once more."

I moved to the opposite side of the cup, holding it in both hands. Silas placed his hands over mine.

Markus cleared his throat. "Drinking from this cup demonstrates several things to the world. First, you are saying that everything that's yours is theirs. Second, you are saying that no one will know you more intimately. And third, and perhaps most important, you are saying that you share their fate come what may, even death itself. Do you assent?"

"I do." Silas bowed his head.

I swallowed. "I do."

"Drink and be blessed!" Markus raised his arms.

The crowd remained silent as Silas drank first, and I followed.

As one connected unit, the crowd howled in celebration and closed

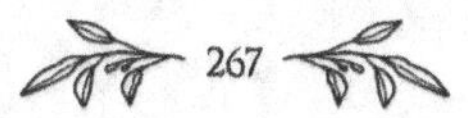

in on us. The chalice passed from hand to hand as a symbol of support from family.

Nash and Andra sidled up next to us. Nash wrapped his arms around my shoulders, squeezing me tight. "Welcome to the family, little sister."

48
SILAS

BEFORE I COULD HUG MY FAMILY or kiss my wife, Lilah corralled us down the path a little ways to the Kitchens. A feast awaited us—spruce bread and blackberry butter, a spread of different fruits and cheeses, a venison and bear roast with fire-roasted potatoes, decadent honey cake and other desserts, and gallons of *kulas* to wash it all down.

To Eden's immense delight, Jacob and Claire had procured some more human things including a few clothing items, coffee for both the reception and her personal use, a camera like Jacob's, along with some film, and a speaker to borrow for the reception. Half of the things were foreign to me, but Eden was elated.

While we ate, people congratulated us from both packs, some leaving all sorts of gifts off to the side of the Kitchens. At some point, Andra urged us to cut the cake. We cut into the honey cake, Jacob snapping a photo, and picked up a piece each.

"It's a tradition to feed each other the first piece." Eden smirked, her hair escaping its braided crown.

The crowd counted down from three, and when they said *one*, I carefully fed the piece to Eden so I wouldn't get her new dress filthy. Eden, on the other hand, had no qualms about mess, and shoved the piece straight into my face.

Sputtering, I wiped the cake off my face amid friendly laughter. "I swear, you humans and your violent tendencies."

After everyone had eaten their fill, we led the crowd back to the Yard. Jacob and Claire snuck up behind us.

"We have a surprise for you." Jacob grinned.

The sound of strings began to play from the speaker Jacob brought, and Eden inhaled sharply.

"Perfect time for a first dance." Claire smirked, nudging us out farther into the clearing to dance to a soulful-sounding song.

"I love this song." Eden sighed, placing a hand on my shoulder and the other in my hand.

As we danced in a very human fashion, a man sang about a lady named May loving a man a little rough around the edges. The man accounts all the good things in his life to Lady May, the springtime and his success and his love.

It hit me that so much had changed in a year, how much had changed in me, too. And I owed a good deal of that to the past three months with Eden. She wasn't perfect, and she obviously wasn't exactly like me, but I figured that's why we fit so well together.

The song ended and a new one replaced it. A muted beat barely had time to start before Eden was jumping up and down, grabbing Nash and Andra from the crowd gathering at the edges of the Yard.

"It's y'all's song!" she squealed.

Despite the weight that held her down since Archer's passing, Andra perked up and surprised everyone with a full laugh.

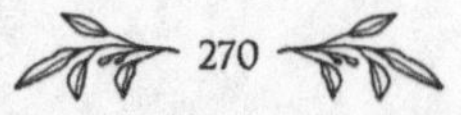

"Never would I have guessed I'd get to dance to Rasputin at an Arcadian wedding with the crown prince." She doubled over in laughter.

"First time for everything." Nash shrugged and started moving his body in ways I never would've dreamed of.

Some Lukosans in the crowd joined in, matching some of Nash's dance moves, but most just watched the dance unfold. Nash hopped up and down, throwing his hands out on either side and clapping occasionally to the beat.

"This is that song they go on about with the cat?" I asked Eden, raising an eyebrow.

The smile painted on her face would be permanent if they kept on dancing. "There isn't really a cat, but yes."

"Was he, like, a ruler or something?"

Eden pursed her lips. "We'll go with or something."

I pulled her closer, leaning down for a quick kiss. "I heard humans go on trips when they have a wedding. Fancy another trip with me?"

Eden scoffed. "Never doing that again. Wildfires and Wendigos and a demon-possessed ring? No thanks. I already lived through it once. No guarantee I'll live through the next one."

I gave her a quick squeeze and turned back to watch Nash. "Do you think they'll end up together?"

Eden didn't respond at first, so I checked to see if she'd heard me, but her eyes were focused on Nash and Andra. Something wise resided in Eden's gaze, and that look reminded me so much of my mother.

"I think they're both hurting, and they'll find the comfort they need in each other." She chewed her bottom lip. "And I think maybe, if we're really lucky, that will lead to something more."

A new song started with a strange mechanical sound and a stiff beat in the background. Apparently, the singer was in a relationship with a crazy woman, but he loved her because she reminded him of his mother. Odd choice, but maybe it was normal for human weddings.

I intertwined my fingers with Eden's and kissed her knuckle with the ring that matched mine, Raven Mocker-free. "I hope they find some semblance of happiness, with or without each other. They've both had such difficult lives and had to grow up so quickly. They both deserve the world."

Eden leaned her head on my shoulder. "And so do we."

49
CAROLINE

Jacob photographed Nash and Andra acting like bears with an itch dancing to that song they loved about the man and the cat, and Markus and I laughed until we cried at the movements they made around each other.

"Are we going to have this much fun at our wedding?" Markus asked, his face red from laughter.

"We can do whatever you want if the ceremony is small." I squeezed his arm. "And as long as you're still wearing this for our wedding."

Markus bobbed his eyebrows, his blond hair flopping in his face and sending me into another fit of laughter. "I love your laugh." He pulled me into a hug. "I can't wait to make you laugh all the time."

"You already do."

"But now that I've won you over with my handsome good looks, I have to keep the humor up." Markus grew serious. "I won't be handsome forever. But humor lasts a lifetime."

I stared at him for a moment before we burst into giggles again.

After a few upbeat songs, Jacob cleared his throat. "I wanted to play one that's been important to me for a long time. It's a bit poignant, but it brought me through some really dark days." He cleared his throat. "In the wake of what we've lost this week and celebrating new beginnings, rain and clouds may come for a while, but they never last long."

Jacob started the song, and the words hit me strangely.

"Now that I have won my freedom, like an eagle, I am eager for the sky," I repeated, muttering to myself. "Because I can see the light of a clear blue morning."

Markus pulled me close, kissing the top of my head. "We're going to be okay, you and me. You remember my theory that you dismissed when we were trying to figure out what was wrong with Eden? What was it that I said weeks ago about the stars?"

I rolled my eyes. "Seers."

"What was that?" he asked, assuming a confused expression. "Did I hear a you-were-right-Markus-you're-so-smart-and-handsome come out of your mouth?"

I shoved him. "You were right, okay? What was it all about again?"

Looking smug, he crossed his arms. "A new beginning at the foot of the Princess. That's you and Eden starting new chapters of your lives. An entry into the kinship of sorrow. That's losing Archer and finding out the truth about Nash."

A silence enveloped us, thick and sticky like pine sap. I still couldn't quite believe that Archer was gone, but each day brought new pains and new growth for all of us.

"What about the love born in the darkness?" I furrowed my brow. "That's not Eden and Silas. And that's certainly not us unless it's not a metaphor and literally means the darkness of the Sage Brush."

"I don't know." Markus frowned. "Love born from the darkness... It could mean a lot of things still. But I was mostly right."

I pushed out my lip in a pout. "You were mostly right, Markus. You're mostly smart and entirely handsome."

He pulled me back for another bear hug, faking laughter. "I will take what I can get. And from you, that still means a lot."

I tucked my head under his chin, breathing in the scent of sage that forever clung to his robes, even this newer one. I'd never get over this feeling that he was mine and he'd be my safe place now until we passed into the Other Realm. And how special it is to love someone that much and for that long.

50
NASH

I SANK DOWN IN FRONT of the balanced stones I knew so well now. "Well, Father, Mother, our Silas did it. He married the most beautiful woman. It was perfect, really. I wish y'all could have been there. Eden's dress was regal, like she'd been meant for royalty this whole time." I smiled to myself. "Did you know that, when you chose her? Did you know, deep down, she was born a queen? Did you know Silas would need someone as stubborn as me to keep him balanced when I'm gone?"

That muscle in my chest tightened, a dull twinge of pain stretching across my torso.

"Right, I forgot to mention I'm leaving. I don't really know where yet, but I can't stay here. And I'm not leaving for good, only a week or two. I think I need some space or fresh air or something. I'm going to miss y'all, but I couldn't leave without—without..."

I sucked in a breath, and it caught in the back of my throat. Everything burned. My chest, my lungs, my eyes...

"I can't say it," I choked, tears blocking any further coherent words.

"Then don't."

I turned to find Andra, still wearing her borrowed ceremonial robe, standing a few feet away. She closed the distance between us, kneeling next to me. She studied the stones, my mother's a little more grown and weathered than my father's.

"I'm sorry I wasn't here for them," she said to the stones. "I wish I could've been here to take care of your pups." Her eyes found mine in the dark. "I'm sorry I wasn't here for you, Nash. But I'm here now, and you don't have to say goodbye."

My eyes drifted to her lips, avoiding her gaze, but I found myself thinking about that moment a little over a year ago when I kissed her by mistake. What would it be like to kiss her on purpose? To choose her intentionally?

I cleared my throat. "I have to leave."

Andra's hand gently rubbed my arm. "No. You need to stay. Stay with your family, the people you love. Try out staying for a while instead of running when things get difficult."

"And if the people I love aren't all in the same place?" I cast my eyes down, afraid of what she might say.

"Leave with the promise of return. Go explore, come see us in Lukosan, or find your own place to call home. But always keep your promises."

"You promised me something." I swallowed. "Do you remember?"

She blinked once, twice before nodding, but she said nothing.

"Are you going to keep that promise?"

Andra cut her eyes back down the path, but we both knew we were alone aside from the *kuslar* dancing in the moonbeams. She met my gaze, her hazel eyes piercing even in the dim light. "I always keep my promises."

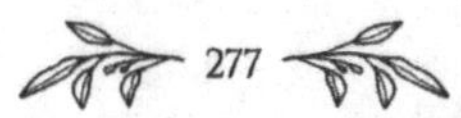

"If you keep your promise, here's mine. Whatever we are to each other, I promise to hold you tight, keep you safe, and always tell the truth."

She raised an eyebrow. "Truth or dare?"

I hesitated. "Truth."

Her eyes glimmered. "Do you think about that kiss last year?"

"All the time."

"Truth or dare?"

I cleared my throat. "Dare."

She grinned. "Do it again."

I slid my hand into her hair, running a thumb along her jawline. Her eyes fluttered shut, and she leaned into my touch. Moving forward with the most confidence I could muster, I pressed my lips to hers.

Her hands were in my hair, tangling in my braid. She leaned into me, almost knocking me over. I broke away, chuckling. "Please don't cause me to strand my parents in the Other Realm by toppling over their stones."

Andra turned red, tucking her hair behind her ear and turning to the stone stacks. "Sorry, Iain. Sorry, Ellie."

I stood, pulling her up with me. "Come on. There's something I need to do."

Her face twisted until I walked her a few paces away and across the aisle to her brother's freshly filled grave, stones stacked by Silas with my assistance. Andra's face dropped, adopting the pale shade that I knew meant she was afraid.

I knelt in front of Archer's stones, his body several feet under the soil. I bowed my head to him in honor. "Arch, I have a question. One of the last things you said to me was to tell Andra I loved her, and I haven't followed through on my promise." I glanced at Andra, who knelt next to me, but turned back to the stones. "And Arch, I wanted your permission to be with Andra. Despite dragging my paws when admitting the truth, you saw that truth before anyone else. So I hope you'll say yes, because I really do love your sister. And life is too short to keep that to myself."

A gentle breeze rustled through the Solomon's seal, caressing our skin and blowing Andra's hair in her face. She chuckled slightly.

"Hey, Arch," she whispered. "Thank you for wanting me to be happy."

As soon as the wind started, it blew away, leaving us staring at a stack of stones on a small path in a valley nestled between a vast mountain range, wondering what this confession would do to our friendship.

Andra cleared her throat. "My offer is still on the table, you know."

"Offer?" I stood, helping Andra to her feet.

"To live with us in Lukosan." She turned her eyes away from me, looking anywhere but my eyes. "I'm needing a new Beta... and possibly another Alpha?"

"Is that a proposal?"

She lowered her eyebrows. "It most certainly is not. That's your job."

"My job?" I placed a hand on my chest. "You'd think the Alpha would do the choosing."

She shrugged. "Unless the other is a lone wolf."

I playfully shoved her arm. "Whatever. If that's what you want, say the word. Your wish is my command, *je kunin.*"

Andra laced her fingers with mine, pulling me back down the path out of the Aisle of Kings. After a minute or so of silence, I pulled her to a stop.

"Andra." I swallowed. "If you're serious about this... I mean, if you're serious about me in Lukosan–"

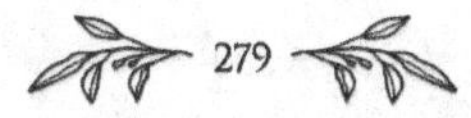

"I don't want to take you away from your family." Andra stared at our feet rather than looking me in the eye.

I tucked a finger under her chin, bringing her eyes up to meet mine. "I think they'd be happy we found someone. I think they'd be happy we were happy, if that's what you want."

"I want to know that you'll be there with me when I wake up." She searched my eyes for something, maybe confirmation.

"I promise." I smiled. "And I never break my promises."

She smirked before resting her head on my shoulder.

"You know," I started, thinking about a conversation I had with Silas about a month ago. "I bet we could start a cross-connection between other packs. I mean, starting with Lukosan is easy. But what about the sea *virlukos* or the pack in the Rockies? Or the small pack in the dessert?"

Andra shifted back to look up at me. "What, like inter-pack relationships?"

I shrugged. "Sure. We get connected to other packs, and eventually we can host them at Arcadia or wherever. I don't know, Silas and I had talked about how what we're doing this month has never been done before in Arcadian history. Not only had we never had humans before Eden, but we'd never had a non-royal presence from any other pack."

Andra hummed. "It could work. It would take some planning. Lots of correspondence. I bet it would practically be a full-time job."

I straightened. "Consider me for the position? It could be my legacy."

The more I thought about it, the more it made sense. I wouldn't have to stay in one place for too long, but I'd always have a home to return to. And it meant I could come see my family and hopefully my little niece and nephews if Lycaon blessed either of my siblings in *Starra*.

But if my plans succeeded, the possibilities would be endless. We'd have friends across the country, and maybe even the world. And it would be all mine.

51

ANDRA

A PIECE OF ME FELT LIKE I betrayed Archer for celebrating. Would he feel dishonored that I smiled so soon after his passing?

But Archer had always been the life of the party. He would be the last one awake, the last one dancing, and the first one back at it again. So maybe he'd be grateful I had something to celebrate, a reason to smile and laugh and dance with the people I loved.

"So, what are these?" Silas picked up the craft Eden and Jacob had been working on along with the other humans from Lukosan and assistance from the *micca*.

"They're Christmas crackers!" Eden squealed, handing one to each of us at the private table in Guardian's Glade.

The rest of the two packs celebrated in the Kitchen and Yard and anywhere else where people could gather. But the royal family plus a dozen invited guests sat around a table where a feast had been set by Eden and Lilah.

After *Joulo* with our fire ceremony, gathering mistletoe, and lantern lighting, we also wrote down our wishes for *Starra* and wedged them in pinecones to burn. But Eden insisted we have a human Christmas since so many humans were visiting Arcadia.

With Jacob's help, they crafted Christmas crackers, played traditional Christmas songs, and even baked sugar cookies with the help of Lilah. And tonight, December 24th, we all sat around a table with the roasted duck, jams, spruce bread, cookies, and endless mugs of warm *kulas* made by Nash.

After his return, the *micca* and *kuslar* and the other creatures of the forest welcomed him back with open arms. He'd immediately started making *kulas* again, eager to help out with the preparation for Caroline and Markus's wedding. But for now, we celebrated Christmas the human way: singing bizarre carols and laughing together as a family.

"So, what do we do with Christmas crackers?" Nash asked from my left. His hand rested on my thigh, warm and comforting.

"Take hold of it like this and cross your arms. Then whoever is sitting next to you grabs the other end so that there's one between each person."

We all followed her instructions, taking hold of our neighbor's cracker until we all had our arms crossed.

"Now what?" Leander asked.

"Pull!" Eden yanked, and all of us joined in.

The sound of crunching and rips and surprise filled the space. Inside each cracker, small gifts escaped. A mussel dropped into my lap.

"Oh, nice!" Nash snatched it from me.

"A mussel?" I furrowed my brow.

"No, it's what's inside." Nash gently opened the mussel and used his thumbnail to wedge a pearl out of the soft tissue. "This is the gift. For you, *je kunin.*"

I held the pearl carefully in my hand. "A freshwater pearl?"

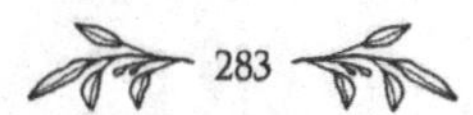

"Yes, ma'am. Good ole Tennessee pearls." He rested his arm on the back of my chair, taking a gulp of his *kulas*.

"What did you get?" I glanced at his plate.

He sat up and passed me a feather. "It's a seagull feather."

"Strange. We both got sea gifts." I swirled it between my fingers.

"Hey, maybe we can visit the sea wolves." Nash perked up. "That can be our first pack to meet."

"What are you two talking about over there?" Markus leaned forward, a few seats down from me and Nash.

I leaned forward. "About our cool gifts. What did you get?"

Ransom frowned. "A literal lump of coal."

"To keep your fires bright." Eden smirked.

"You know, I could get used to having more humans around," Silas said around a bite of sugar cookie. "I know what I used to say about y'all, but–"

Eden choked on her *kulas*. "Did you just say 'y'all'? I might die from shock."

The table erupted in laughter, and Nash's hand found its way to my hair, brushing the strands behind my ear.

"You know, Arch would've loved this." I sighed.

"But his feast has to be so much better than ours." Nash smiled, kissing my temple.

"Are you two official yet?" Aubrey raised her eyebrows. "I'm beginning to think it's no longer a secret you both are madly in love."

"Oh, please, it was never a secret." Eden waved a hand in the air. "You can tell. They just gravitate to each other."

Nash cleared his throat. "Actually, there's something I've been meaning to tell y'all."

The table quieted, everyone turning their attention to Nash, including me. I raised an eyebrow.

Nash shifted in his seat. "As you all know, the past week has been

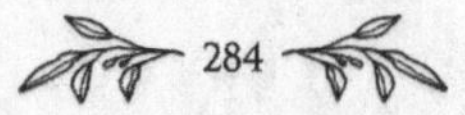

a lot for us all, some more than most." His hand found mine under the table and squeezed it like his life depended on it. "I've decided that, in a few weeks, when Lukosan packs up and heads out for *Starra*, I'm going with them."

"What?" Caroline sat up straight.

Nash met my gaze, a soft smile on his lips.

"You're coming with me?" I couldn't quite believe it.

Nash shrugged. "If you'll still have me."

I swallowed, still unsure if I had dreamt all of this.

"Nash." Silas leaned forward on his forearms. "Are you leaving for good? If I did something–"

"No." Nash laughed. "No, it's something I should've done last year when I had the chance."

"Fate had other plans," Ransom said before finishing off his *kulas*.

"But you'll visit, right?" Eden frowned. "I still have three books to read, and I'd hate to lose my narrator."

Nash raised his hands in surrender. "Yes, I'll visit. I'm just up the plateau somewhere, so I won't be too far."

"Are you two…" Markus pointed between us.

I shrugged. "I don't know what life has in store for us."

"Nor should you." Aubrey shook her head. "Sometimes I wish I could be rid of Sight some days."

"Speak for yourself," Leander chided, which earned a round of laughter from everyone gathered.

I was going to miss this camaraderie, but I couldn't wait to set out on my own again with Nash by my side. My life would be forever changed without Archer, but I had someone who loved me to ease my worries on the difficult days.

And that would be enough.

The perfect Christmas gift.

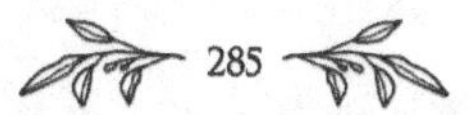

52

ARCHER

I STUMBLED OUT OF THE TREELINE, bare like the day my mother birthed me.

Funny, I never remembered leaving *Atagahi.*

The air surrounding me warmed my clammy skin. Wasn't it winter? Had I stumbled back to Arcadia without realizing it?

Where's my sister?

Where's Nash?

I blinked in the bright light, my surroundings coming into full clarity. Ahead of me, a stone gazebo stood in the center of a clearing, illuminated by a light source I couldn't see. Everything shone from that light and reflected colors I didn't have names for, but my focus zeroed in on the gazebo.

I approached, resting a hand on the ancient runes carved deep into the stone. They appeared fresh, some of the dust clinging to my palm.

"Je lyco," a voice rumbled around the clearing, trees swaying in its wake.

I spun, coming face to face with a great, white wolf. I found myself speechless in His presence.

"Rauha, my trusted son. You have excelled in your tasks. Be at peace among these trees and worry no more." He phased, and I realized the light emanated from Him.

Somewhere deep inside of me, I knew Him. I knew His name. And He knew mine. He'd called me well before I knew the sound of His voice, so it was no wonder I found myself here in this clearing by His side.

I swallowed. "I'm dead."

The shining man nodded.

"And they're out there." I furrowed my brow. "And I'm here."

Another nod.

I ran a hand through my hair, as soft and fresh as if I just bathed. "What do I do next?"

The man smiled. "First, we feast and celebrate your job well done."

"And then?" I dreaded the answer. What would I do without my sister? My pack?

A smirk lit the man's face. "And then, a long-overdue reunion."

As I tried once more to recall His name, two wolves bounded into the clearing—wolves I knew better than myself.

"Mother." I crumpled to my knees while she circled me, licking my ears and hair and every inch of skin she could reach without tackling me to the grass.

"Father," I cried, and my father joined in, rubbing his chin on my head, his muzzle into my shoulder.

Both my mother and my father whined, their words unintelligible, spoken over top of each other.

The man whose light illuminated the clearing laughed with His entire body. "Come on, my son. Your feast awaits you. And then, eternity."

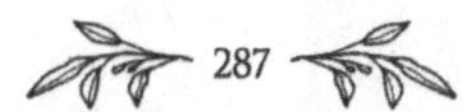

EPILOGUE
THE GREAT MOUNTAIN

T HE WOLF MOON HUNG ABOVE ME, her light casting my slopes in an ethereal glow, the world hushed and waiting. My daughter and son were coming to visit.

A sound like rippling water filled the silence of the witching hour, followed by shushing.

"You're going to wake the Wildcat," a playful growl said, cutting through the laughter.

"You don't want to be seen with a human?"

"Please. I want to be seen with you everywhere. All of Shaconage will hear about my wife. I'll howl it from the mountaintops."

"Who's going to wake the Wildcat now?"

My daughter, my son.

"Just a little farther." My son with his new bride on his back traversed the snowy landscape, tail wagging. *"The trail is past the cabins."*

They skirted the edges around the sprawling buildings of LeConte

Lodge, most of them empty aside from the Wildcat long asleep in his winter home. Had my daughter been walking and not riding on the back of a *virlukos*, the snow would've been past her worn hiking boots.

But the king maneuvered deftly over the fallen logs hidden under blankets of snow. He scrambled up crunching ice, clinging to crumbling slate before rounding the bend in the trail. The expanse of sky and earth and space unfolded beyond them, a mastery of creation extending as far as the eyes could see.

"Woah," the new queen breathed, her words forming white clouds in the atmosphere. Creation begetting creation.

My son's whiskers gathered frozen droplets, and his bride slipped off his back. *"Those are what we call the Cairns, although I think humans call them Chimneys. And beyond is Kuwohi."*

They talked of simple things, the Seers expecting pups in the summer and the Elder's and Beta's wedding. They talked of the son of Iain leaving with the daughter of Lukosan. But most of all, they spoke of life—vibrant and glowing life.

They both gazed up at the Wolf Moon, a stark white against the swirls of navy and starlight. With a mischievous glint in her eye, my daughter howled as loud as her human voice could project. My son, a rumbling laugh escaping him, followed suit. A stone-rattling howl echoed against me and reverberated over the earth for all to hear.

My roots deep below the lakes and the villages and the valleys rippled with some unknown magic, some ancient thing long before the electric lights and migrations and wars. That primordial enchantment woke something in my stone heart, that forgotten feeling of venturous and untamed love.

And what is love if not wild?

Acknowledgements

The end of an era. I can't believe this trilogy is complete. As I sit on my porch writing this, I think back to where I was when I began the first draft (of many) of *To Live Among Wolves*. My husband and I had moved back to our hometown for a job that wasn't what it claimed to be, living with my parents, and not sure where God was leading us. It took us eventually to a vastly different town with entirely new jobs that turned out different than we thought it would be which led to me throwing all of my free time into these characters.

Fast forward to writing *To Breathe Beneath Stars* from a time of needing an escape after hitting burnout at the last job and us moving back in with my parents. So before *TLAW* was in print, I'd started this new adventure, and it filled me with creative energy.

And then, in a rented house on a hot September day, I started the chilliest and spookiest part yet when I started drafting *To Dance With Spirits*. We moved (again) and bought a house, both started new jobs (yes, again), and even found out I was pregnant with our first child! We also grieved the diagnosis of several illnesses in our families (spurring me to write myself yet another escape), celebrated engagements and weddings of friends and family, started doing weekly trivia with friends, and I also started a publishing house (shoutout to Michael Westmoreland for being an excellent business partner through all of my crazy).

And so, I come to the end which is just the beginning for our beloved characters, and I've run out of words to say. Or perhaps I haven't run out. I simply don't know how to express my gratitude to the multitudes of people who supported me along the way.

To Jordan Comeaux, Emma Hill, Reagan Waddell, and McKenzie Melody—you four shaped this series in more ways that you know! Your insight and knowledge of the strange things (bones, cryptids, and folklore being just a few) helped me craft a world you want to slip into. And for that I am eternally grateful.

To Caitlin Miller—your editing abilities when my words feel sloppy and my plot stretches thin in places always astounds me. Somehow when I have given up on my words and want to throw in the towel, you see the magic in them and inspire me to make them even better. Without you, this trilogy couldn't be what it is today!

To Maria Spada—your designs are the reason people pick my books off of shelves. You so easily captured the magic and wonder of these stories, and I couldn't be happier with the result. And now they're all three together on my shelves!

To Julia Scott—formatting is not a skill I have, and I have been so grateful for your expertise. After a last minute panic with *TLAW*, Madeleine Elizabeth recommended you to me, and for that reason, this trilogy is as special as it is. Your work is amazing, and you're amazing for being so patient with me.

To my unofficial Street Team—I'm so grateful for your continued support. Words cannot describe how much it means to have people read my books and then share about them. 'm honored to have my dedicated readers who will read anything I write. Are y'all down for one more in Spring?

To my parents—y'all know I wouldn't be here without your guidance, right? My love of reading came from your encouragement, and you all gave me space to create all those years. And even now when y'all know I'm on a deadline or struggling to market, you still ask how you can help out. I love you mucho.

To my in-laws—it always blows my mind how many people y'all tell about my books (from the dog groomer to work friends to extended family). Y'all have taken me into the family, and I am so, so grateful to be your daughter-in-law.

To my husband—thank you for taking care of our little menace dog so I could finish this book. I should have known naming a rescue Wolfadoodle Nash would wreak havoc on our house, lives, couch, etc. But I love it, and I wouldn't have it any other way.

And last but never least, to my Lycaon—Somewhere deep inside of me, I knew You. I knew Your name, and You knew mine. You called me well before I knew the sound of Your voice, so it was no wonder I found myself writing these words and this story. I always hope I capture some aspect of Your nature in my silly, little books. It seems ridiculous to try to capture Your image in a fantasy book, but aren't we all made in your image? Your will be done with this trilogy as with every piece of writing I send out to the world. You've blessed me to do this task, and as long as that continues, I will keep writing.

Soli Deo Gloria.

ABOUT THE AUTHOR

A story lover at heart, Morgan has always been crafting stories. Growing up in East Tennessee in the Great Smoky Mountains, their mystery and beauty have inspired many of her tales. She's a big fan of rain, stargazing, coffee, and taking the long way home.

Currently residing in East Tennessee, Morgan lives with her husband, writing books and exploring the mountains. When she's not reading or writing, you'll find Morgan outside foraging among the plants or trying new coffee shops.

Keep in touch with Morgan at
WWW.MORGANHUBBARDAUTHOR.COM
and on Facebook or Instagram @morganhubbardauthor

9 798986 398143